When Libby Met the Fairies

And Her Whole Life Went Fey

When Libby Met the Fairies
And Her Whole Life Went Fey

*To introverts and outcasts and
people who don't think they belong.*

One

For two and a half glorious days, my plan seemed to be working.

I'd moved out of the country to get away from people. Not all people, all of the time. Not my boyfriend, Paul, for example. Just most people, most of the time.

You know that feeling, right? The feeling that the world is crazy and people are crazy and you just want a little more space, a little more breathing room to center yourself, get back in touch with who you really are—and who you know you really want to become.

But then I took a break from unpacking and went for a walk.

ψ ψ ψ

I hiked up the hill from the house.

It was early spring. The ground was muddy and beaten-looking, and it didn't take an expert to see that nothing had been grown there for a long time. Well, except hay. Poor, weedy hay. So poor that the farmer who'd baled the last cut hadn't even bothered to take it all. He'd left several bales, disks of hay almost as tall as me, sitting there, all rolled up and wrapped with nylon twine.

But—another big reason I'd moved to the country—I was finally following my dream.

I was starting over.

As a farmer. An organic farmer.

So I didn't care how my land looked that day. What mattered to me was that I'd torn up my old career and I'd thrown the torn-up pieces to the four winds. And now, I was going to transform this weedy, muddy, winter-killed ten acres into a lush Eden with neat rows of lush market vegetables and maybe some adorable white chickens wandering around, pecking and clucking and fluffing their feathers.

I walked past one of the rotting hay bales.

And then I saw it.

A fresh, new, blaze-orange "Posted, No Trespassing" sign, stapled to a tree bordering the south end of my property line.

⚘ ⚘ ⚘

I admit, I was a bit shocked.

I stood for a moment, staring, trying to figure out if I was actually seeing what I was seeing.

Because I have no problem with Posted signs. I have no problem with a neighbor letting me know I was supposed to stay on my side of the property line.

But that brand new, blaze-orange sign was in the wrong place. It was stuck onto a tree that was on MY property. On MY side of the tumbled down stone wall that marked the end of my property and the start of the woodlot beyond.

Not cool.

And then I saw that it wasn't just one sign. There were more. All along the tree line. I counted seven, altogether.

They hadn't been there three days ago.

Over where the shade of the trees had protected it from the sun, there was a little snow left on the ground, and there were fresh footprints in the snow. Big boot prints.

No way Big Boot Person could have missed the survey markers, bright ribbons tied around the trunks of trees along the line.

I followed the footprints to where they disappeared at the far south-east corner of my land. And me without my bloodhound, ha ha ha.

I pulled out my cell and phoned my realtor.

"That's not legal," she said. "Posted signs have to be on the poster's own property."

"Can you find out who did it?"

"They should have a name on them."

Right. They did. Unfortunately, the signatures were illegible.

"I'll send you a pic," I said. "Maybe you can decipher them. But they look like they were signed by a doctor."

"I'll look into it."

"Okay, but in the meantime," I said, "I'm taking them down."

The signs had been mounted using a staple gun.

I fetched a screwdriver and got to work, prying the staples loose.

And when I was done—because I'm a nice person, and who wants to start off her new life by getting into a fight with a neighbor?—I stacked the signs on a flat stone near the road, went back to the house, tore a flap off one of my moving boxes, and wrote a note on it.

If you really feel you need these, please hang them on your side of the property line, not mine.

I left the note on top of the stack of signs, weighted down with another rock.

And that should have been the end of it.

⚘ ⚘ ⚘

But it wasn't the end of it. A week later I was dragging my garbage can down to the end of the driveway and are you kidding me?

Big orange Posted signs. Back again. And on *my* trees, again.

I marched to the house to retrieve my screwdriver.

Argh.

Where was that screwdriver?

I was sure I'd left it on the kitchen counter near the door.

I was positive I'd left it there. Positive. I was positive, in fact, that I'd seen it not ten minutes ago as I stuffed broken-down boxes into my recycle bin.

But it was gone.

What the heck had I done?

Bumped it on my way out? Had it fallen into the overstuffed recycle bin as I wrestled it through the door?

And also, how annoying is that? When you know darn well you left something someplace and now it's gone, and it wasn't like there was someone else in the house I could blame.

And I had other tools, but they weren't unpacked, yet, and wow, was this annoying, and how much more aggravating could this morning possibly be?

And you know what? Eff it. I didn't need a screwdriver.

I'd just tear those stupid signs down.

The weather had turned chilly and wet, but it wouldn't take long, right? So I didn't even bother putting on a jacket or gloves. I went back out and marched back up the property line, ripping signs down as I went.

And I was making good progress.

I was halfway up the hill, yanking a sign stapled to a white pine tree.

Then it happened.

A massive bellowed "ra-RAUWF" hit my body so hard my diaphragm thrummed.

I whirled around.

I let out a shriek.

A huge, brindle Mastiff. Galloping toward me.

Galloping. He was the size of a small horse. And his brow was furled, and his mouth was hanging open, all red and dark and full of long white canine fangs.

So yeah, I panicked. I spun back the other way and dropped the signs and grabbed the lowest branch of that pine tree and hoisted myself up off the ground.

A minute later I was 15 feet up, looking down at that enormous dog, now leaping again and again against the tree trunk below me, and every time his paws jabbed the tree, it made the whole thing shake.

And his head looked massive.
And I'm thinking OMG, now what????

Two

He finally stopped barking. He finally dropped all four paws on the ground and began sniffing around the base of the tree.

He pawed at one of the Posted signs I'd dropped there.

I like dogs. I like petting dogs. Even strange dogs, when they are, say, on a lead at a park. But being treed by a dog—a very, very large dog—is not an experience I'd put at the top of my bucket list.

I was shaking so much the needles on tree were trembling. Water droplets were shaking off the needles through the air around me and down, down, down to the wet ground below.

So okay. Focus, Libby, focus.

My glasses were wet, and a dead brown pine needle was clinging to one of the lenses. I cautiously let go with one hand and brushed at the pine needle, which, of course, smeared the lens.

Which caused me to realize that my fingers felt tacky, and I could smell the pungent odor of pine pitch.

I'd climbed a pine tree.

And I'd just smeared pine pitch on my glasses.

Great.

I looked down, through the smear, at the dog.

He was wearing a collar. So at least he wasn't a feral dog.

But where the hell was his owner?

I peered through the branches toward my house. I could see the saplings and brush between it and my fields, and beyond the saplings and brush, the dark gray shingles of my roof.

I craned my neck to look north. Empty fields. Scraggly hedgerows of buckthorn and crabapple, leafless still because it was so early in the spring. I could see through them, all the way to Einbeck Road.

Not a soul in sight.

No apologetic dog owner running over, leash in hand.

I looked south. Forget about it. A thick, dark mass of tree trunks, gray and purple and algae-green. Nothing else. Not even a chickadee.

Just me and the dog.

Great idea, Libby. Moving out to the country to get away from people.

The dog was sitting, now, at the base of the tree, surrounded by the scattered pile of torn-down Posted signs.

He didn't look like he was planning to go anywhere, soon.

Something pulled at my hair, and I turned my head and—great. My hair, which had gone all frizzy in the wet, had also started to come loose, because my scrunchy was old and stretched out. So now long strands of hair were sticking to the globs of pine pitch oozing from the tree trunk.

Great.

I looked back down at the dog.

Maybe he'd listen to me, if I told him to go away?

I took a breath and tightened my grip on my branches. "YOU!" I said in a loud, firm, take-charge-of-the-dog voice. "GO HOME! Right now!"

Epic fail.

WOOF! He jumped back up against the tree, making it shake again, which startled me enough that one of my feet slipped, and a fresh shock of adrenaline zapped my guts as, for a split second, I felt like I might fall.

The dog sat back down.

I regained my balance. I reminded myself to breathe.

My hands were getting stiff and achy from the cold.

How long was I going to be stuck up here, treed like a cartoon varmint in a not-really-that-funny cartoon nightmare?

And then something else caught my eye.

A man. Standing on the other side of the stone wall, maybe 20 yards away. Motionless in the trees.

"Hey!" I yelled, "I could use some help, here!"

WOOF! WOOF!

The guy didn't move.

I blinked and let go with one hand, again, to make another useless swipe at my glasses.

Was it possible the guy couldn't hear me?

"HEY!" I waved maniacally with my free hand, feeling my boots slip slightly, again, on the branch under my feet. "HEY, I need some HELP here!"

He heard me. He was looking right at me. No question about it.

Why wasn't he coming over?

And then it hit me.

Of course.

It was my neighbor. The one who'd put up the Posted signs. And he was annoyed that I'd torn them down, and this was his revenge: to leave me stranded, treed by a humongous dog.

Well. That was IT.

I lost it. I'd had enough. "Damnit!" My voice came out more like a squeal than a yell. "Get over here! Get me down!"

He was too far away for me to really know if he was laughing.

But he started walking over, and as he got closer, I could see well enough—even through my smeary glasses—to catch the look of amusement on his face.

Yeah. I was pretty sure he'd been laughing. I was pretty sure he thought this whole situation was absolutely hilarious.

Three

"C'mere, Bo."

AH HA!

The dog? It was HIS dog.

I watched the guy step over the stone wall. Just like Bo, he was big. Not fat. Just big. He had a beard—a little too untrimmed for my taste—and was wearing a Carhartt jacket and big heavy work boots, and a red and black plaid hat with flaps down over his ears.

The hat looked like it was probably warm.

Really warm.

I waited until the man had a firm grip on monster dog's collar.

I climbed down the tree.

"That animal should be on a leash," I said, brushing bits of pine bark off my sweatshirt.

"Bo won't hurt you," the man said. "Unless you've done something wrong."

Right. When you have a sciences background, few things are more exasperating than people who project human thinking processes onto animals. "He's a dog," I retorted. "He's incapable of distinguishing 'right' from 'wrong.' Humans, on the other hand, do, and it's most definitely wrong to let your dog terrorize other people."

Maybe I hit a nerve.

He let go of the dog's collar.

Uh oh.

But this time I stood my ground. Not that I had much of a choice. There was no time to scramble back up the tree. Plus there was the little matter of my dignity. Or anyway, what was left of it.

Bo loped up to me.

He pushed his muzzle into my hand.

He gave it a sweet doggie lick, his tongue hot against my chilled fingers.

I pulled my hand back. "This changes nothing. Are you the one who's been putting up these Posted signs?"

"Are you the one who's been pulling down them down?"

The man snapped his fingers, and Bo returned to him.

I pushed aside a twinge of guilt. I actually like dogs. I could have petted the dog. After all, it wasn't Bo's fault that we'd gotten off on the wrong paw. It was this rude person, here. This person who, apparently, owned the land next to mine.

Well. No time for guilt about the dog. "You can't post signs on someone else's property." I pointed at the pine tree I'd just climbed. "This tree is on my side of the line."

"You might have said something to me, rather than just yank them all down," he said. "I'm right next door."

Next door. Next door, country style.

The nearest driveway was a half mile away.

"How was I supposed to know that?" I scowled. "And by the way, I couldn't read your signature. Your handwriting is appalling. And I also left you a note."

"A note?"

"I piled the signs down by the road and left a note on top."

"You talking about that piece of cardboard that sat outside for a week in the rain? If there was a note on that, it was long gone by the time I saw it, lady."

Lady?

How old did he think I was?

"I'm sure my note was easier to read than your handwriting!"

He shrugged.

An impasse.

I realized I was shivering.

The drizzle had switched to light rain, and rain was now dripping down from the tree branches overhead. I felt it hitting the top of my head. I felt an ice-cold rivulet run down the back of my neck.

"Look," I said, hugging myself as my teeth began to chatter. "You are in the wrong here. You're posting 'no trespassing' signs on my property, but the only one trespassing is you."

"All you had to do was stop by and ask me to move them," he said. "That's what neighbors do."

He put a tiny little emphasis on the word "neighbor."

Making it clear that whatever I was to him? "Neighbor" was not it.

Like I cared. Because I'd seen enough to know. Because, give the guy the benefit of the doubt, he might not be a big bad wolf. I could guess what kind of person he was, though. A big bad woodchuck. Living in a shack with his collection of torn tee shirts and piles of Genny empties and baby pot plants growing in drywall buckets. Harmless enough if you overlook his vast assortment of firearms.

Yeah.

I knew the type.

I turned toward my house. "Look. I'm freezing. Just move the signs onto your property. If you really think you even need them, because, trust me, I have no plans to encroach on it."

I picked my way through the brown, broken-down weeds between me and my field and started down the hill.

I felt Bo's muzzle touch my hand again.

And suddenly, the man's big heavy Carhartt dropped over my shoulders.

"Hey." I started shrugging the jacket back off. "I didn't—"

"Take it. Your lips are blue."

"I don't—"

"Take it. I'll stop over in a few to get it back."

I gave up. I was tired of arguing. And besides, the warmth of the coat was already calming my shivers. "Fine. I'll leave it on the stoop."

The man nodded.

I watched as he walked back to the pine tree and started gathering up the Posted signs from the ground.

Well!

Look at that.

Mark one in Libby's victory column.

I thrust my arms through the jacket's sleeves and pushed my cold-stiffened hands into its pockets. I crossed the field and threaded the path through the saplings and brush between the field and my house.

I stopped short.

Why was a battered old Ford Escort parked in my driveway?

Four

I didn't drive a battered old Ford Escort.

I drove a not-so-battered old Toyota Corolla.

Then the front door on the driver's side of the battered old Escort flew open, and a jeans-and-tee shirt-clad person skipped up toward me. "Auntie Em! Auntie Em! I'm home, Auntie Em!"

I stared. "Maisey?"

I hadn't seen the girl in years. Four years, at least. Which made her, what, nineteen now?

My friend Gina's kid.

She grabbed me in a hug. "Wow, I bummed when I knocked and you weren't home! I fit all my stuff in my car, do you believe it? Did you get my message? Did you talk to Mom? What's with that jacket, have you gone native? What happened to your hair?"

"What? What message?"

"Mom said she talked to you. Didn't Mom talk to you?"

Oh dear. I'd been so busy! So yes, Gina had called me a few times, but the calls never seemed to come through when my phone was handy. And I'd texted her updates about my new place, and I'd listened to her voice mail messages. So I knew she'd met a guy, she was moving to Hawaii, some sort of business venture, something about how sexy the new boyfriend was, something about him being a Tantric sex coach...

Right. I had only the vaguest idea what that meant. But I still felt a twinge of jealousy. I get the cheating husband and the divorce and then

Paul, who was perfectly nice, but he was…Paul. While kooky Gina gets a Tantric sex coach.

I mean, I was happy for her, because she was an old friend, maybe my oldest friend. But she could also wear me out. I'd learned that small doses of Gina were best.

And now I was getting the sinking feeling that I may not have listened to those voice mails closely enough.

"You've got room, right?" Maisey said, her eyes on my house, sizing it up. Farmhouse, circa 1870, obviously at least three or four bedrooms.

"Room? What do you mean, Maisey?"

"I can stay here, right? Mom's gone to Hawaii. I need a place to stay. Not for long. Just through the summer."

I suppressed a groan.

"Lemme get my stuff," she called over her shoulder.

I looked up at my new house.

Holy Old Friends And Their Daughters, Batman. My house was shrinking. Right before my eyes.

☙ ☙ ☙

I found my phone where I'd left it, next to a half-empty box of paperbacks, and sat on my couch and listened, again, to a bunch of Gina's voice mail messages.

Sure enough, she'd asked if it was okay if her daughter bunked with me for a few months.

How had I missed that?

Maisey passed the living room doorway, dragging a huge roller board suitcase.

"Take the last bedroom on the left!" I called out.

I had an old saved message from Paul, too, one he'd left weeks ago, back when I was still sleeping in my apartment.

I hit the play button. His voice was a rock of calm after the morning's nuttiness. "Hey, babe. Sorry I missed you." The message was a relic, left over from our old routine, when Paul would come over to my place at 5:45, give or take five minutes depending on traffic. And then he'd take me out to eat. And then back to his place...

I heard a clunking noise, which sounded like Maisey was throwing bricks or something around one of the upstairs bedrooms. I looked up at the ceiling toward the noise as if I had super ceiling-penetrating vision powers, which I do not.

I rubbed my forehead. So much for getting away from people. So much for my new, quiet, country life out here with no company except some plants and birds and maybe a raccoon or two.

And why wasn't the girl in college?

Suddenly a pounding on the door thudded through the house. A loud pounding.

"Who's *that*?" Maisey had come back downstairs, and her head appeared in the living room doorway. "Sounds like somebody is PISSED!"

The jacket!

I was still wearing the jacket.

I leaped up. The pounding had sounded pretty loud. And my doorbell was broken. Which meant Posted Sign Guy had been standing out there in the rain, pressing the button for goodness knows how long. No wonder he'd given up and started pounding.

I remembered that he was a big guy.

I ran through the living room and the kitchen and yanked the door open with one hand while I eased my other arm out of the jacket sleeve.

Posted Sign Guy didn't look very happy.

I held the jacket out to him.

But instead of looking at me, he was looking past me, a hint of curiosity passing quickly over his face.

I glanced back. It was Maisey. She'd followed me. "So it's your jacket," she said, and then suddenly let out a squeal and practically knocked me over as she pushed past me, through the door, and out onto the stoop, where she knelt and threw her arms around Bo's neck, stroking his head and crooning ecstatically.

A tattoo—a dandelion head with a few seeds blowing away—was visible over the collar of her shirt.

I pushed open the storm door again. "Maisey, the man wants to leave now."

"What's his name?"

Maisey meant the dog. And was asking Posted Sign Guy, not me.

"The dog's name is Bo," I said. "Now why don't you finish unpacking your stuff, okay?"

The teen stood up, rolling her eyes for the benefit of her audience and saying, "Bye, Bo," in a dramatically regret-filled voice.

She pushed back past me again.

"Thanks for lending me the coat," I said.

"Your doorbell's broken."

"I know."

"And there's something in your hair."

The pine pitch. I reached up without thinking and my fingertips touched the wad of pine-pitch-clumped hair on the side of my head.

Great. So I looked like a freak. Just great.

I watched the man walk down the drive.

"So, who is that?" Maisey was back. "He is gorgeous. And so's the dog." She giggled.

"Shush!" I closed the door. "He'll hear you."

"So? What do you care?"

I scowled. "Maisey. No bedding my neighbors."

"Yeah right, like I'd sleep with a senior citizen."

Ouch. "Maisey! He's my age! And if you think that's old, you just wait. You will be, too, before you know it."

"Yeah, sure. And anyway, I have a boyfriend."

That little disclosure should have set off a whole slew of fresh warning bells.

It didn't.

"I'm gonna go finish unpacking," she called over her shoulder.

I put on a kettle for tea and went into the downstairs powder room to look in the mirror, twisting my head to try to see how bad the pine pitch situation really was. And ugh. My hair is thick and wavy and not very obedient even on good days, never mind days I'd been out climbing trees in the rain. And sure enough, the glob of pine pitch had, by that point, captured an entire fistful of hair and woven it into a nice messy tangle that, of course, also stuck out in a demented mass, just to make sure nobody could miss it.

I went back the kitchen. Fortunately I had some mayonnaise. Mayonnaise gets pine pitch out of hair.

I dug a spoonful out of the jar and began rubbing it into the tangle.

Better to smell like a sandwich than pine pitch.

I thought about what Maisey has said.

Gorgeous? Was he gorgeous?

Yeah, well, maybe. Tall enough, anyway.

No, I stopped myself. *Stop it.*

Maisey's not the only one who's got a boyfriend.

🌿 🌿 🌿

I'd left my cell on an overturned box in the living room.

Moving forty-odd miles south of Rochester had meant big changes in my routine. Mine and Paul's. No more Paul stopping by after work every night.

Instead, we had to schedule dates. Make advance plans to meet in the city.

It would be so nice to hear his voice.

I dialed him at work.

Five

Paul didn't pick up until the fourth ring.

That was kind of odd.

He'd been promoted. So, of course, he was busy. But he'd also been moved to a real office, with a real desk. And when Paul was at his desk, he was a first ring kind of guy.

Yeah. A real office. Actual walls. Not a cubicle. Back when I'd started working there, Paul had had neither. He was in the lab, like I was. That was where we'd met, two biologists, part of Cal4 Laboratory's crack "benign skin conditions" research team. Or as we called it, Psori-Ops. Short for Psoriasis Operations. Ha ha ha.

Anyway, in the lab, the phone was almost always out of arm's reach, and even if one of us happened to be near it when it rang, we resented being interrupted. We had more important things to do. We'd almost always let incoming calls go to voicemail.

But then Paul had made the jump from research to marketing.

That was a year ago.

He deserved it.

And around the same time, I separated from Wallace. Paul and I started seeing each other, but when Paul got promoted, I'll be honest, the office gossip started to get to me. Another reason to follow my dream, trade the office politics for a new life.

I didn't sever my ties with Cal4 entire, though. They'd given me a side project to do while I was in the lab, a little marketing e-newsletter called *Skin Tones*. I'd hated doing it, at first, because a lot of the work involved calling complete strangers and interviewing them. Out of my comfort zone. But when I quit nobody else wanted to step up and take over, so I struck a deal with them to keep doing it on a contract basis.

Which made Paul extremely happy since, now that he was marketing, he was in charge of the thing. When I agreed to keep doing it, it was one less headache for him.

And for my part, I realized it was a blessing in disguise. The *Skin Tones* contract would bring in a little money to cover the bills while I got my farm up and running.

🌱 🌱 🌱

"Hey, Libby. What's up?" Paul said when he finally picked up his phone. He sounded funny. Distracted. "Well, you know. Getting settled in. Are you busy?"

"Not really."

"So guess who just showed up, looking for a place to stay? Maisey."

"Who?"

I wondered if calling him at work was a mistake. "You know," I said. "My friend Gina's kid. The one she had when she was back in high school. I've told you about her. Maisey. I used to babysit her sometimes."

Right. Babysit. Gina used to leave Maisey with me for days at a time. I was still in college, but Gina had graduated, and had gotten a job selling med supplies. She was doing a ton of travel to cover her region. But I was glad to help her out.

Of course, that was long before Paul. But I'd told him the stories. "I used to take Maisey to soccer games, remember?" I prompted him. "And that one time she had mono and—"

"Yeah, sure," he said. "Mono, I remember. Right."

Something was going on. "Paul, what's wrong?"

"Uh, I'll tell you later. I'm not sure. They're calling us all together this afternoon. Right at 4:00."

Uh oh.

Cal4 upper management had a formula for announcing layoffs.

A 4:00 p.m. company meeting was not a good sign.

And here I'd expected sympathy because I'd inherited an unexpected house guest.

"Hang in there," I said. "Robbie loves you. You'll be okay." While in the back of my mind I couldn't help but wonder, oh man, if there's another big shake-up, there goes *Skin Tones*. There goes my only source of income.

"Look," Paul said. "I'd better go. We're still meeting for dinner, right?"

He sounded so distracted.

"Sure," I said. "Can we do Thai tonight? It's been a while."

"I was thinking ribs, actually."

Okay. So the least I could do was let him pick. "Okay, we'll do ribs. And good luck, Paul. You'll be fine."

Honestly, I couldn't really say Paul was happier since jumping over to the marketing side of the shop. In some ways, it was more stressful. Even though he was a bit closer to the decision-makers. The researchers used to joke, in the lab, that the Cal4 execs didn't even know the researchers' real names. We used to write our names on labels—the labels we used for samples—and stick them on our foreheads, and joke it was a new corporate policy to help Robbie and his son keep us straight.

I set down my cell and grabbed a box of files to take upstairs to my office.

Maisey must have brought an air mattress, which was a good thing, considering that I didn't have a spare bed.

She'd pushed it up against the wall beneath a window and was sitting on it, puffing an e-cigarette.

"I'm heading to the city," I said. "Need anything?"

"No, I'm good. You going on a date with Paul? Want me to braid your hair?"

I shook my head. "I just need to get the mayonnaise out of it."

I also needed to unpack another box of clothes. I hadn't bothered to unpack any of my dressy clothes, yet.

I went down the hall to my bedroom and—okay.

That was odd.

The screwdriver that I swore I'd left on the kitchen counter?

There it was. On the pillow of my bed.

Was I losing my mind?

"Wow," I muttered.

This is what the stress of moving had done.

I'd carried my screwdriver upstairs without even realizing it.

Six

Paul was a little late meeting me at the restaurant, which made me nervous. Was that a bad sign? But he arrived finally and leaned over, pecked my lips, and slid into the booth across from me.

"So. Who's gone this time?" I closed my menu.

"Nobody," he said. "You're never going to believe this. We've been acquired."

"Acquired?" Okay. That was different. Not that rumors didn't flare up from time to time. But Paul and I both knew enough about the company's bottom line. Cal4 wasn't exactly the coveted jewel of the nation's biotech industry. "Who by?"

"A cosmetics company."

"Oh, Paul, you're kidding me!"

"Nope. Dormet Vous Lustre. 'Making your skin like yesterday's, today.'"

I'd seen their ads. Late-night cable. And website pop-ups, too. Yech.

"Apparently," Paul said, "they think some of our IP will be good for their, ah, wrinkle creams and stuff."

I rolled my eyes. "Robbie."

"Robbie," Paul echoed knowingly.

The owner. Robert Donavan. He was a smooth talker, that man. Could sell a comb to a frog.

"Is it a done deal?" I asked.

"For sure. He introduced our new masters during the meeting. We're officially a wholly owned subsidiary. Robbie's been named President, and Junior is VP of Operations."

"Business as usual, in other words," I said, thinking to myself, well maybe *Skin Tones* will be safe after all.

"Yeah, except that we're not out to save the world anymore."

That's how we labbies had coped. We'd told ourselves that we were saving the world. And we'd had a point. There was a chance our research might help people live more comfortably. Or cure them of some embarrassing skin condition, even.

"Well," I said, "For a woman who wants to look her best, I suppose wrinkle cream is kind of important."

I remembered Maisey's "senior citizen" crack.

I pushed it out of my mind.

"Anyway, Paul, if it's business as usual—" I started to say, but with exquisite timing the server stopped by for our order.

Paul asked for a combo special, full rack and barbecued chicken. Plus dessert. He overate when he was stressed, and I'd noticed he'd been ordering dessert more and more often these days. Hopefully his relaxed fit dress pants were relaxed enough to withstand Dormet Vous Lustre.

"So anyway," I said after we'd finished ordering. "It'll be all the same products, right? Only the market is different."

He sighed. "Yeah. That's all." Because now that he was in marketing, he'd bear the brunt of "only the market is different".

The waiter brought our drinks. Decaf Earl Gray for me. Cola for Paul. More calories.

"It might be fun," I said supportively. "It's a change, anyway." I dunked my tea bag in the hot water. "And, uh—*Skin Tones*. You'll still need the newsletter, right?"

He glanced up. "Oh, that's right. *Skin Tones*." He hesitated for a moment, avoiding my eyes, and I felt a twinge of nervousness.

Even though I shouldn't have been surprised. He wouldn't have had time, yet, to think about my project.

"If you need time to figure it out, I understand," I said.

"No. No. Why don't you just go ahead with the next issue. You know. Business as usual, until we hear otherwise."

He knew how much I was counting on the money.

"Are you sure?" I asked.

He nodded. "Yeah. It's in the budget, right?" He reached for his cola.

"I've got Internet at my place now," I said. Making a mental note, as I spoke, to get the next issue out the door and invoiced as fast as I could.

Before someone from the new company barged into Paul's office with different ideas about that budget.

Seven

But I didn't get to work as early as I'd planned. I still had so much unpacking and organizing to do. It wasn't until late the next day that I finally forced myself to settle in and begin planning the next *Skin Tones* issue.

And I tried to concentrate. I really did.

Because this was important. There was no way I'd make any real money farming in my first year. Not by a long shot. I didn't even own a tractor, yet. Just some hand tools.

In fact, my plan was to let most of the land lay fallow year one. I'd hire someone to plow a smallish plot—a quarter acre or so. I'd choose a few things to plant there and maybe undersow it with white clover. The clover would add nitrogen to the soil and then serve as a green manure. Compost, basically. And by fall, I'd have a tractor, so I could plow the clover into the soil myself.

That was the plan.

That, plus get my organic certification. The document that would mean I could charge organic-level prices for my produce.

It was a plan I'd been working on for a long time, even before I left Cal4, if you count daydreams. I'd joined a CSA farm—that stands for Community Supported Agriculture—while I was still in college. I'd worked there in exchange for a discount on produce, spending hours every summer helping with the planting and mulching and weeding. And I'd made friends with Susan and David, the owners, and had picked their brains about the business—not the CSA piece, I didn't want to do a CSA—but about the farming part. What to grow, how to market, how to make it a viable business.

And switching to farming didn't seem like a big stretch for me. Growing things is still biology. Granted, it's not peering at cells through a microscope or running analytics on test results. But I believed in the whole local food idea. That fresh, locally grown vegetables are better for people. Hey, I'd become a biologist to help people live healthier lives. Organic farming would do the same thing. It wasn't such a stretch.

Plus, with the divorce, I found myself with an extra chunk of cash. Not a huge chunk. But combined with my savings and the money from my *Skin Tones* gig, it would be enough.

Hopefully.

I ate my leftovers from last night's dinner. I alphabetized the paperbacks in the living room. I drank some tea.

I decided that *Skin Tones* could wait.

It would be dark, soon.

I needed to get outside, go for a walk, get some fresh air.

🌿 🌿 🌿

I climbed up to my first field.

I turned and faced the west.

The wind was blowing in, hard and biting-cold against my face.

The valley was vast, wide. Simple and naked-looking from this height. Vast because it had once channeled the Genesee River, before glaciers had scoured a new course further to the west, leaving only a creek winding the course the river had once followed.

And above the valley, a boiling line of clouds, dark as a bruise, had begun to mount upward into the sky.

The Posted signs were back, but now they were stapled to trees on the other side of the tumbled wall.

No longer on my property.

Good.

I continued to climb.

I reached the easternmost edge of my land.

I turned around and looked down again.

Clouds now blocked the last rays of the setting sun.

This was my new beginning. Because, as I stood there, on that ground, I could see that I hadn't lost anything. It had simply changed shape, that's all. Wrecked dreams into new dreams.

The alchemy of divorce.

I was okay. I was okay.

I started back down.

The darkness closed around me as I walked, more quickly than I'd expected it to, and as I reached the edge of the field closest to the house I slowed, picking my footing carefully over the uneven ground.

I remembered that there was a little ditch there somewhere, running along the edge of the field closest to the house. Someone had dug it long ago to channel rainwater into what had once been a shallow pond at the other end of the field, probably to water long-ago cows.

I peered now into the darkness as I walked, looking for the ditch.

There it was.

And then there was a movement. A very strange movement. As if the shadows in the little ditch suddenly formed and became three dimensional and moved.

My mind thought *animal!*

But it was not an animal. I could see that it was not an animal.

It was a little man. Standing up from the ditch.

I stumbled back a step, clamping my hand over my mouth, and that shriek I heard was me, shrieking through my fingers.

He'd stood up from the ditch. And, yes, it was dark, but not too dark to see him. Not too dark to know that, without question, it was a little man, a man about two feet tall, with eyes that seemed to gleam out of his face.

And my mind was telling me *this can't be. I can't be seeing this.* And I wanted to just turn and run but I couldn't move. I stood there, staring, shaking.

And then he spoke. "You're rude."

If he'd said anything else—"I come in peace," "take me to your leader," even "don't be frightened"—I probably would have lost it completely and run, screaming, to my house, locked my door, run to my bed, and pulled the covers over my head.

But to be insulted? Indignation kicked in. "I am not rude."

"You weren't watching where you were going."

I was calming down enough to pay more attention. I saw that he was perfectly proportioned, a little on the thin side, and whatever he was dressed in, it looked like paper—like a paper bag, creased all over.

"What are you?" I said when I could speak again.

"*What* am I?"

My brain hadn't yet caught up. I wasn't yet conscious of the sensible explanation, which was that I'd somehow blundered into a waking dream of some kind. Or, less graciously put: a hallucination.

But my instincts were still working.

No way was I going to refer to this thing—this phenomenon—as a "who".

"I said, *what* are you?" I repeated.

"I look after this." He gestured with his hand so I'd know "this" meant the land around us.

My property.

"Do you?" I said. "Well, this can't be happening."

He laughed. Perhaps because when you tell your hallucination it can't be happening, you tickle your hallucination's funny bone.

And that laugh was exactly what I needed.

I could move again.

Not that I dared to try walking right through him. I chickened out and walked around him, instead.

And I didn't look back. I concentrated—hard—on walking at a natural pace, when what I really wanted to do was to sprint away.

Then I heard his voice again, behind me.

"Watch where you're walking, Libby."

My palms were sweating inside my gloves.

That hadn't been real. That had not been real.

What was real, unmistakably self-evident, was that I, Libby Samson, wasn't as sane as I'd thought.

On the contrary. I was finally, truly cracking up.

Eight

The light inside seemed strangely yellow after the dark gray outdoors.

And the air felt hot, and the lingering smell of the warmed-over ribs I'd had earlier hung heavily in the air, almost sickening.

I pulled my gloves off.

My hands were sweaty.

I couldn't think.

"Hey, Aunt Libby!" Maisey yelled. "You're back! Come here, look who's here. You won't believe it!"

I froze.

My heart started pounding again.

He's here. The little man. With Maisey, in my living room.

I leaned on the kitchen counter to steady myself.

Get a grip, Libby. There is no little man.

I stood back up and forced myself to walk to the other room.

It was not a little man.

It was a scrawny teenage boy.

He stood up from the couch when I walked in, and Maisey stood up next to him, grinning ear-to-ear. "It's Tyler, Aunt Libby! My boyfriend I was telling you about. He finally got here!"

I felt my body go a bit limp with relief. "Hi, Tyler," I said, looking at Maisey and then back at the boy.

That would have been a goatee on his chin, I supposed, if he were old enough to grow a real beard.

Tyler ducked his head and shrugged in the nouveau-hippy equivalent of a handshake. "Thanks for giving us a place to stay."

What?

I sucked in my breath. "Sorry? What?"

The kids exchanged glances, and I could almost hear the whir of the gears in Maisey's head as she considered what to say next. "He doesn't know anyone, Aunt Libby. He doesn't have anywhere to go. He doesn't even have a car."

Tyler, picking up on the strategy, gave me a lost puppy look.

"And he's kind of short of money at the moment, right, Tyler?"

I sighed. Skinny kid. "You hitchhiked from Seattle with no money?"

"I had some when I started." Tyler shoved his hands into his jeans pockets and pulled them back out again. In his left hand, a jackknife, a strip of rawhide with some glass beads strung on it, and a compass. In the other hand, a few bills. "I got some left. Let's see. Seven dollars. And thirty, fifty, fifty-five—some change."

I shook my head, and something else occurred to me. "Uh, Maisey?" I said. "Does you mom know that you're planning to…" I trailed off, unsure what words to use. Shack up with your honey? Cohabitate with a boy who's just started to shave? And I was also thinking, in the back of my head, *Gina had Maisey when Gina was only sixteen, and maybe she'd be a little concerned about her daughter following in her, er, footsteps?*

But Maisey was nodding her head vigorously. "Mom's fine with it!" she said. "She's met him. She loves Ty!"

I wondered if "fine with it" included making sure her daughter was using proper protection during sex. And yeah, I'd babysat for Maisey when I was in college, but it's not like I was exactly qualified to be a full-time parent.

This was all happening a bit too fast for me.

"And Tyler's a great cook!" Maisey was chattering on, still happy as could be. "He cooks Tex-Mex. His enchiladas are to die for, right, Ty?

And he knows computers! If you ever have any problems, you know, with your computer, he can—"

"No! No computer help, no!" I yipped, a little horrified. I couldn't do *Skin Tones* without my PC! The last thing I needed was to walk into my office and discover my computer had been turned into a gaming system. Or was loaded up with spyware from questionable websites. "Please, you guys, don't touch my PC—"

"Oh, no worries, Aunt Libby! We'd never do anything without your permission, right, Ty?"

He smiled and pulled Maisey toward him in a hug.

"Well," I said weakly. "I guess if your mom is okay with it."

I went to hang up my coat.

And, as I pulled it off, I suddenly remembered I'd been for a walk, and it all came back in a flash: the little man standing up from the ditch—and talking?

Talking?

My heart began to pound again, and my mouth felt dry.

I went to the kitchen sink and turned on the water, watching it stream into the basin and over the rust stain that had formed from years of well water hitting the chipped white porcelain.

I filled a water glass and took a drink.

I'd tell Paul.

That's what I'd do.

I'd tell him, and he'd say...

What?

I wasn't sure.

All I knew is that I had to tell him. I had to hear his voice. I had to hear him say that there was a perfectly rational, logical, scientific explanation for what had happened to me.

I looked at my cell phone on the kitchen counter.

Paul was having dinner, tonight, with Josh something-or-other, his new boss, the guy that Dormet Vous had put in charge of marketing. They'd be sitting down right about now.

And I was going to interrupt him to tell him I was seeing magical beings that don't really exist?

No. Better to wait a little while.

⚓ ⚓ ⚓

I holed up in my office after dinner, and it calmed me down a lot, to sit there, alphabetizing the folders I used to manage the *Skin Tones* project: interview prospects, future story topics, past story notes…

There had to be some logical explanation for that hallucination. Stress. Some psychological trigger.

I thrust a folder marked "Billington, M.D." behind another labeled "Babcock & Sons", noticing how real the folders felt to my fingers.

I should have walked right through him, right through that little… hallucination.

I headed back downstairs.

There was laughter coming from inside Maisey's bedroom.

My quiet little country house was apparently now a not-so-quiet B&B.

Okay.

It was late enough to phone Paul. And I wasn't sure what I was going to tell him, but I was glad I'd waited, because I was calmer now. And if I was calm about it, he'd be calm about.

"Hi, snookums," he said happily when I answered my cell.

Snookums? "Well, hi. Sounds like your dinner went well?"

"Free dinner, Libby. What's to argue with a free dinner. Good dinner, too. Porterhouse. And cheesecake. Coupla pieces of cheesecake."

A couple of pieces?

I decided not to say that out loud. "So what did Josh have to say?"

"You were right, Libby, my darling."

"I was?"

"What you said the other night. About how much women need to look their best."

"Oh, that."

"This is big, Libby. It's important. Women—when you women get old, you just want to die." And he giggled.

He *giggled*? Was I hallucinating again?

"Who said that?"

"Women do. I'm not sure about men."

"Women want to die because they might get wrinkles?"

"Die before they get old. Like in The Who song—" He made some "ner ner ner, ner ner ner" guitar sounds and launched into song, "What a draaag it is getting old."

"That's the Stones, not The Who."

"Mmmmm," he said, and then, "Libby, I was wrong."

"What do you mean?"

"This isn't a step backwards. Not at all. Looking good is important for a woman's self-esteem. And without self-esteem, there would—Libby?"

I frowned.

"Libby, without self-esteem, there'd be no steam at all."

He giggled again, and I hoped he hadn't offered this bit of philosophical insight during the dinner.

I was also hoping that he'd had enough sense to take a taxi.

"Ribby?"

"Yes, Laul?"

"I'm going to bed."

"Yeah, good idea."

"I love you Ribby." Giggle. "I said 'Ribby.' That makes me—Rastro! Ry ruv roo, Ribby!"

We hung up.

So much for unburdening myself to Paul.

I sighed.

Okay. Maybe it was for the best.

Maybe the better path forward was to keep quiet and avoid going for walks for a while.

Maybe, if I just avoided going for walks for a while, this whole thing would go away.

Nine

March was almost over.

And I'd kept to my new plan. I'd stopped walking my land.

And it was a perfectly fine plan. Because after all, it was far too early to really get anything done up there. The ground was too wet and cold to work. It was winter, still. Never mind what the calendar said. Never mind that instead of snow it had been raining on and off all day. It was cold out, still.

And it's not like I didn't have other things to do. I had a bunch of online forms I needed to complete to apply for my organic certification. And later, the certification people would do an on-site inspection. I needed to get that scheduled.

And *Skin Tones*. I was very busy with the next issue of *Skin Tones*.

It was an amazing newsletter, if I do say so myself. Filled with inspiring stories of people who had been helped by Cal4's research. Imagine a story about, say, a little boy who could finally swim in the family pool without triggering a full-body eczema outbreak.

That's the kind of thing we published.

We put it on our website and also emailed it out, mostly to the trade—wholesalers and distributors, hospitals, dermatologists, companies who licensed Cal4 research—but also to consumer and health publications.

Sometimes editors used excerpts of my articles for their stories. That's what made *Skin Tones* such a brilliant idea. It wasn't promotional, at all. But it made Cal4 look positively angelic. Of course, Robbie, the big boss, always grumbled about it. When he was in a bad mood, he called it *Sappy Tones* or *Stink Tones* and complained about how much it cost. But on good days he knew it was a fabulous way to get positive PR. And he got calls from people about it all the time, which helped. Media bigwigs, some of them. Then afterwards, he'd be all gung-ho again and call it *Spin Tones*—his idea of a joke—for a couple of days.

This month, the newsletter's main story featured a woman who'd been misdiagnosed. She'd been told she had skin cancer, but it turned out it was a garden variety of seborrheic dermatitis that responded to topical ketoconazole.

The only odd thing was that the woman didn't seem to understand it had never been a malignancy. She seemed to think the ointment had cured her of cancer.

Of course, I left that out of the article and focused on how ecstatic she was about her skin clearing up. Nothing about the idiot doc who'd said the C-word and scared the poor woman almost out of her mind.

But I thought about it a lot afterward, about how others' skewed interpretations of the so-called facts could become other peoples' nightmares. Like that doctor who'd examined the woman. Something had happened. But what? What had made him decide he was looking at a malignant cancer instead of a benign and fairly common dermatitis?

There were two kinds of people in the world. People who were faithful to the facts, and people who weren't.

I knew what camp I belonged to. So why was I still thinking about that little man?

Why was I wondering if there might be times when something steps between the objective world of facts and my own two eyes?

I sat in front of my computer screen, pushing the hair back from my face as if to push away the thoughts that crowded unpleasantly into my mind.

My marriage. Something came between the facts and my eyes.

Only instead of seeing a malignancy that wasn't there, I'd had made the opposite mistake. I'd seen a fascinating, energetic, faithful husband when what was really there was something else entirely.

"I gave him the benefit of the doubt," I muttered out loud. "I loved him."

He used to come home late. Tripping across the bedroom floor in the dark as he kicked off his shoes. He'd started showering at night. He never used to shower at night. He used to shower in the morning.

And was that a hint of strange perfume lingering on the collar of his sports jacket?

And when I emptied the pockets to get it ready for the cleaners, why was there a business card in the pocket for an interior designer?

We hadn't talked about hiring an interior designer.

And later that week when he was outside mowing the lawn? If I hadn't picked up his cell phone and called the interior designer's number? Would we still be married?

I pushed back from my desk and stood up.

I knew the answer to that question.

If I hadn't called that number and heard that woman's voice on the other end—the sultry "hello" that switched instantly to tight-voiced denials when the woman realized it was not Wallace, but Wallace's wife placing the call—then I, Libby, would not be here now, on the farm.

My farm.

My future.

I went downstairs and walked to the window in the kitchen, the one over the sink that looked back out toward my fields.

The rain had started again.

It was cold near the window.

I found my sweater where I'd left it in the living room, and went back upstairs and sat at my computer.

Maisey and Tyler had gone out somewhere in Maisey's car—when you live in the country, you pretty much have to be out in a car if you're going to be out at all—and I was editing a newsletter feature story for about the fifth time when the door slammed.

"Aunt Libby! Come here! You should see what it's doing outside!"

I looked back out the window.

Everything was gleaming faintly.

Shiny.

And then it hit me: I was looking at a glaze of ice.

Maisey clattered up the stairs and into my office. "It's totally freezing rain out there! We almost went off the road, like, fifty times!"

☙ ☙ ☙

I worked a while more, massaging my article into shape.

I looked out the window again.

A bit of late afternoon sun had broken through the clouds.

The ice coating the trees along the road was catching the sunlight and shimmering. A coat of lacquered gold.

Rain and sun at the same time…

There had to be a rainbow in the sky in the other direction. In the east.

Right?

I stood up.

So tempting to take a break. Take a walk. Get out there and look for the rainbow amidst all that shimmery gold…

Maisey and Tyler were standing in front of the stove, pressed up against each other and looking down into a frying pan.

"Going for a walk?" Maisey asked.

"Yeah," I muttered. How long had it been since I'd last taken a walk? "I won't be gone long."

I couldn't live like this.

A prisoner in my own home. Too scared to walk my own land.

And that…thing…that I'd seen?

An anomaly. Had to be.

I'd never see it again.

I zipped up my jacket and pulled a hat down over my hair, and stepped outdoors, and turned up the hill.

I'd missed the sun. It had already gone back behind the clouds.

No rainbow for me.

Which means no gold. No pot of gold...

I pushed the thought aside angrily.

It was ridiculous, the way I was letting this stupid...episode... haunt me. Keep me away from the very life I'd chosen when I'd quit my job and moved out of my apartment and away from Paul. Kept me from being outside, spending more time outside, close to the land.

Whatever had triggered that episode, it was a fluke. A once-in-a-lifetime thing.

I was fine.

The rain was still falling, light and steady. Beneath my feet, the ice coating on the blades of grass crackled as I walked, and when I turned and looked back, my footprints had made dark splotches in the pale iced lawn.

I reached the shallow ditch.

There was nothing there.

Of course there wasn't.

I breathed deeply, deliberately.

It's going to be okay.

I turned to follow a deer path along the edge of the property, near where the Posted signs had been hung.

And there he was.

The little man, sitting on one of the rocks from the tumbled-down stone wall.

Barely five feet from where I stood.

My heart began hammering. I felt the color drain from my face.

So okay. I was losing it.

Losing my mind.

I whirled and began walking quickly back the way I'd come.

"If I were you, I'd move my car, Libby."

Crazy.

Craziness.

I started to run. Feet crunching the ice, my stomach hurt like I'd been punched, my eyes suddenly burning with tears.

I nearly lost my footing on the steps of the stoop. They were glazed with ice. But I caught myself on the handrail and a moment later burst into the warmth of my house.

I stood there, pulling off my gloves, trying to catch my breath, to calm my shaking hands. My glasses had steamed up, and I took them off and pressed the backs of my hands against my eyes.

He said my name.

He'd said it the other time, too.

Which proves it's a hallucination. Living inside my head.

I draped my jacket over the back of a kitchen chair, grateful that Maisey and Tyler weren't downstairs where they could see me like that.

A moment later I closed my office door behind me, sat on my work chair, and clamped my arms around myself.

And I sat there, shaking, without making a sound.

Ten

CR-RACK.

It was pitch black.

I sat up in bed.

What was that?

My heart pounded.

CR-RACK.

There it was again.

And more odd sounds as well. Popping noises. Some close, some distant.

What the heck?

I tossed off my covers, fumbled on my nightstand for my glasses, walked out into the hall—and ran smack into Maisey.

"Aunt Libby, do you hear that?"

I flicked the light switch.

Nothing happened.

And then I knew.

The noise was tree limbs, breaking.

"It's the ice," I said. "It must still be freezing rain out there. The weight of the ice is breaking the trees."

"Tyler's up, too," Maisey said.

"What time is it?"

"A little after 3:00."

We went downstairs.

Maisey and Tyler had lit the pillar candles on the fireplace mantel, and now Tyler sat up on the couch, wrapped in his blanket. He opened it up, inviting Maisey to join him.

I pressed my face to a windowpane.

I couldn't see much.

I went to the kitchen and got a flashlight.

There was another, huge CRACK—this one so close and loud I literally jumped—followed by the sound of breaking glass.

It took me a second to realize what had happened.

The cars.

I had no garage. Our cars were parked outside, at the top of the driveway. Right under an ancient maple tree, which happened to have quite a few enormous limbs that were either dead or close to it.

I ran to the front door, opened it, and stepped out onto the stoop. The stoop was slippery under my feet and the air felt weird, a swirling mix of warm and cold and dampness and stinging rain. The sound of the trees snapping, now that I was outside, was vivid, sharp, like gunfire, sometimes close, sometimes distant, constant and arrhythmic.

My flashlight beam was just strong enough that I could see my car. And it was not good. A big chunk of the maple had snapped off, and my Toyota had taken a direct hit. The roof looked pretty much crushed.

"Oh, Aunt Libby!" Maisey said. She and Tyler were standing in the doorway behind me, still wrapped in the blanket. "Your car is soooo totaled!"

"C'mon," I said. "We need to shut the door. It may be awhile before they get the power back on. We don't want to the house to cool down."

"Good thing you have the fireplace," Tyler said.

I shook my head. "The chimney hasn't been cleaned or inspected. We can't use it. But fortunately, it's not below freezing out there. We'll be fine." I paused. "There's nothing we can do until morning. I'm going back to bed."

"Should I call the power company?" Maisey asked.

"Yeah, sure. But don't spend too much time on the phone with them. Save your battery."

I climbed back into bed.

I was thinking about the little man.

If I were you, I'd move the car, Libby.

I lay there, listening to tree limbs crack, and wondering how the hell a hallucination had known that a tree limb was going to break off and fall on one particular spot—my car—nine hours in the future.

Eleven

When I woke again it was light, but it still wasn't quiet. Tree limbs were still snapping under the weight of ice.

I rolled out of bed, shivering.

I checked a light switch.

Nothing.

I put on my robe and headed downstairs.

"Morning, Aunt Libby. Guess what Tyler's doing? Making coffee!"

If anything could have made me change my mind about my two unexpected houseguests, those last words came pretty close. "How's he doing that?"

"Gas grill," Maisey said proudly.

"Ah." I'd forgotten but yeah, an old gas grill had come with the house, along with a lot of other junk I hadn't had a chance, yet, to clear out. It had been left uncovered, up against the shed, and I'd barely paid attention to it, much less considered trying to run it. It was pretty rusty. "What did he use for water?"

Maisey looked at me like she was asking a dumb question. "What do you mean?"

"Did he use tap water?"

"Well, yeah."

"Okay." I hesitated, wondering how worried I should be. "Look, we need to be careful with using the water. All the water we have, now, is whatever's left in the compression tank in the basement. The pump on the well can't refill it until the power is back on. Once the tank is empty, we're out."

We watched Tyler from the kitchen window. He and the shed and the grill were the only things out there that still had their normal shape. Every plant, bush, tree was disfigured, drooping under the weight of ice, and where the sagging branches had touched the ground, they were fused to it by a shield of ice, pulled by the ice down from the sky and trapped against the Earth.

"There must be an inch of ice, at least. Has the plow gone by?" I asked.

"Not that I've seen."

Tyler came in, carrying the coffeepot, a white enamel stovetop percolator I'd picked up at a garage sale because it was decorative, country chic. Little had I known it might actually come in handy.

Tyler poured coffee into the three mugs lined up on the counter. I bent over to inhale its sharp smell. My glasses fogged, but the warm mug felt incredible in my chilly hands.

Maisey glanced at the fridge. She took milk in her coffee.

"No." I stopped her. "If we keep the door closed, stuff will keep for a few hours, until the power's back on. Otherwise—"

I hesitated again. Was it realistic to think they'd have the power back on in a few hours? Or even within 24?

"Ty," I said. "How much propane is in the tank, you think?"

"Dunno. Half a tank, maybe?"

Another tree branch snapped near the house. We listened to the clatter of ice shards against the ice-clad ground.

"Ty, would you mind walking out to the road to see if the plow's been by to salt the road? Stay away from the trees."

We watched him walk down the driveway. He had trouble keeping his footing.

On the way back he took a little detour and looked at my car.

"There's a power line down across the road," he said when he was inside again. "No sign of a plow."

"I'm calling Paul," I said.

I tried his office landline first. Fast busy signal. But I got through on his cell. "Hi! You got power?"

"You're joking, right?" he said.

It was not the answer I expected. "No."

"The whole area got slammed. Aren't you listening to the radio?" he asked and then, before I could answer, "Aw, Libby, don't tell me. Living out in the middle of East Jeepers and you don't have a radio?"

"Paul, it's the 21ˢᵗ Century. Not 'Little House on the Prairie'."

My voice sounded less jovial than I'd hoped, and I noticed Maisey and Tyler were paying close attention to everything I said.

"I'm sorry, Libby," Paul was saying. "But this is bad. Really bad. State of emergency. People are in a panic. And you—you're too far away for me to—"

Here we go, I thought. He'd wanted me to buy a place in the city. Actually, he probably wanted me to move in with him. But I wasn't ready for that yet.

"I'm *fine*," I said.

Then I remembered my car.

"Well. Except my car."

"What happened to your car?"

"Tree fell on it." My voice, now, definitely didn't sound jovial at all.

"Aw, no. Drivable?"

"I doubt it. But Maisey's car is okay."

"Okay. Good. When they open the roads, Maisey can bring you back to the city."

So the roads were closed. Of course. It was a state of emergency. The authorities would need to close the roads.

I hated to admit it, but Paul did have a point about the radio.

"You've got a fireplace there, right? So you can keep yourself warm?"

"Yeah," I lied. "And there's firewood stacked by the shed. And a gas grill. We had coffee this morning."

"Okay." He sighed. "Better save your cell."

"Yeah."

"Sorry I snapped at you, Lib. I'm a little stressed. I've got a ton of crap to do at work and I've only got about an hour's worth of charge left on my effing laptop."

"They'll get this sorted out by tomorrow."

Famous last words.

I looked at Maisey and Tyler. "Roads are all closed. I'm going to put on something warmer. And hey—don't flush the toilets. We may need to dip the water out of the tanks. It's drinkable."

Maisey made a face, but Tyler said, "Sure, man, it's like, ultimate survivor mode. Cool."

Twelve

Being without power can be kind of fun for a couple of hours. With the right attitude, it can be an adventure when it lasts for a day.

We got creative. After the freezer began to melt, we moved our perishables into a big cooler and gathered ice to keep it cold. We cooked on the gas grill. We played cards and checkers, and Maisey borrowed one of my paperbacks to read.

By day three, it started to get old.

The house smelled like it had before I'd moved in—that dank, chilly, unlived-in smell empty houses have because the heat isn't on and the windows are all closed. It was eerily quiet, too. No refrigerator hum. No furnace fan. Nothing, except the occasional creak as the foundation shifted and settled.

Outside, it warmed up into the forties. The ice began sliding off the trees and their branches, released from the weight, were trying to spring back. But they didn't look right. Nothing looked right, nothing looked normal. So many limbs had been snapped, or torn off, or left bent, disfigured. It looked like someone had rolled a giant bowling ball over everything in sight.

Maisey and Tyler decided they'd had enough. They were heading to the city. Maisey had found a friend who was home from college on spring break, and her parents were one of the few lucky ones who hadn't lost power. "We'll be able to take hot showers!" Maisey grinned. "You should come, too, Aunt Libby. They said it's fine."

I shook my head. I'm uncomfortable around strangers. The thought of popping up on the doorstep of someone I'd never met? No, thanks.

And this couldn't possibly last much longer, could it?

Paul had a different idea. He thought I should catch a ride with Maisey and Tyler and have them drop me at Cal4. That's where he was now. The office park's power had come on the day before, so now he was camped there along with a handful of other staffers.

"I'm eating Lean Cuisine," he'd said, mumbling through a mouthful. "Piping hot."

"Does Barb know?" Barb, one of the labbies, kept a stash of Lean Cuisine in the office freezer.

"She's stuck in Sodus. She won't mind. So what do you say? I'd feel better if you were here."

But I didn't want to go.

I didn't want to leave my place. I didn't dislike my former co-workers, not at all. But I didn't want to live with a bunch of them twenty-four hours a day.

And this couldn't last much longer, right?

Plus what if Robbie saw me hanging around? You could never tell with Robbie. If he saw me, he might get the bright idea to start talking about the fate of *Skin Tones*.

Out of sight, out of mind. My little freelance gig was definitely safer that way.

"You know the forecast, right?" Paul said. "It's going to get cold again."

So what? I'd dress in layers. "I'm fine. I have food and I won't get bored. I have a ton of books."

I helped Maisy and Tyler carry their stuff to Maisey's car and watched as Tyler used a piece of garden hose he'd found somewhere to siphon off the gas from my tank into hers.

"We'll pay you back for the gas," Maisey said.

"Be careful," I called out as they got into the car. "If you see any downed power lines, turn back. You can live another day without showers."

Maisey grinned and waved and they were gone.

🌱 🌱 🌱

I took stock of my food supply. We'd cleaned out the cooler, which was just as well, since the ice had all melted. But I had some dried beans. Lots of calories in dried beans. I had matches to light the stove. I could boil water from the creek up the road. And I had about half a five-pound bag of carrots.

Between that and my canned food I could last for a long time, yet. Right?

And, like I'd told Paul, I had a ton of books. I was enjoying that a lot, actually. I was going back and forth between my books on organic farming and my novels. Paperbacks, picked up at garage sales. Historical fiction, mostly. And thanks to the power outage I'd finally gotten around to arranging them on my living room bookshelf. They were now all alphabetical by author.

Order, imposed.

And as bad as things were, the power would come back on any minute now.

My only regret was that I hadn't printed out the forms I needed to submit to apply for my organic certification. They were all online.

But a few days' delay in submitting the paperwork wouldn't matter too much. Hopefully.

The power was bound to come on soon, surely.

I thought about going for a walk.

But that reminded me about the little man.

Where had he sheltered during the ice storm?

Was he okay?

I quickly shoved that treasonous thought from my head.

Little man. Right.

Cuckoo, cuckoo.

If I were you, I'd move my car.

Had I taken his advice, my car would still be okay.

What was cuckoo, then? Hearing the voice?

Or not listening to it?

ψ ψ ψ

Somebody was banging on my door.

I'd piled all the blankets I owned onto my bed and had burrowed under them. It took me a few minutes to burrow out again, so by the time I got to the door, he was walking back down the driveway.

It was Posted Sign Guy.

Walking with Bo.

He didn't hear me open the door. Bo did, though, and, when the dog stopped and looked back at my house, Posted Sign Guy did, too.

He walked back up my drive.

"So. You're still here," he said.

"Where else would I be?"

He pointed his thumb toward my Toyota. "Bad luck with your car."

"Yeah."

"Where's your daughter?"

I shrugged. "She's not my daughter. She went to a friend's."

"She left you?"

I shrugged again.

"Why didn't you go, too?"

"Why should I?"

He shook his head. "You don't have a woodstove, do you?"

I didn't have to answer. I was bundled into enough clothes that I could have passed for a caterpillar. A big fat caterpillar with glasses and unkempt hair frothing down from my Polartec cap.

He frowned. "You do know it's supposed to get down into the teens tonight?"

"I'll be fine."

I seemed to be arguing that point a little too often lately.

"Look. You'd better come to my place. I've got heat."

"I don't even know who you are. But thanks for the offer."

He looked like he might try to argue, but he didn't.

"Suit yourself."

He turned north at the end of her drive. Not toward his property.

He was heading up the road toward the next house. He was checking on all the neighbors.

I went back to my bedroom.

Okay. So it was going to fall into the teens. That was—that was cold. People-dying-of-hypothermia cold.

I blew a faint plume of breath into the air and pulled my hat more snugly over my head.

Surely being bundled up in fifty layers and my head inside a Polartec hat would be enough.

Right?

And okay, maybe it hadn't been so smart to stay here instead of catching a ride to Rochester with Maisey.

It was time to swallow my pride.

I'd call Paul. Tell him to come fetch me.

I swiped my cell.

Nothing happened.

I pressed the power button.

Oh, no.

I told myself to calm down. The phone had over 30 percent battery the last time I'd used it. No way could it be dead.

I held the power button down for longer. Still nothing.

And my scientist's brain knew the truth.

It was the cold.

The cold had sucked the last juice from my phone's poor old battery.

Deep breaths. Deep breaths. No need to panic.

I'd made my decision. I was going to be fine. Just like I'd been saying.

I crawled back under my covers, covering everything except my nose.

Damn, it was cold.

$$\psi \quad \psi \quad \psi$$

Banging on the door again.

I got up. More quickly this time.

It was Posted Sign Guy, again. "The name's Trevor Dean Milbrant." He held out his hand. "I go by Dean."

"Libby Samson," I said, shaking his hand. "Let me get my boots."

A few minutes later we walked together up the road.

We didn't talk.

He wasn't a talker.

We reached his driveway.

It was long and forested on both sides, and clogged with fallen limbs and, in places, entire trees, some with trunks bigger around than me. Only when we had almost reached his cabin, I saw that he'd started clearing it. Bright piles of sawdust dotted the ground where he'd been cutting up fallen trees.

Thirteen

"Oh gawd." It slipped out without my intending it to. "*Heat.*"

I'd never been in a place heated with wood before, so it was my first time experiencing wood stove heat, which is real heat. Blast you in the face when you first step inside heat, and then warm-you-to-your bones heat as you peel off your outerwear.

I slipped off my jacket and hung it on the coat rack by the door.

And then I remembered. Underneath the jacket and the two sweaters and the sweatshirt and the sweatpants? Flannel pajamas. And yep, that means the gal was braless.

"Everything okay?" Dean asked.

I felt my face get warm. "I just realized—I'm, uh, in my PJs."

He rolled his eyes. "And me, without a tux."

I left the sweatshirt on. I could take being a bit overly warm.

"Hungry?" he said.

I stifled another "oh, gawd," and nodded instead. "I could eat."

He ladled something into a bowl from a pot on top of the wood stove. Steam rose from the bowl as he walked over to me. "Hope you like venison."

I'd never had venison. "Sure. Love it."

🌱 🌱 🌱

Bo slept on the rug by the couch. I heard his snuffy breathing every time I woke in the night, and sometimes he woke too and scratched himself, or got up and circled around and then lay back down again.

I don't sleep well in strange places. And Dean's house counted as a strange place. A log cabin, perfumed by wood smoke. Although the inside walls had been planed, they were rough, and the dim light coming from the little glass panel on the front of the wood stove cast rough, wavering shadows across everything in the room.

And no sooner was I able to get to sleep than I was startled awake by a clanking noise.

I half-rose from the couch.

Dean was bending down in front of the stove, putting another log on.

I lowered myself back down.

At least lying awake gave me a chance to savor being warm. All over warm.

And then the next morning, another luxury. Dean had a back-up well with a hand pump in the front yard. After days of conserving water, I finally got to wash my hair. He even offered to warm some water for me, but I said no. A mistake, I realized a few minutes later. The water from the pump was so cold it practically knocked the wind out of me when it sluiced down over my head.

I came back indoors, and he took the towel from me and handed me a comb.

I sat by the stove while my hair dried.

"I should check on my house," I said when I was warm again.

"Bring your cell phone back with you, if you want to charge it," he said.

I tilted my head in surprise. "How?" I asked.

"I have a generator. I run it a couple hours a day. Got a freezer full of venison."

"Oh wow."

"Oh, and when you get to your place? Don't be surprised if your pipes have burst."

So I wasn't.

⚜ ⚜ ⚜

My house was bitterly cold.

I shut off the water valve to the house. Then I went to the second floor and shivered as I changed, as quickly as I could, into clean clothes—flannel shirt and sweater and jeans. I packed a duffel bag with toiletries and a clean pair of pajamas and a pile of books.

When I got back to Dean's, I heard a generator motor running from somewhere behind the cabin.

Dean was in his recliner by the woodstove, listening to his radio.

I dropped my duffel on the floor.

He didn't look up.

I found an outlet in the kitchen and plugged in my phone, then took a seat on the couch. He had the radio tuned to a local talk station, and the DJs were in full hunker-down mode, relaying information about shelters, passing along tips, taking calls from people with stories to tell.

And as I listened, the enormity of what had happened started to sink in. There were no generators left in the stores, no chainsaws, precious little bottled water. The local power companies were overwhelmed, and although dozens of out-of-state utilities were mobilizing crews to come in and help, it was going to take time—weeks, perhaps—before everyone's power was restored.

Dean stood up and switched off the radio.

He didn't say anything or look at me.

He put on his jacket.

Bo followed him outside.

I went to the window.

Man and dog were starting down the driveway.

Dean was carrying a chainsaw.

He disappeared behind the trees, and a moment later I heard the growl of the chainsaw motor.

I pulled a sweatshirt over my head and went outside.

I stood watching him for a moment.

Then I circled around a limb he was cutting and went to work dragging the smaller stuff off the driveway. And, when he finished cutting a bigger limb, I helped him carry and stack the pieces.

It was slow going. But faster, I guessed, than if he'd been working alone.

"Won't be buying firewood this fall," he said to me at one point.

And a little later, "I'm gonna go shut the generator off. Think your cell has enough charge for now?"

But, other than that, we didn't speak.

I wondered if it was because there was no point in trying to talk over the noise of the chainsaw or because he was so focused.

When you're handling a chainsaw, it's probably a good idea to forgo chitchat and pay attention to what you're doing.

We quit around dusk.

By then I was so exhausted and hungry I wouldn't have wanted to chitchat even if he'd been a gabber.

My hands were scratched and aching.

My knees felt wobbly.

And we still hadn't reached the road. We'd been working for hours and there was still more driveway to go.

We went back to the cabin.

I unplugged my cell and dialed Paul's.

"Libby! What in the hell! Where have you been? I've been trying to reach you since yesterday!"

"My battery died. I'm okay."

"You should have come up with Maisey. You should have—I was all set to drive down there myself, you know. I've been sick with worry—aw, shit, hang on a second."

I heard voices, Paul's and someone else's, not distinct enough to make out what they were saying.

"Libby? You still there?"

"Yeah, I'm here. But I can't talk long, I'm only at 30 percent. I'm staying with a neighbor."

"What neighbor?"

"Dean, he's—"

"Is that where you are now? Hold on a sec. We've got some shit going on—"

"Are you still sleeping at the office?"

"Yeah," he said. "And as long as we're all here everybody's working late—this better be worth it. Hang on, hang on—"

Clunking noises, then, "Hey, Randy," Paul said to someone in the room with him, "Slow down, you brought the wrong thing. No. Not those. The mock-ups—the agency dropped off mock-ups this morning. Well, they said they were going to drop them off. Aren't they here? Aw, for—hang on. Libby, can I call you back?"

"Tomorrow, Paul, it's fine. I'm fine. I'll be able to get some more charge tomorrow."

"Aw, look, Libby, I'll come and get you. I'll come tonight. We'd only need to stay here at the office for another day or two. They'll have the power back on at my place by Friday at the latest. Where did you say you are?"

"Paul, there's no need. I'm fine."

He'd begun talking to someone else again. "They're not here? Did you call them? You need to call them. I'm supposed to have them for Josh tomorrow at our nine o'clock—Libby? You sure you're okay?"

"I'm sure."

"Okay. If you're sure you're okay. I love you, babe."

"I love you, too."

Dinner was stew, again, warmed on the top of the woodstove.

I didn't have any trouble sleeping that night.

Fourteen

The next morning, after breakfast, Dean handed me a pair of work gloves.

They were huge on me. But plenty welcome for my sore hands. And we made it to the road that afternoon.

I followed Dean back down the driveway to the cabin.

He'd taken his jacket off, and the back of his shirt was split down the middle by a dark streak of sweat.

Inside, I took off my sweatshirt and picked up my paperback from where I'd left it on the couch.

I expected to hear Dean come in as well, but he didn't, and after a few minutes I got back up and went to the window.

He was loading his chainsaw and a couple plastic gas cans into the back of his truck.

He got in and drove off.

I sat, looking at the words on my book, but not reading.

Wallace, my ex, had been what they call a "good communicator." He'd always told me where he was going, when he'd be back. If he was going to be late, he'd call and let me know. And then, if I asked him how his day had gone, he always had some new story to share. Usually a funny one.

The bright hard sanity of Wallace's stories had comforted me. It had made it easy to pretend I believed his lies.

He'd been a talker, a born salesman.

A charmer.

The kind of man who'd come home from a night with a girlfriend bearing jewelry for his wife.

And I let him do it.

A wave of rage washed over me.

Wallace.

But no, it wasn't Wallace I was angry at.

It was me.

I did the best I could do.

I stood up and looked out the window, down the driveway.

I knew, somehow, exactly where Dean had gone. He was driving around with that chainsaw, maybe to the neighbors', maybe to a friend's, maybe to a stranger's, and when he found someone who needed help, he was doing whatever he could.

And how odd was that? Dean hadn't said a word, yet I knew more about where he was headed than I'd known the whereabouts of my own husband.

Maybe what matters most when two people communicate is what they don't say. The thought had never occurred to me before, and I stood up, because I didn't like the way that idea made me feel.

One wall of the cabin's living room was practically all books. I began scanning the titles. A lot of history books. A few novels.

A hunk of glass obsidian the size of a football served as one bookend.

Another row of books was held in place by a lidded pitcher that looked Mideastern in design and pretty old. It was copper but had long since acquired a dull greenish patina.

I found myself standing at the foot of the ladder to the loft.

I really shouldn't...

I stepped on the first rung.

Just a peek...

I climbed to the top of the ladder and stood on the rung, scanning the room. There was a platform bed with a Shaker headboard. King-sized. No surprise, the guy had to be six-six.

And then I saw that there was a desk in the corner. With a computer.

I admit, that surprised me a bit.

For a moment I considered climbing the rest of the way into the loft. The impulse grabbed me to climb up, open the desk drawers, peek inside. Find out more about my peculiar neighbor.

I stopped myself.

The man had given me food and a warm place to stay. And I was considering *snooping*?

I backed hastily down the ladder and returned to my book.

But I still couldn't read. I just sat there, staring at the open page.

ॶ ॶ ॶ

The next morning, for the first time, I got up before Dean.

And I knew what to do, from watching him do it: first, light the gas stove (matches in the cupboard above the sink), scramble six eggs in the cast iron pan, light the broiler to brown the toast.

I heard the ladder creak as he climbed down from the loft.

He stood, watching me for a moment, in the kitchen doorway.

"You need to charge your cell?" he said, and I nodded. A moment later I heard the generator come back on.

We ate in the living room, near the woodstove.

My duffel bag on the floor next to the couch was gaping open, and when he passed it to take his plate back to the kitchen, he noticed it and did a little double take. "You're welcome to borrow books," he said.

"I'm good." My face felt suddenly warm, for some reason. The heat from the woodstove, probably.

A moment later I watched him hoist his chainsaw into the back of the truck, open the passenger side for Bo, and drive off again.

I opened one of my paperbacks.

ॶ ॶ ॶ

It was starting to get dark when he got back.

He came into the cabin and climbed up to the loft, and a few minutes later passed me again, this time carrying a towel.

By leaning forward from where I was sitting on the couch, I could see him at the water pump in the front yard.

He started to strip.

I leaned back again—quickly—and opened my novel. And, when he returned a few minutes later and walked past me again, I kept my head down and eyes fastened on the pages of my book.

Fifteen

Saturday morning.

Still no power.

Bo had learned that if he came over and stood by the couch while I was reading, and laid his head in my lap, I'd scratch his neck. There was a place under his collar that he adored having scratched, and he'd stand there for as long as I was willing to keep at it, so relaxed and blissed out that his back would sway slightly from the movement of my hand.

I'd just reached the place in my novel where the heroine has to escape from the hold of a merchant ship, so I didn't notice at first that Dean was standing inside the front door.

But then, suddenly, I was aware of him.

I wondered how long he'd been standing there.

It was because of Bo. He was watching Bo, how he had his head in my lap.

I didn't say anything. I was becoming used to not speaking. And it would have sounded strange, my voice rattling on, and what if Dean didn't answer?

I'd feel like a dope.

So I turned my attention back to my book, still scratching Bo's bliss spot.

I heard the door swing shut as Dean went back outdoors.

ꙮ ꙮ ꙮ

He stewed a chicken for dinner that night.

I watched him work, then went in and filled my plate when I saw him fill his.

We ate, as usual, near the woodstove.

Then, about midway through the meal, he suddenly set his fork down. "You probably think I'm not very friendly."

I dipped my fork into the well of melted butter that had formed on top of my mashed potatoes and dragged the tines to channel the butter. "You've been more than nice," I said. "I don't expect to be entertained."

"I appreciate you chipping in. On the driveway. And bringing firewood in. And helping with the dishes."

"It's the least I can do."

"I'm out of practice."

For a second, I wasn't sure what he meant. Out of practice doing dishes? Then I realized he was referring to being sociable. Or entertaining people, maybe.

But I didn't really know how to answer that, so I ate a bite of potato instead.

After dinner he went to the kitchen and I stood up, scanning his books, wondering if I dared take him up on his offer and borrow something. His novels were all hard covers. I pulled one down, opened to the first page, and found myself being drawn in by the words.

I didn't notice he'd come back into the living room.

"Whine?" he asked.

I started. "Excuse me?"

"Glass of wine?"

I realized he was holding a bottle and two wine glasses. But, instead of answering, I kind of stood there like an idiot. Because one of the reasons this had worked, until now—one of the reasons I hadn't said to Paul, yes, please, come down, get me, I want to stay with you—was precisely because Dean kept a good distance. In every meaning of the term.

I looked away, feeling nervous all of a sudden.

"It's not poison," he said, a trace of irritation in his voice. "Quite the opposite. It's a very drinkable Burgundy."

"No. No, thanks. I don't care for any. Thanks."

He looked, for a split second, like he might say something, but then he shrugged and took the bottle back to the kitchen.

I heard a cork squeak and then pop as he pulled it from the bottle, and a minute later he sat down in the leather recliner opposite me, swirled the wine, smelled it, and took a sip.

He smiled slightly, stroking his beard. "Don't say I didn't tell you. It's very nice."

I looked back down at my book. The guy was a misanthropic, pick-up driving woodchuck living alone in a log cabin. With a wall of books. And a state-of-the-art computer.

And—a wine cellar?

From the corner of my eye I saw him pull the lever on the side of the recliner and extend the footrest and put his feet up.

He was wearing slippers. Leather, moccasin-style. And something about the slippers. He didn't look like a person with ulterior motives.

"Okay," I said. "I'll take a glass."

In a few minutes it would be too dark to read, anyway.

"Help yourself."

I went into the kitchen. He'd left the second glass next to the bottle on the counter.

ψ ψ ψ

"I really appreciate you—taking me in this way."

"No problem," he said.

There was nothing, really, to talk about. It wasn't like I felt comfortable jumping in with a bunch of chitchat: so what did you pay for this place, how long have you had Bo, and hey do you have any family?

Something about this, the way he lived. That habit of privacy he kept wound around himself, his thoughts. It was like those No Trespassing signs all over again.

But then he cleared his throat. "It's good, isn't it?"

"Sorry?"

"The wine."

"Yes. Very good."

He nodded. "Good."

I took another sip.

He uncrossed and recrossed his legs. "Can I ask you something?"

I looked up at him, a bit shocked. He'd actually asked a question?

He must have taken my non-answer to mean yes. "Why did you buy that place?" he said. "The Stowe Place?"

"I'm going to farm it."

"Oh, really?" He sounded skeptical.

"Yes, really," I said, feeling suddenly a bit defensive. What was he implying? That a woman couldn't run a farm?

"It won't grow anything. It's been worked to death."

Oh.

I thought about the way the fields looked. Bare and brown. The tired, thin topsoil. But I knew exactly how to fix that. Science knew exactly how to fix that. "I'm aware of the condition of the soil," I said quietly. "I'm going to restore it. I'm going to bring it back."

And I thought about the little man.

I wondered, suddenly, *Was it possible that Dean had seen him?* This quiet man who lived out here by himself in the middle of the woods?

And did I dare to ask?

But I couldn't. Of course, I couldn't.

I pushed the thought back out of my mind.

ᗯ ᗯ ᗯ

He'd moved to the floor and was scratching Bo's head.

Since the cabin was surrounded by forest, dusk passed quickly into night, and the room was now dark save for the wavering firelight. I'd noticed a couple of oil lamps, one on his kitchen counter, another on the stand beside the couch, but Dean had never lit them. He didn't need to, even in the middle of the night when the firelight was low. He moved around the place in the dark like someone who had been living somewhere for a long time.

I took another sip of wine.

Bo appreciated the attention he was getting and sighed heavily with pleasure.

I'd begun to feel more relaxed, helped along by the wine.

And Dean had asked me about why I'd bought my farm. So asking him about his place was fair game now, right?

I shifted my weight. "So—how about you. Have you lived here a long time?"

I didn't entirely expect him to answer, but he did. "Seven years."

"Did you build it?"

He nodded.

"I've never seen a log cabin quite like it before."

"Most of them are kits."

"Kits?"

"Companies sell plans and the logs. You hire a contractor who puts them up for you."

"This one's not a kit?"

"No."

"It's almost gothic-looking." I tilted my head back. The ceiling's high peak was nearly invisible in the dark.

"I like the lines. I lived out west for a long time. The lines remind me of the mountains."

"What mountains?"

"A lot of different mountains."

Okay. Apparently, some subjects were off-limits.

On the other hand, Dean hadn't lied about the wine. It was very drinkable, and a glassful later, as I sank into that buzzy feeling where talk becomes easier, I decided to try again. "So, okay." I gestured with my wine glass around the room. "You built a house that reminds you of various mountains. But you could have built it anywhere. So why here? Why live like this?"

"So I'll be ready if there's an ice storm."

I tucked my feet up under myself on the couch. "Right. Only until now, there hasn't been an ice storm like this in our lifetimes, and we'll never see one again." I glanced at him, wondering how far I could push. "So there has to be more to it than that." I took another sip of wine. "Also, not answering only makes me curiouser."

"Curiouser isn't a word."

He stood up and put another log in the stove. I watched as he pushed the log into place with the poker iron.

Sparks chased each other toward the flue.

I couldn't see his face well enough to tell if I'd crossed a line with my questions. But when he sat back down, he answered. Sort of. "I like the quiet. People have forgotten how to be quiet."

They sure have.

I looked down at Bo.

The dog had fallen asleep on the rug.

What a relief it would be, if someone besides me had seen the little man...

"Dean?" I said.

He nodded.

I took a deep breath.

No turning back, now.

"I'd like to ask you—I mean—not 'ask' exactly." I cleared my throat. "It's about my property. Kind of."

"Shoot."

I took another deep breath. "I haven't mentioned this to anyone else."

If my words piqued his curiosity, he didn't show it.

"I've seen something—peculiar. A couple of times. In the field, behind my house."

He nodded, as if seeing peculiar things was a perfectly normal topic of conversation.

"A person," I continued. "I mean, sort of a person. Not a human."

I watched his expression, trying to discern his response, but the light from the fire was dim, flickering. His face was partially in shadow.

But he didn't seem put off, as far as I could tell. So I kept going. "He was about this tall." I held my hand a couple of feet above the floor. "And he spoke to me."

Dean nodded again.

"So—have you—have you ever seen it?"

My voice sounded shaky in my ears, and it dawned on me as I spoke how important it was, to hear his answer. And how very much I was hoping the answer would be yes.

But he shook his head. "No."

I slumped back onto the couch. "You think I'm crazy," I muttered. "I shouldn't have told you."

"Kind of late for that."

I stole a quick look at him. His brown eyes were studying me. Sizing me up.

"So what happened?" he asked.

At least he wasn't laughing.

"It's actually happened more than once." My hands were trembling, so I set my wine glass on the table at the end of the couch. I wasn't sure I could trust myself not to spill it. "And he's spoken to me. I don't remember the first time very well except that he seemed—I guess, sort of offended. I mean, I was freaked out. I didn't exactly clap him on the back and invite him home for dinner."

"Can't say as I blame you."

"But here's the thing." I leaned forward. "The last time I saw him? It was the day of the ice storm."

I paused.

Tears began to well up in my eyes. "Dean, he told me to move my car."

A log popped in the woodstove and in the sudden flare of light I saw his face.

He was frowning. "No kidding," he said thoughtfully.

"It was Tuesday evening," I said. "It was about 6:30. He said, 'If I were you, Libby, I'd move my car.' That's what he said."

The flare died down and it was again too dark to see Dean's eyes.

"I'm telling the truth." I passed my sleeve over my face to wipe my eyes. "It's—I'm not happy about this." I shook my head. "I'm a biologist. A scientist. Things like this? They don't happen. I don't know what I'm going to do. I don't want to go for walks any more. I'm freaking out. I'm—scared."

There.

I'd done it. I'd told someone.

But was it a good idea?

I didn't know this man. Not at all. What if he told someone? Nothing could be worse than that. Nothing. For people to know that I was some kind of freak, having some kind of mental breakdown.

"You won't tell anyone, right?" I whispered.

"I won't tell anyone."

My eyes welled tears again, and I realized that I'd been fighting to hold them back. And not just that evening. I'd been fighting to hold them back since I'd stood on my porch and shone the flashlight beam on my car and realized that freaky little creature that was apparently haunting my property was somehow able to predict the future. "You're sure you haven't seen it?" I said in a quavery voice. "You haven't seen the little man?"

He didn't answer.

He stood up, left the room, returned with a box of tissues, and sat on the couch next to me while I pulled a tissue from the box.

I blew my nose.

He settled himself against the back of the couch. "Let's take a look at this head on, okay?"

"Okay." I wadded the tissue into a ball in my fist.

"First off. Why does it scare you? Has he threatened you?"

"No."

"Did he have horns?"

"Horns?"

"You know, devil horns." He put the tissue box on his lap and made horns on his head with his index fingers. "Like this." He wiggled them.

"That's not funny."

"You're smiling."

"To be polite."

"Well, did he? Have horns?"

"No. Of course not."

And suddenly he reached out.

He touched the back of my head.

Stroked my hair.

My eyes met his.

And then he was kissing me. A long, slow, delicious kiss. A dizzying kiss.

And for a moment I let it happen. I let the deliciousness and the dizziness grab me and carry me and—

And then I realized what I was doing.

I jumped up. "I—I can't."

I felt giddy from standing up so fast.

"I'm got a—I'm in a—a Paul."

"You're in a what?"

My cheeks went from flushed to broiling hot. "I'm in a relationship."

He looked away. "Ah. I'm sorry."

"No, don't be. It's a good relationship."

He laughed. Forced it a bit, maybe. "I'm sure it is." He got up. "Here. You can have your seat back."

I realized I was rubbing the space over my breastbone and stopped myself. "It's okay," I said. "I mean—it's okay that you—I just don't want you to think—"

He stepped over Bo, waking him, and the dog raised his head to watch Dean for a second before flopping his head back down again with a big doggy sigh.

Dean picked up his glass from where he'd left it by his chair. It had a finger of wine or so left in the bottom, and he tipped it back and drained it. Then he looked at me. "As far as your little man," he said, "whatever it was, it sounds to me like he was trying to help you."

Help me?

"I suppose that's true," I said slowly, thinking in the back of my mind, *Libby. You're a scientist. Trained to look at the facts. And wasn't it a fact, that the man's words were pretty good advice?*

"So, as far as I can see, maybe you could just, you know, be curiouser. Instead of scared. And see what happens."

"Curiouser isn't a word," I said.

We stood for a moment, facing each other.

Not talking.

I wondered if he wanted to kiss me again.

I pushed the thought away.

"Goodnight," he said, and he turned and climbed the ladder to the loft.

Sixteen

Exactly six days after the kiss—not that I was counting—Dean and I were eating breakfast when his refrigerator suddenly hummed back to life.

The power.

It was back on.

Our eyes met, but I quickly looked back down. Pretending I was deeply interested in my scrambled eggs.

And a little while later I was hiking back up the road to my house, duffel bag over my shoulder. Telling myself that this was all good. That everything was finally back to my new normal. That the kiss was a distant memory, pushed completely out of my mind.

And I had so much to do. So many people were in the same boat as me, digging out from fallen trees and property damage. It took me days to land a plumber to fix my broken water pipe, and even longer to find a tree guy to clear the limb that had crushed my car (and yes, Dean had offered to do it, but I politely declined—I was beholden enough to him already). The tow truck showed up finally and took my car away, and I put a sticky note on my computer screen to call the insurance adjuster back. I needed to get the claim settled ASAP, because I was driving a rental now, and the cost of that wasn't covered by my insurance.

And then Maisey and Tyler moved back in. And, surprisingly, I didn't mind having them around. Their chatter didn't bother me as much as I would have thought. It was kind of pleasant, actually.

Oh, I also started my organic certification paperwork, finally, and set up a May date for my on-site. That was a little later than I'd originally planned, but fingers crossed, everything would fall into place before I harvested my first crop. Which would be greens of some kind, because greens grow from seed to harvest pretty fast. They're one of the first market crops in the Northeast. And I needed something that would be ready to harvest sooner rather than later. Between the deductible on my house and car insurance, and the cost of the rental car, my savings account was dwindling faster than I'd planned.

Then Paul texted me on a Saturday morning that he had some news about *Skin Tones,* and he'd tell me all about it at dinner.

That made me a bit nervous. But I told myself it would be fine, there was nothing in his text to suggest Cal4 was pulling the plug on the thing, and around three I showered and blew dry my hair so that it looked halfway tamed and drove to Rochester.

And then I was sitting across from him and a big platter of poutine. Which, if you've never seen poutine, is french fries topped with gravy and melted cheese.

"Can we do Thai next time?" I said.

"Yeah, why not."

I stuck a straw in my glass of ice water and took a sip. "So what's the news on *Skin Tones*? You liked the last issue, right?"

"Oh yeah." He made a scoop out of a row of french fries and scooped up a glob of melted cheese. The scoop was almost too big for his mouth, but not quite.

I waited while he chewed and swallowed.

"We want to keep the format," he said. "And the name. In fact, the only change we want is that instead of stories about sick people getting better, it'll be stories about old—I mean, about differently-aged people finding ways to feel better about themselves."

I sighed. But it was a quiet sigh. Because, honestly, I'd pretty much expected this. And since Paul was, technically, my boss on *Skin Tones*—off with the boyfriend hat, on with the boss's—I had to be professional. "Sounds good, Paul," I said. "Does Dormet have the contacts for customers? People I can interview?"

"Yep. They have a kick-ass customer database." He angled another cluster of French Fries into his mouth with one hand, and, when one started to fall, he caught it with the other hand just before it hit his plate.

The server slid our entrées onto the table.

"You should be happy about this, you know," he said. "I was kind of worried they'd make it a glorified sales letter. But they got it. The whole concept. That it's marketing but instead of a hard sales pitch it's all about stories from customers who love our stuff and are seeing results from using it."

I was happy about it. Only mostly, I was happy that they weren't going to get rid of it. "Thanks for doing this," I said to make sure he would know that I truly was grateful.

"Yeah," he said, and began sawing at his steak. "So how d'ya like the rental car?"

"It's fine," I said. "It's not a Toyota."

"Pretty crazy, your car getting smushed like that. At least you didn't owe anything on it."

"Yes, I did," I said. "I had two payments left."

"That's nothing."

Not to you, maybe, I thought.

But it was my car and I loved it and it had almost been paid off.

⚜ ⚜ ⚜

I'd met Paul at his condo, and we'd talked about maybe going to a club after dinner. But I felt tired after the meal and begged off.

He walked me to my car.

"I don't like you living so far away," he said, wrapping his arms around me.

My mind was wandering. I was thinking about the next issue of *Skin Tones*, and about all that organic certification paperwork...

And about the little man.

I'd been wondering if I should tell Paul, that night, about the little man. After all, it was kind of a big deal, and I'd already told one person, and Paul was my boyfriend.

But for some reason, I couldn't quite figure out how to broach the subject. Not over dinner, not during dessert, and certainly not now, as his hands wandered down the small of my back.

My forehead was starting to throb. Maybe the meal hadn't agreed with me.

"I hate to say this," I said, pulling away, "but I'm not feeling that great. I should get going."

"It's too much for you, dealing with that place all by yourself."

I shook my head. "I'm fine. I'm getting caught up."

I hated to leave, in a way. But I was also glad to be in my rental car, alone again with my thoughts. There was no traffic on the highway once I got south of the city, so I put it into cruise control and switched on the radio.

A moment later, I switched the sound back off.

I was thinking, again, about the little man. About what Dean had said. About how maybe I needed to become curiouser.

Okay, then.

Fine.

I was going to face this thing. I was going to march out there, onto my land, and find that little man. On purpose, this time.

I'd be a scientist. I'd gather more data, and when I had more data, I'd be able to talk to Paul about it.

I reached up and rubbed my forehead, feeling the tension ease and the headache start to lift.

ψ ψ ψ

I spent the next day keeping myself as busy as I could.

The certification paperwork was pretty involved. I had to draw up maps to show where I was going to plant and how the adjacent land was being used. I had to answer questions about whether my land might get hit by industrial run-off or herbicide drift from crop dusters. I had to document where I was buying seed and what sort of fertilizer and pest control I planned to use.

And then I noticed the dust in the living room and ran the vacuum cleaner.

I pulled some weeds that had sprouted by the front stoop.

I decided to make a meatloaf for dinner.

Annoyingly, when I got ready to chop an onion, my favorite kitchen knife was missing from its spot in the drawer.

I hunted around for a few minutes. It wasn't in the drainboard or in any of the other drawers.

Damn it.

Maisey and Tyler. They'd used the knife and stuck it somewhere.

I finally gave up and chopped the onions with my least-favorite kitchen knife, but maybe I was nervous about my plans for later. Or maybe I was just generally in a bad mood. Because I was still grumbling to myself about the knife when I heard Maisey's car pull into the driveway.

"Guys, where did you put my knife?" I said accusingly as the two of them came through the door.

"Is that dinner? It smells great," Maisey said. "What knife?"

"The one with the blue handle." I pointed to the drawer. "It belongs there. In the knife block."

"I haven't used that knife," Maisey said.

She'd noticed how annoyed I was, and I felt a little twinge of guilt. She looked uneasy.

Tyler, meanwhile, had come into the kitchen and I heard the sound of the drawer as he pulled it open.

"This knife?" he said.

I turned around.

He was holding up my blue-handled knife. Okay. So that was really, really strange. "What? Where did you—?" I broke off, unable to understand how he could possibly have found the knife. Not there. Not in that drawer.

But he was pointing, now, at the knife block. "It was right there."

I swallowed.

I wasn't sure what was worse. Realizing that I'd accused Maisey and Tyler of misplacing something when obviously they hadn't?

Or knowing that the knife had most certainly not been in the knife block when I'd looked an hour ago.

"Okay," I managed to say. "My bad. I must have missed it, somehow."

Tyler slid the knife back into the block and shut the drawer.

But after they left the room, I opened the drawer again to see for myself.

The knife was sitting there, in its usual place, blade tucked into the wooden block. There was no way I could have missed that knife when I had opened the drawer earlier.

The screwdriver. Remember how you were sure you'd left the screwdriver on the kitchen counter and—

No! No way.

I was careless, sometimes. That was all. I let myself get distracted and careless. I could be absent-minded. I'd been anxious about my plans to go look for the little man. And instead of focusing on the knife I'd been thinking about the little man, and I'd overlooked it in the drawer.

There was no way that objects in my home could possibly do that. Disappear and then re-appear, again, a little later.

I took the meatloaf out of the oven and called out to Maisey and Tyler that dinner was ready.

But my stomach felt funny.

No way was I going to be able to eat.

🌱 🌱 🌱

I choked down a few bites, in the end.

And then I put the leftovers away, and insisted on doing the dishes even though Maisey offered, and then finally I couldn't put it off any longer.

I put on a sweatshirt and grabbed a blanket.

Maisey and Tyler were curled up on the couch watching TV.

I made a cup of decaf tea and poured it into a Thermos, and told the kids I was going for a walk and would be back in a little bit.

Outside, I grabbed an old boat cushion that was hanging in the shed and made my way up the hill. Through the hedgerow. Over the little ditch.

I sat down and wrapped myself in the blanket.

I waited.

It would serve me right if Dean blabbed my story about seeing a little man all around town, and I ended up labeled That Crazy Lady Up On the Hill.

On the other hand, his response had been helpful, in a way. There was no real reason for me to be afraid, right? On the contrary, I needed to face this thing head-on. Go out and look for that little man and ask him what he wanted of me. And Dean—a man who kept to himself like that—what were the odds that he was a blabberer? Not very high.

I poured a bit of tea into the Thermos cap.

I waited a little longer.

I started to feel silly. Because of course. Now that I'd decided to look for the little man, he was nowhere to be found.

Which might actually prove that he was a hallucination of some kind. Like when you're dreaming and suddenly it occurs to you something bad might happen, and just like that, the dream shifts and begins to turn into a nightmare, the thing you were dimly aware of being afraid of suddenly arises, takes shape. Begins to snarl, to chase you.

And then you wake up and poof. The scary disappears.

Maybe hallucinations work the same way. Maybe I'd woken up.

ψ ψ ψ

The sky was getting darker. When I looked straight up, it had turned a deep royal blue with stars piercing the blue like diamonds.

The air smelled damp and earthy.

I finished the tea.

I was chilly and a bit stiff. But also relieved.

It was over, right? I'd never see that little man again.

I stood up and draped the blanket over my shoulders and picked up the boat cushion.

But I hadn't gone ten paces when a voice said, "So? What do you want?"

Only it wasn't the same voice.

It sounded more female. Kind of reedy, and not as low-pitched as the other's had been.

I looked intently in the direction of the voice.

I couldn't see anything.

My heart was hammering. "Who's there?" I said. "Where are you?"

No answer.

The sky was darker now. A half-moon had risen behind me, and in front, Venus dangled just above the tree line, a bright jewel in the southwest sky.

I plunked my cushion back down on the ground again and sat back down. And I may have gotten a little drowsy. Because all of a sudden, I realized someone was sitting cross-legged on the ground in front of me.

It was a woman, this time.

She was the same size as the little man. Same dark clothing. Leggings, not a dress. But her face was softer, and for some reason I could see her eyes quite well, despite it being so dark.

"You've calmed down a bit," the little woman remarked.

I'd thought a little bit about what I was going to say. Only now, of course, I remembered none of it. "Who are you?" I blurted out, instead.

The little woman was studying my face. "I believe you know the answer to that," she said. "We're what you call 'fairies'."

Fairies? I suppressed a groan.

"But you don't have to think of us that way, if it bothers you so much."

"I don't see as I have much choice."

The little woman stood up. "Things you see with your eyes can sometimes take different shapes. They are representations."

"That doesn't make any sense."

"Doesn't it?"

She didn't exactly disappear. She didn't dissolve or blink off. But I didn't see her walk away, either. It was more like the night became a little bit thicker and I could no longer make out the little person's form enfolded within the darkness.

I sat, waiting to see if the little woman would come back.

But nothing else happened.

I gathered my things back up and returned to the house.

Maisy and Tyler were still on the couch in the living room, but I avoided them because I was afraid they might see something in my face and start asking questions.

And I wouldn't have been able to stand it, if they'd started asking questions.

Seventeen

Late April. It was finally spring. Time to plow.

Only it took longer for me to pick a spot to plow than to actually plow it. Because Al Butterman had different ideas about where to plow than I did.

Al ran a thirty-head dairy farm a mile down the road. He was in his 60's, and I could tell he thought I was bonkers to try to grow vegetables on the Stowe place.

He also had strong opinions about how I should try to grow vegetables on the Stowe place. And he seemed to think if I would only take his advice, it would save me from complete and total ruin.

First, he thought I should plant close to the road on the northernmost boundary of my property. "It'll be easier to load your produce," he said.

But I didn't want to plant down by the road. I wanted to plant on the field closest to my house. And in retrospect, that wasn't particularly logical, and it was maybe bad form, for a scientist, to be illogical. But I liked my idea, and it was a decision I'd made, and for some reason having this old, weathered, tobacco-chewing guy tell me I should being doing it differently? It brought out my stubborn side.

Finally Al gave up and drove his tractor to the field closest to my house. Just like I'd asked him. Then we got into another argument, about what part of the field he should plow.

His opinion: plow the whole thing. Then I could plant anywhere I wanted.

Right. I was starting to feel genuinely irritated by then. I didn't want to plow more than I was going to plant, because that would expose topsoil needlessly which would mean erosion and that the rain would leach nutrients from the soil.

"Better get it mown, then, if you're not going to plow it," he warned. "You'll have trees growing here next year if you don't."

"Got it," I muttered, thinking to myself I had plenty of time next year to worry about baby trees. "So please plow half this field," I said. "Starting up there." I gestured toward the highest part of the field.

"Soil will be better down there," Al answered, tipping his head in the other direction.

"Up there. Thanks, Al."

And to his credit, Al charged me only twenty dollars, which probably didn't cover his fuel, considering how long his tractor had idled while we'd argued.

Then afterward he maneuvered the tractor back through the break in the hedgerows, and I listened to it mutter away down the road toward his place.

I nearly ran back up the hill to my field.

Plowed!

I inhaled the smell of the newly turned earth. And for the first time, it seemed real. That I was actually doing it.

Starting a farm. Starting my new life.

⚘ ⚘ ⚘

"So, did you decide what you're going to plant?" Maisey asked.

I was sitting on the living room floor, surrounded by seed catalogs. "Yeah," I said. "Lots of things. But to start, mostly tatsoi."

I was looking for one catalog in particular. And naturally, it was missing.

I decided I didn't need it. No way was I going to get dragged into a missing-catalog mystery this morning.

"Tatsoi?" Maisey asked. "What's that?"

"Tatsoi. It's like bok choy, only the leaves are smaller." I opened one of the catalogs. "There's a picture in there, somewhere."

"Mom and her squeeze are growing pineapples."

"Oh, really?" Gina hadn't mentioned that this new business venture of hers was an agribusiness. Or if she had, I'd missed it. And where was Gina lately, anyway? I hadn't heard from her in—how long? Weeks. She'd called Maisey after the power had come back on. Maisey had handed her cell to me so I could say hi. But other than that—

"He's got some new kind of pineapple he invented," Maisey was saying. "It's called 'honeyham'."

Honeyham? What, a *salty* pineapple? Or pink, perhaps? Nitrates sold separately? "What do you mean, 'invented'?"

"He, like, crossed one kind of pineapple with another kind, or something. Well, more than once."

So he'd bred it. "Is he from Hawaii, then?"

"Yeah. He didn't grow up there, though."

I leafed through another catalog, thinking about Gina and her boyfriend and that I really needed to forget about Gina and her boyfriend and get my seed order in.

Oh, all right. I admit it. I was feeling, once again, a teensy bit jealous. Because suppose it turned out that Gina's boomer boyfriend who owned a pineapple farm on Hawaii was rich—which he'd have to be, to own a pineapple farm on Hawaii, which meant Gina was now living in an island paradise? Surrounded by honeyham pineapples?

Not that I wanted a rich boyfriend and an island paradise.

But running a farm was *my* dream, not Gina's.

Unfair. I know. But as I said, we were exact opposites, and this wasn't the first time I'd noticed that my friend Gina had found the easy door to a thing I wanted but struggled to get. Like she could leave her car parked *on top* of a fire hydrant for six months and never get a ticket. While, meanwhile, if I so much as glanced at a handicapped-only parking space, a SWAT team would rappel down a nearby skyscraper and plaster my windshield with $80-dollar tickets.

Well, okay. That wouldn't ever actually happen. But you get my drift.

Tyler walked into the living room and handed Maisey her breakfast. I was pretty sure it was supposed to be an omelet. It looked more like something yellow he'd scraped off a tire.

But Maisey smiled sweetly and said, "Mmmmm," and he smiled back, and then returned to the kitchen. To scrape another tire for himself, presumably.

"Hey, Aunt Libby," Maisey said, stabbing at her eggs, "you ever hear from that Carhartt guy?"

I pretended not to notice the question. I flipped to the next page of my catalog and studied a description of a pie pumpkin. I needed to pick something to plant that would mature later in the season, unlike tatsoi that would be ready to harvest early.

"Aunt Libby? Have you heard from that Carhartt guy?"

"No. Why would I?" I flipped to the page with squashes.

"Well you were living with him! For, like, over a week!" She giggled. Prurient fascination with her mother's friend's personal life, clearly. "And why does he live like that? All alone in the woods, like that?"

"I have no idea. He likes the quiet." I looked back down at the catalog, hoping the girl would get the message. Maybe I'd wait on ordering the pumpkin seeds, or was it squash seeds...

"So what's Paul think of you moving in with a stra-aaaange man like that? He knows that's where you were staying, right?"

"Of course," I said smoothly. I began re-stacking catalogs.

Tyler had returned and Maisey moved over to make room for him. "He's probably some sort of Ted Kaczynski type," she said. "He's probably holed up writing a manifesto about the evils of society, about how corporations are stealing our souls."

"Maisey, I thought you figured he was hiding out because of a broken heart?" Tyler mumbled through a mouthful of eggs.

"Corporations do not steal peoples' souls," I said, pushing the catalogs back under the end table where I was storing them, and carefully re-straightening the stack. "Corporations buy souls, not steal them. And not all corporations even do that." I stood up. "And how do you know about Ted Kaczynski?"

"Ty and I are going to go visit him, aren't we, Ty?"

I was halfway across the room when I heard that, but now I paused and turned around. "Visit who?"

"Ted. The Carhartt guy."

"Ted? You mean Dean? His name is Dean. You can't visit him."

"Why not?"

"He doesn't want visitors." But as the words left my lips, I wondered if that was true. Or, even if it was true, what was going on behind that wall of solitude he'd built up? Maybe he pretended to not want visitors, and yet secretly wished someone would drop by?

Like, maybe, me?

"I want to see Bo," Maisey was saying, nodding vigorously as she spoke.

My stomach lurched slightly. "You can't just drop in on people. You need to be invited."

"He's a neighbor. We have to be neighborly. And I want to see his cabin. I love log cabins."

I opened my mouth to try to argue, but what was the use? Plus, if I kicked up a serious fuss, it might seem...strange. Woman-thou-dost-protest-too-much strange.

Better to drop it. Chances were Maisey would forget the whole thing. It's not like teenagers have record-breaking attention spans.

So I dropped it.

But I didn't like it. This whole mixing two worlds thing. Which was how I'd come to think of it. Because my life had seemed so off-kilter. Ever since the divorce, if I was being perfectly honest. And then selling our house, and then the move, and the ice storm.

Sleeping on Dean's couch.

The last thing I needed was for that little interlude—the interlude I'd spent sleeping on Dean's couch—to intrude on my new-normal life.

Hopefully she'd forget the whole thing.

And I'd help, by ignoring it.

I had more important things to think about. I had an issue of the fully re-imagined *Skin Tones* to write.

⚘ ⚘ ⚘

"Hi, this is Libby Samson, editor of Dormet Vous Lustre's newsletter, *Skin Tones*. Is this Angela? I understand you've tried our 'Tight By Tomorrow' nightly facial crème, and I was wondering if I could profile you for our upcoming issue?"

"I guess so."

Cold calls like this were never my favorite part of the job.

"Is now a good time to talk, Angela?"

"I guess so. Who did you say you are, again? Did I win something?"

I repeated my intro spiel and then launched into the interview. "Let's start with the basics. I've got a little bit of information about you from a survey card you filled out. But tell me in your own words, why did you decide to try 'Tight By Tomorrow'?"

"Well, a woman always wants to look her best."

I made a suitably sympathetic murmur.

The woman went on a bit more, about how she'd noticed a difference right away. Diminished wrinkles, tighter skin. I frowned. She sounded suspiciously like she was reading Dormet Vous copy off the Dormet Vous box. So much so that a picture of her formed in my mind: there she was in her pink sweatshirt with the pictures of Persian kittens silkscreened on the front, sitting on a dilapidated sofa, cell phone in one hand, and in the other a 'Tight by Tomorrow' box that she peered at through her drugstore reading glasses as she spoke.

I fished around for a line of questioning that would give me a real story. I needed to get to the pain. The humanity. "Tell me, Angela, when did you first start to worry about how old you look?"

"Oh! I don't look old! My friends say I look very young for my age. Who did you say you were, again?"

Whoops. Backtrack, Libby! "No, of course you don't look old! Our customers are all—what I meant was—uh, when did it become important to you to 'look your best'?"

"Oh, I've always wanted to look my best. Doesn't everyone?"

Oh, boy.

I wondered if Dormet Vous was going to keep funding the newsletter once they realized my articles were lifted, word-for-word, from their product packaging.

Eighteen

Oak trees are the slowest trees to leaf out in the spring, and the trees on Dean's property were mostly oak, so when I looked up from my planting, it didn't look like May. It looked April-ish. But the sun was hot on my back already at 10:30 in the morning, and the soil was definitely dry enough to work.

Not that there was much soil to work with. To my horror, when I finally got my seeds and got out there and down on my hands and knees, I realized exactly what I was dealing with.

And it was worse than I could have imagined. This soil had been hammered. The layer of topsoil was super thin. There was hardly any organic matter, and what was left had hardened into rock-like clumps.

Not good.

I began to wonder if maybe I should have taken Al's advice.

Only one way to find out.

I swallowed my pride and walked to the downhill end of the field. I pushed my spade into the ground, flipped it over, then shoved the spade in again and lifted out another shovelful of dirt.

The topsoil there was a good foot deep.

I looked up at the higher end of the field—the end Al had plowed.

I looked back down at my feet.

And I smacked my forehead, literally, hard enough that my glasses slid partway down my nose.

The topsoil on this field had been eroding downhill, probably ever since someone had first started farming here. So every time someone had plowed and it rained, soil had washed down from the highest end of the field to the lowest.

Al Butterman had been right.

I stood there, considering what I should do next.

I could phone the guy, ask him to come back and plow a new spot.

But no. It was too late. Planting in newly plowed sod isn't a good idea. As the turned-over sod decomposes, the bacteria eating it temporarily suck all the nitrogen out of the soil. I'd end up with thin, yellow, sickly tatsoi, instead of green, healthy tatsoi.

Yellow, sickly tatsoi doesn't sell too well. Not a good way to launch my operation.

Option two: wait another month before planting. But that meant putting off any hope of farm income for another month. Plus, if the weather turned warm, it might affect the tatsoi's flavor. Make it bitter.

I thought about my bank account. Which was also on the verge of becoming thin, yellow, and sickly.

I had only one other option. Raised beds.

I walked back up the hill.

Building raised beds is hard work. Hard work like digging trenches is hard work. In fact, it's exactly like digging trenches. You dig trenches and pile the soil from the trenches into long mounds. The trenches became the paths, and the mounds, a little over two feet wide, become the growing beds.

It was slow going. It took me two days to build enough beds for my first crop.

Then I had to mulch them. Which turned into another ordeal as I started to shop for straw and learned that the closest place I could buy any was in Spencerport, an hour's drive away.

I made two trips in my new-to-me car—my insurance settlement had finally come in—to transport bales of straw.

My new-to-me car now looked like a straw beast had slept in it while shedding his winter coat.

And when I got the straw back to my place, I had to haul the bales to my beds with my wheelbarrow. And yes, I grumbled as I pushed the wheelbarrow up the hill. I really, really needed to get myself that tractor, and oh by the way, ol' Al also had a point about planting closer to the road.

I spread some of the straw along the flanks of the beds and reserved the rest for mulching the tops.

At long last, I was ready to plant.

Tatsoi seeds are tiny, so I didn't bother with furrows. Just walked down the side of the beds scattering the seed, then made another pass with a rake, raking the surface of the soil, very lightly. Then a third pass, on my knees this time, patting the soil, and then a fourth to lay down a light covering of straw.

I planted three beds. It would be a lot of tatsoi, but Sally and David had promised I could offer my crop to their subscribers.

So I'd have customers.

I'd actually be generating some income from my farm.

I tossed the last handful of straw into place and straightened back up, rubbing the stiff places in my lower back.

"You might have asked first."

It had been so long, at that point, since I'd last seen the little man, that for a split second I assumed it was someone else speaking.

Dean.

But it wasn't Dean. I knew it wasn't Dean.

It was the little man. Sitting on the ground, not far from where I'd seen him the night of the ice storm.

"Asked what?" I said, not very enthusiastically.

"About what to plant."

"Look. No offense. But—please. Go away."

"There are choices that would have been wiser."

"Oh, for crying out loud," I muttered quietly. But then I remembered my beloved Toyota, crushed by the maple tree, and sighed, and looked back over at the little man. "All right. What, exactly, are you trying to say?"

He regarded me thoughtfully.

I waited.

He plucked a piece of grass from the ground and examined it.

"Look," I said. "I'm sorry, but I'm really tired. It's late. I need my dinner. I need a hot bath."

I wondered if he knew what a hot bath even was. Do supernatural-slash-hallucinated beings bathe?

"Lamb's lettuce would have been a wiser choice."

"Lamb's lettuce?"

"Mache."

Great.

I felt a little stab of concern tweak my guts. "But tatsoi will be a big seller," I said, thinking to myself that even though they might bathe, supernatural-slash-hallucinated beings are quite unlikely to understand the dynamics of modern commerce. "My friends said so."

I picked up my tools, laid them across the wheelbarrow and began wheeling down the hill toward my house. "I have to go."

And if the little man answered, I didn't hear.

And anyway, it was only a bizarre coincidence that my car had gotten crushed. And hey, how could tatsoi get crushed? Look at that sky. Perfectly clear. No hailstorms coming. No fiery meteors streaking down toward my field.

"There aren't any tree limbs hanging over my beds," I comforted myself as I pushed the wheelbarrow into the shed.

It was ridiculous. I'm a biologist, a scientist. I'd put a lot of thought into what I was going to plant. What did that...*thing*...expect me to do?

No way was I going to take farming advice from a hallucination.

⚜ ⚜ ⚜

"Aunt Libby?"

I opened my eyes just as Maisey touched me on the arm.

I must have fallen asleep on the couch.

"Your phone's blowing up," she said. "Someone's trying to reach you. Are you okay?"

Paul. Had to be Paul, trying to call me.

I sat up for a second, then tipped back down onto the couch. Wow, was I tired...

I'd left my dinner plate on the coffee table. The smears of sauce from my microwaved enchiladas had started to dry.

Maisey had a concerned look on her face. "You've been working awfully hard. Mom says—"

I held my hand up, signally stop. "Nothing personal, Maise. I love your mom. But I don't need advice from her at this very moment."

"Yeah." Maisey grinned. "I know what you mean. Me, neither."

My eyelids were drooping. *I should go to bed.* So warm in the house. *So drowsy...*

"But seriously."

I opened my eyes again. Maisey was still there? And she looked seriously concerned. "You look kind of funny. You should go up to bed. I'll wash your plate, okay?"

"I'm fine," I said out loud, while on the inside I was noticing how my body ached all over. How all I wanted to do was drop sideways on the couch, tuck the throw pillow under my head.

I'd be able to sleep for about a week. Easily.

I yawned. "I've been pushing hard is all. And that weird little man—"

I started, suddenly wide awake.

What had I just said?

Had I said that out loud?

"What?" Maisey looked strangely alert as well. "What do you mean, weird little man?"

"Nothing! Nothing!"

Too late, Libby. Maisey dropped down next to me on the couch. "Aunt Libby! You're hiding something! Tell me. Is it Dean? Is he, like, stalking you while you work?"

93

"No! It's got nothing to do with—"

"It's DEAN. But he's not *weird*, Aunt Libby. He's a dish! Oh my gosh, you like him, don't you! Oh wow, Paul is going to just flip OUT."

"Maisey. Stop that. It is not Dean. You aren't even close."

Maisey didn't believe me. Not for a second. The teen's eyes danced.

And so yeah, I panicked. Because Paul was coming to visit on Saturday. His first visit. Which meant he'd be around Maisey.

I could see it now. Maisey running off her mouth, dropping some silly comment about Dean stalking me—

So I made my horrible, awful, worst mistake. "Maisey," I said. "You are to tell *nobody* what I'm about to tell you. Do you understand? Not a *soul*."

Maisey's eyes widened. "Sure, Aunt Libby."

"This place—my property—well, it's kind of like—it's like it's haunted."

"Oh! Oh, shit!"

Shit is right. I'd scared her. *Bad Libby. Bad, bad Libby.* Backtrack, quick. "No! No. That's not—I shouldn't have put it that way. That's not right. Not haunted. They're not ghosts."

"What? What's not a ghost?"

I sighed. "Look, let's just forget about this, okay? But it has nothing to do with Dean—that's the important thing for you to unders—"

"Aunt LIBBY. You have GOT to tell me what is going on." Maisey's face was white, and she was trembling, and her mouth was set in a way I'd never seen before.

"Aw, dammit. Dammit. Okay. Okay. I'm seeing—I'm seeing what I guess are—" I hesitated.

And then I said it aloud. "Little people."

"Little people?"

I said the other word aloud. "Well, I guess—fairies."

"What do you mean, 'fairies'? Like, with wings?"

"No, they don't have wings. They are—they're little people. I can't really describe it. They're about this tall. I've seen them a few times when I've been out back."

"Whoa. Whoa. Aunt Libby!" She didn't look scared any more. Which was good, I guess. Now, she looked awed. "This is soooo cool!"

I made a face. "Not exactly."

"Oh! Yes, it is!"

I reached for my plate. "Look, just remember your promise. You're not to tell anyone. Not even Tyler."

And in that moment, Tyler cleared his throat.

Gentlemanly of him. He was standing in the living room doorway. He'd heard every damn word.

I groaned. "Ty? I thought you took Maisey's car to town!"

"It's okay, Aunt Libby, I think it's way cool, too. I don't think you're crazy."

Gee, thanks for that. "Look, you two. This is a secret. It's not to leave this room."

"You're like that lady from Virginia," Tyler said.

"I have no idea what you're talking about."

"Machaelle Small Wright. She, like, talks to nature spirits and stuff," he said. "And—"

"Oh man! I want to see them!" Maisey broke in. "Do you think they'd appear for me, too? Oh man, this is so cool!"

"They give her advice on how to grow her garden," Tyler said. "Like, where to put crystals and stuff."

"Have they given you advice about your farm, Aunt Libby?" Maisey asked.

"No. I mean yes, kind of. I think." I rubbed my forehead again.

"Wow. What did they say?"

"I don't know!" I slumped back into the couch. "Something like planting some other salad green. Instead of tatsoi."

"So did you?"

"Of course not. I don't have the right kind of seed. And I'd already planted the tatsoi."

"But don't you think you should?"

"No!" I yelped. "I'm not going to take advice from what is probably a hallucination."

"It's not a hallucination!" Tyler gestured excitedly and took a seat on the rug in front of the couch. He had dark brown eyes, almost black, and his face was so young and earnest, he looked almost fawn-like as he gazed up at me. "You got to, Aunt Libby. They're like—they're like tied to the land and shit."

"I don't 'got to' do anything."

"But they're like—you need to read that Virginia lady's books."

I groaned again. "Look, you two, enough is enough. This subject is closed." I stood up. "I'm going to go take a shower."

"You could experiment," Maisey said. "You could plant some of that—whatever they said to plant."

"Yeah," Tyler said. "Do that, Aunt Libby."

"No," I said. "And both of you: do *not* forget your promise. This has to stay a secret. This is private. Very, very private. Do you understand?"

They nodded their heads.

Very solemn.

Very sincere about this being totally private.

Nineteen

Paul stood in the driveway next to his Lexus, squinting up at my house. "So, this is it, huh? Needs a coat of paint. I suppose you want me to help you paint it?"

"What?" One reason Paul lived in a condo was so he wouldn't have any house maintenance responsibilities. He definitely wasn't a paint-a-house-on-weekends sort of guy. "I never—no, Paul—"

"Well. I'm your man, right?"

"I'd never ask you to do that!"

He nodded. "Lemme know if you change your mind."

I noticed he sounded a bit relieved that I hadn't said yes to his offer. But I also noticed how shabby the house looked. The paint was peeling and chipped, especially on the north side.

Funny how an old farmhouse that looked like paradise most of the time suddenly looked a little run-down when I was seeing it through someone else's eyes.

"Hiya, Paul!"

I turned and looked down the driveway. I hadn't seen Maisey coming. She must have been out for a walk. I eyed her suspiciously. "Maisey? Where have you been?"

"Visiting Bo."

"Who's Bo?" Paul asked.

"Dean's dog," Maisey said.

"Who's Dean?"

"My neighbor," I said.

Paul looked over at me, his expression unreadable. "The guy you stayed with during the ice storm?"

"After the ice storm," I corrected him. "Because he was kind enough to take me in so I wouldn't freeze to death. C'mon, I'll show you around."

I gave him a tour of the house. The kitchen with its charming bead-board cupboards, the dining room—empty because I couldn't afford dining room furniture, but the brass chandelier was also charming. The living room with the brick fireplace—which I still hadn't used—and painted built-in shelves. And then upstairs, the cozy bedrooms with their old-fashioned windows, and old glass panes that had tiny bubbles in them.

And Paul seemed strangely quiet during the tour, which, in retrospect, was a red flag. Because when you're in a relationship, and you veer away from certain subjects, it's not because the subject at hand is sensitive, necessarily. It's because you both know that there's a nerve right there below the surface.

"So that's the house," I said when we'd finished looking around inside. "Want to see my growing beds?"

"Of course."

It had rained the day before, and the air felt hot and humid, especially after we emerged from the little grove of trees and brush that separated my house from my fields, and could no longer feel the western breeze. Summer was definitely around the corner.

"Hear that?" I said, pausing for a moment and cocking my head. "Yellow warbler."

Paul nodded. He was wearing jeans and his face was flushed.

We hiked up the hill, and I smiled to see my planting beds, how they looked so clean and neat with their bright straw dressing gleaming in the sun.

But then we got a little closer, and I saw something awful.

I broke into a run.

I knelt by the nearest bed.

"Lib? What's going on?" Paul said as he caught up to me. "Is something wrong?"

Wrong? I'll say something was wrong!

I couldn't see any tatsoi. Only then I did. Or rather, I saw what was left of the tatsoi.

"Libby?" Paul asked again.

"I can't believe it," I moaned. "Something's been *eating* my tatsoi!"

My baby plants. Yesterday, they were fine. They'd had their third or fourth set of true leaves. Sturdy, green, happy.

And now: where the leaves had been there was nothing left but green lace. Green lace and stumps.

I stood up and walked along the bed, stunned, and then I noticed something else: tiny little insects, shiny black insects, hopping everywhere. Hopping off of what was left of my baby plants.

"What happened?" Paul said from where he stood at one end of the bed. "Rabbits?"

"No," I said miserably. "Bugs of some kind."

"That's what's put the holes in the leaves?"

Yeah. Holes. Holes upon holes until there was nothing left except the holes.

I stepped over the bed to the next one, my guts knotting, hoping against hope that this plague, whatever it was, hadn't spread to every plant. But as my shadow passed over the bed, I could see the little black insects skitter and hop. There were hundreds of them. Thousands.

"Some of the plants look okay," he said.

"No. None of them are okay. Every plant. Every plant."

I knelt and cupped my hand around one of little insects, trapping it against the ground, and pulled a Kleenex out of the pocket of my cut-offs.

The insect wasn't hard to catch.

I folded the tissue around it and stood back up. I needed to figure out what these things were.

I'd almost forgotten Paul was there as I started down the hill.

"Figure out what it is?" Maisey asked.

I was on the living room couch. I'd dropped the insect into an old mayonnaise jar so I could see it clearly and was turning the jar in my hands and watching it hop around on the glass.

My stack of gardening books and insect field guides was beside me.

"Yes," I said sadly. "It's called a flea beetle."

"A flea? Ugh."

"No, not a flea. It's not related to real fleas. It's a beetle. But it hops like a flea."

Paul had left me to my books and my bugs and had gone out to his car to get his cell phone. He came in now, talking animatedly to Josh. Dormet Vous had reorganized Cal4, and Josh was now Paul's boss. Although Paul wasn't allowed to call him a boss. Josh's official title was "mentor", because Dormet Vous Lustre management believed in mentoring, not bossing.

Of course, you were still expected to do whatever your mentor told you to do. Minor detail.

"Yeah, she can work with that," Paul was saying into his phone. "Pop that collateral into the regions and our numbers will dance, man."

He rounded the corner into the kitchen which, thankfully, put a wall between me and his phone call.

"Well. What are you going to do?" Maisey said.

"I don't know. It says here that they go after members of the cabbage family." I set the jar back down. "And tatsoi is in the cabbage family. And you know those weeds with the yellow flowers that are growing everywhere I haven't plowed? That's wild mustard, which is also a member of the cabbage family."

And I'd been thinking how pretty the mustard had looked, all bright in the May sun. And how mustard was actually good for fallow soil, it helps condition the soil.

Turns out, my little plot of tatsoi was surrounded by an enormous flea beetle nursery.

"If I replant, I'm going to have to treat the plants. Dust with diatomaceous earth, I guess, or pyrethrum maybe."

"Diatom-what? Are you allowed to do that?"

I nodded sadly. "As long as I use something that is okay for organic farmers." I was wondering how much I'd need. And how much it would cost.

Maisey lowered her voice. "Why don't you ask your fairy what to do?"

I shot her a sharp look. "Shhh!"

I listened a moment. Paul was still talking on the phone in the kitchen.

Maisey's eyes widened as she noticed me glance in that direction. "Paul doesn't know?"

I shook my head and put my finger to my lips.

Her eyes widened further, and she nodded to let me know she understood, then leaned toward me and lowered her voice to a whisper. "But what I was saying is, the fairy—what was the stuff he told you to plant? Is it cabbage, too?"

"What's going on?"

I jumped. It was Paul. His call was over, apparently.

"I'm trying to figure out what to do," I said, shooting a *keep quiet* look at Maisey. "I can either replant the tatsoi and try to treat the beetles." I paused. "Or I could try, uh, planting something else."

Maisey was looking at me. Her eyes were dancing. "That's what I was saying to her when you walked in, Paul," she said excitedly. "My idea! I thought she should do that, plant something else. And so did Tyler."

My palms felt sweaty. *Please stop chattering, Maisey.*

But Paul let out a derisive snort. "That's great. Blind leading the blind."

What?

"Excuse me?" I said.

Paul's face changed. "It was a joke, Libby."

Maisey shrank down into the couch, opened a field guide, and started looking at the colored plates of butterflies.

"It was not a joke. It was an insult."

"Geez, Libby, take it easy. You're a beginner, that's all. You're bound to make mistakes."

Except that I couldn't afford to make mistakes. And not just for financial reasons. And so I did it. I went there. "You have never believed this was a good idea," I said, standing up.

"Oh come on, Libby!" He gestured around the room. "Be logical. You've got a beaten-up old farmhouse out in the middle of nowhere. You move out here all by yourself, and you honestly believe you're going to turn it into a working farm? Well, it was a working farm, once, and what happened? Where did they go? You ever think there might be a *reason* it wasn't a farm anymore when you got here?"

Because it had been a dairy farm, I thought to myself. Because small, family farms are so easily crushed by forces they can't control: the economy, the perversions of modern age markets.

But what was the use of arguing? Because this wasn't about the farmers who'd lived here before me. And we both knew it.

"Hey, Tyler's home!" Maisey ran from the room.

"You ought to be supporting me."

"I do support you, Libby," Paul said. "I saved *Skin Tones*, remember?"

"That's not what I'm talking about."

He didn't understand what it meant. To want, so badly, to have a solid foundation under your feet. And to know, at the same time, that it was an illusion. That the foundation was strung together by the most fragile of threads. So fragile that a beetle the size of a millet grain could destroy it in a matter of hours.

We stood there, glaring at each other.

And then something shifted.

"I'm sorry, Lib," he said. He moved over to me and put his arms around me.

He smelled sweaty from the walk, but not strongly so, and the familiarity of his smell calmed me down in spite of myself. "I'm sorry," he repeated. "I didn't mean to piss you off."

"It's just a setback, Paul. I—I need to do this. It's important to me. Just like your job is important to you."

I stepped away and looked him in the eye. "Like we always said. We need to tie our dreams to something big, to helping others. This is my way of doing that."

He wasn't convinced. I could tell. But good old Paul, he nodded anyway. "I do support you, Libby. I really do."

I straightened my glasses and rubbed the back of my neck.

"So, can you take a break from this for a couple hours?" he asked. "I'll buy you lunch."

Twenty

Losing my tatsoi, it turned out, caused problems in more ways than one.

Not only did it set me back as far as potential income—and, of course, puncture my pride.

There was also the matter of the organic certification inspection people. They like to see crops actually growing when they do the on-site. And my inspection was scheduled to happen in two days.

I had no choice. My growing beds were bare. Bare.

I called to reschedule. It would be another month, now, before there would be anything actually, you know. Growing on them.

🌱 🌱 🌱

"Replanting?" Dean asked.

I hadn't seen him coming, but when I heard his voice, I looked up and saw Bo bounding toward me.

Like the day he'd chased me up the tree.

This time I didn't run, although the dog shoved himself against my bare legs so hard, I nearly lost my balance.

"Bo!" Dean scolded gently. He'd caught up with the mastiff, and now grabbed Bo's collar to guide him away from the planting beds.

Dean was wearing jeans and a black tee shirt.

There was a leaf in his hair that begged for someone to reach out and pluck it off...

I dropped my eyes and knelt back down. "Yes," I said. "I'm replanting."

"So you lost your first crop."

I frowned. "How did you know? Did Maisey tell you?"

"No. It was pretty obvious. There wasn't much left."

Ah. So he had been coming by my place. Just not to the house.

I turned back to my work. I could hear Bo panting.

"About Maisey," I said. "I've told her not to bother you."

"They don't."

They? Great. That meant Tyler must be joining Maisey's little jaunts to my neighbor's. Well. As long as Dean knew I had nothing to do with it.

"Look," I said, standing back up. "I don't mean to be rude. But I have to get this done."

"Is there anything I can do to help?"

"No!" It came out a bit louder than I'd intended. But at least he didn't ask again.

Only he didn't go away, either. "I came to tell you that I appreciated the note," he said.

I felt a slight blush crawl up my face and ducked my head a bit lower over my work to hide it. Because, okay. I'd sent him a thank you note. I guess I'm old-fashioned that way. And he had been awfully nice to me, bringing me into his house like that.

It had been a while since I'd sent the card.

And of course I hadn't expected him to acknowledge it.

"It was the least I could do," I said. "You were very kind of you to take me in like that."

My words felt weird.

Stiff.

It's because he kissed you and you want to forget about the kiss. And you've tried to forget. But you haven't.

I moved down the row, edging away from him. But out of the corner of my eye I could see him take a few steps, too. "How about the other thing?" he asked. "Have you seen the little man again?"

My face flushed hotter. I shouldn't have told him about the little man, either. "Not really. Only once."

"Have you thought about asking them what to plant?"

I stood up and stared. Dean's face above his beard was more tanned than it had been that spring, and he'd just had a haircut, it looked like. His beard was shorter than it had been. Trimmed down, neat.

But I knew exactly why I felt so unnerved, having him standing there, holding Bo by the collar. Looking at me. And yes, he was a very good-looking man, but that wasn't the problem. It was the topic of our conversation. Talking about those fairies? It made me uncomfortable. It would make anyone uncomfortable.

I crouched back down to my work. "I don't know why you'd ask something like that."

"Ah," he said. "I see."

"Sorry?"

"You're doing it right now. You're planting something they told you to plant."

How had he guessed that?

"I needed to try something different, that's all." I stepped a little further down the row.

"Of course." He cleared his throat. "You're welcome to stop by sometime, for dinner, or something."

What? And why was my heart now pounding in my chest?

"Thanks," I said. "But I don't think—maybe in the fall. I'm very busy right now."

"Sure," he said. "Okay."

I turned my head a moment later and watched as the man and his dog stepped over the stone wall and disappeared into the woods.

My heart was beating so hard it almost hurt.

ψ ψ ψ

There was an empty Mountain Dew can on the desk next to my computer keyboard.

I don't drink Mountain Dew.

I picked up the can and knocked on Maisey's bedroom door.

"Come in!"

She and Tyler were sitting on the air mattress, their heads pressed together so they could listen from the same iPod earbud.

"I found this on my desk, guys," I said, waving the soda can.

The earbud fell onto the mattress between them.

"Uh, I must have left it there," Tyler said.

I gave them an exasperated look. "I think I told you, once. I really don't want you guys on my computer."

"We're sorry, Aunt Libby," Maisey said. "Tyler was just doing some stuff on his Instagram. For his job."

"Jobs," I answered dryly, "Are those things with paychecks at the end of the week."

"Oh no, Aunt Libby! He gets paid!" Maisey said.

"Yeah, Aunt Libby. I'm an influencer. People send me stuff and I post about them and I get money. Yeah. I like, get paid."

"I know what an influencer is," I said.

"I can do most of it from my phone, but sometimes—" He grinned his charming-guy smile. "I'm working on getting my own computer. But it'll be a few more weeks."

Must be the "revenues" weren't exactly in the six figures.

They were now both looking at me with puppy dog, don't-punish-me eyes.

I gave in.

I mean, they were nice kids.

And what could possibly go wrong?

"All right. But you may only use it when I don't need it. And you must exercise extreme care. No loading software, no messing with the files on my hard drive."

They nodded.

"And Tyler, get your own computer ASAP."

"Thanks, Aunt Libby," Tyler said, grinning. "I'm sorry I didn't tell you—I forgot what you'd said—"

I tossed the Mountain Dew can at him. "And no drinking soda at the desk."

Twenty-one

"Okay. I planted mache," I said.

It was just past sunset.

It had been another warm day and I could feel currents of warm air coming off the earth.

A cardinal whistled from the edge of Dean's land, and a car shushed by on the road.

I waited, listening.

Although, to be honest, I wasn't sure I wanted them to answer.

Yes, I'd been forced to accept the fact that maybe this little venture of mine was going to be harder than it had looked, on paper, when I was working in the lab and dreaming of the day I'd have my own farm.

And that maybe these fairies, or whatever they were, could help me.

Because what if this little venture of mine failed? Then what was I going to do?

Crawl back to Rochester with my tail between my legs?

Marry Paul?

It's not that I didn't figure we'd get married at some point, of course. But this meant everything to me, this dream I had of building a working, profitable market farm. My whole life was invested in it.

And I'd turned 31 last fall. That might have been part of it. I was at the age when you start to realize how quickly time moves, how you might be running out of chances to feel young, to feel like you were starting out new, starting out fresh.

I'd married so young. Just out of college…

My choices for most of my adult life had been joint decisions. Decisions I'd made with Wallace. But not anymore. Not with this farm. Now the whole thing was on my shoulders.

I'd either carry it off gracefully, or I'd stumble and fall.

And I'd started to have serious doubts. Failure will do that. Even little failures. Like choosing tatsoi. It had had seemed like such a perfect idea on paper. Fast growing. Nutritious. Met an established demand!

Yeah, it had been perfect.

Except for the part about being a big mistake.

Which is how I found myself, standing in the evening chill, hoping an imaginary being would give me some more free advice so that I wouldn't make another big mistake tomorrow.

"Are you there?"

Clouds had been moving in from the west for the past hour, and as they thickened overhead it hastened the growing darkness.

I tried some humor. "I need some free advice. That doesn't suck. Hey. That could be your marketing slogan. Free advice that doesn't suck."

"It helps if you're relaxed."

I turned around.

I couldn't see a thing. "Hello? Are you there? Would you mind—"

"And less…hostile."

Hostile? I wasn't hostile. Was I?

And by the way, have you ever noticed how when someone accuses you of being hostile, it tends to make you feel—wait for it—

Hostile?

I scowled. I considered quitting, right then and there. Quitting everything. Just walk down to the house, Libby, phone Paul to tell him you were wrong, he was right. Put the place back on the market.

Clean out half the closet, honey, I'm moving in.

I unclenched my jaw. "It's hard to be relaxed when I'm talking to a disembodied voice. If you don't mind."

"Give us a moment."

Us?

I squeezed my eyes shut, hard, and opened them again, trying to make out if there was anything there, in the direction of the voice.

After a moment there was a brush of movement in the darkness and there he was. Standing about 10 feet in front of me. "We don't meet in a physical location so much as a mental one," he said. "If you're a bit more open, it's easier for me to find the juncture."

"I'm sorry. I have no idea what you're talking about."

He was carrying a little staff, this time, and he shifted it from his right hand to his left and thrust it against the ground. But not impatiently. Deliberately, like the gesture would help make a point. "Can you dream while you're awake?" he asked.

"Are you saying this is a dream?"

"No. But it has elements in common with the dream state. So it helps if you're a bit more relaxed."

I'd taken some yoga classes, once. Kind of a waste of time, I thought at the time. But I remembered what the instructor had said, and I took a couple breaths from my diaphragm and dropped my shoulders a bit.

There. Relaxing... Because if this...dream-thing...could help me, I supposed the least I could do was to try to cooperate.

"How's that?" I said.

He didn't answer.

I squinted into the darkness. Was he fading out?

"Please don't go!" I said. "I've planted the lamb's lettuce. I was wondering if there's anything else—"

His form seemed more solid, now.

"I mean, if there's anything else that—you know. That I should do."

I waited.

"Yes," the little man said finally. "The crystalline structure of the soil is distorted, which is causing certain...drainages to occur. You need to correct its alignment."

My heart sank. "I'm not sure what that means. Sorry."

"The crystalline structure of—"

"I heard you." I paused to collect myself because I was aware that if I didn't, I might sound like I felt. Discouraged. And yes, also a teensy bit annoyed. Not hostile! Annoyed. Because: crystalline structure of the soil out of alignment? Hogwash.

Only I no longer dared ignore it, the advice I was getting from these fairy things. "I'm sorry," I said, trying to be as humble as possible. "I have absolutely no idea what you're talking about."

"Boil a peck of horsetail in five gallons of water for three hours. Cool the solution."

"I don't underst—"

He turned around and spoke, now, over his shoulder. "Then sprinkle it on the field. Two thirds on the beds, the rest on the fallow section. That should do it."

"Hey, where are you going? That makes—I'm a scientist. That makes no sense. Please, I mean, I have some more questions."

It looked like he'd crouched down into a sunken spot on the ground, but suddenly I could see him again. "Horsetail, the plant," he said. "Not horsetail from a horse."

"Where am I going to get—I don't even know what—"

"Check the ditches."

"Ditches?"

But he was gone. I couldn't see him anymore.

"Ditches?" I called out.

But he didn't answer.

ψ ψ ψ

Tyler was on my computer when I got back to the house.

He sprang to his feet as soon as heard me come into my office. I guess it was something about the expression on my face. He knew better than to do anything but get out of my way.

I Googled horsetail.

Equisetum Arvense. Also known as bottlebrush. A relative of the fern, descended from treelike plants of the Paleozoic period.

I paged through the photos on Google images. Some of the plants in the photos looked vaguely familiar. I'd seen horsetail around, for sure. I just couldn't remember quite where.

Tyler was with Maisey in the kitchen when I passed it on my way to the basement.

"Okay if I get back online?" Ty asked.

I nodded without speaking.

I had several peck baskets stored somewhere. I'd picked up from a garage sale because I thought it would be a pretty way to display produce, if I ever joined a farmer's market.

A peck.

I scanned the rusty metal shelves lining my basement walls, trying to remember where I'd put the baskets.

Thinking ha.

My fairies?

Obviously, pre-metric-system fairies.

֎ ֎ ֎

Well.

Turns out the little man had steered me right when he said "ditches." I found horsetails growing thickly in the drainage ditch along the road, up by Dean's property.

Filling a peck basket with horsetail, however, was harder than I'd expected. Horsetail leaves aren't exactly leaves. More like long, flimsy, scrawny pine needles.

And the little man's recipe?

He hadn't explained if "a peck" meant a peck of horsetails tamped down, or just tossed in loosely.

I thought it over.

I'd get to "a peck" a lot faster if I didn't have to pack them down.

In the end I compromised. I tamped, but lightly.

Twenty-Two

"What is that SMELL?" Maisey squealed.

I would have preferred to prepare my fairy brew while she and Tyler were out.

However, the recipe had the "boil three hours" step, and my two houseguests were homebodies. It was a rare day they were absent for three whole hours straight.

Young kids, you'd think they'd have better things to do than hang around a house and watch movies and listen to podcasts.

At least they tried not to make too much trouble. And I also had to admit that they were cute together. Although Maisey wasn't being cute at that particular moment. Her face was wrinkled up and she was holding her nose.

"It's horsetail," I said. "It's for my soil."

They'd gone grocery shopping, and Tyler was pulling stuff out of a reusable grocery bag. But when he heard my words he stopped, and his eyes got huge. "Oh, wow," he said. "Did you talk to them? Is this a fairy recipe?"

I didn't answer. Which, of course, they took to mean "yes."

"Wow!" Maisey said. "So you *have* talked to them again!"

And once again they took my non-answer as a "yes," and started chattering at me, both at the same time. "When did you see them? Was it the same one as the other times? What did they say? How come they want you to cook that stuff up?"

The brew was at a full boil now. Greenish steam rose in a cloud over the pot. "It's really not that big a deal, you two."

I turned the burner to medium-low.

The kids were still jabbering at me.

"Aunt Libby!" Maisey was saying. "What are you talking about? It's ha-yuge!"

"You're like—it's like, you've been *chosen*, man," Tyler chimed in, shaking his head in wonder. "It's like being one of the Prophets from the Bible or something. You're a modern-day prophet. Have they said anything about the climate?"

I put a slice of bread in the toaster.

Me and my big mouth.

"Okay, kids. I'm not a prophet. So you can just—"

"We've been talking," Tyler interrupted, "and you know, these fairies might have an important message for the world, or something."

I opened the fridge to get some butter, and when I turned around again, I saw their eyes, wide open. And earnest. And oh so young. Had I once been that young?

"Sorry to disappoint you," I said, shaking my head. "Nothing like that is going on. Not even close. Whatever these—this phenomenon is, it's not like that, at all."

"Have you told Paul about it yet?" Maisey asked.

Argh. That was getting a bit too personal. But I kept my cool. "As I told you, I haven't told anyone else, besides you two. Well—"

I'd told Dean...

And wouldn't you know it. Maisey caught my little slip. "Someone else knows?" she breathed excitedly. "Is it Mom?"

Oh Jeez. I didn't even want to think what Gina's reaction would be if she ever got wind of this whole little people thing. "No, your Mom does not know. In fact, she's been too busy to pay much attention to me at all since she got to Hawaii with Pineapple Man."

My toast popped up.

"So who else knows then?" Maisey continued to press.

"It doesn't matter."

"Oh, my God. You told Dean!" she gasped, and started hopping up and down. "Am I right?" Maisey said.

Why, why did I not teach myself how to lie? "Yes, you're right," I sighed. "But Maise? Ty? This is not a big deal."

I put my toast on the plate. The crust was black and smoking slightly. One of them, Tyler or Maisey, kept turning the dial too high.

"So it's okay to talk about it with Dean, then, right?" Maisey said. "Since he knows?"

"No!" I answered snappishly. "It's not okay."

"Why not? He already knows. You just said!"

"Just don't discuss it with him. Do you understand?" I didn't mean to be like that. And it wasn't just the whole little man thing. I mean, that was bad enough. But there was something else, too.

Something about how much I dislike the idea of the three of them talking about me. What else might they say? And why did Maisey think she had to be friends with the guy, anyway?

I scraped some of the burnt crust off my toast into the sink, and when I finished, I saw Maisey's face.

She looked hurt.

"Look," I said. "Don't you have better things to talk about?"

Neither of the kids answered me. But Tyler put an arm around Maisey like he was comforting her, which made me feel like a jerk. So, of course, I made it worse. "Also, would you guys please turn the toaster setting back down to medium when you're done with it? This is the third time this week I've burned my toast."

They apologized meekly for the grave sin of turning the toaster up to medium high.

I felt even more like a jerk.

I went up to my office.

I turned on my computer and waited for it to boot up, munching on the toast, telling myself that I was perfectly within my rights to react as I had, and what I really should do is tell the two of them that their time was up and how about they moved out into a place of their own.

Because I didn't want them talking about me and this weirdness that had happened in my life. Because okay, I'd experienced something unexplainable. I'm not the only one, right? People see UFOs. Ghosts. Yetis.

But now it was different. Now I was actually looking for them, trying to talk to these…beings. Plus I was actually now following the crazy instructions they'd given.

I'd crossed a line.

I didn't want to think I was crazy.

I didn't feel crazy. I didn't feel different than how I'd always felt.

Which was part of the problem. It would have been easier if I'd felt different. Special. Or like I'd been singled out for something, like Tyler had said. If the clouds had parted and a booming voice announced I'd been chosen to bring a Message to All Humanity.

Instead, I was getting weird gardening advice.

Nothing else had changed.

I was still just Libby Samson, 31-year-old, childless, almost-broke divorcée.

Dull as a Monday.

I plucked a tissue from the box on my desk and wiped my fingers so I wouldn't get my keyboard greasy.

And once again the thought crossed my mind, maybe it's time to tell Paul. Maybe it's time.

Because I was now interacting with this phenomenon in a rational way, right?

Which meant I could present my story—the evidence—to him in a rational, neutral way.

And then I hit on an idea.

After my first harvest.

That's when I'd tell him. I'd get to my first harvest. I'd get to an actual success that I could obviously attribute, in part, to advice from magical beings that only I could see.

And then I'd tell him.

He'd see that whatever was going on, it was a net positive.
Maybe he'd even help me understand it.
It would be nice, to understand it.

Twenty-Three

Finally, the big day arrived.

The day the organic certification inspector was coming to my farm.

Was I excited? You bet. I woke up at five. I threw on some cutoffs and a tee shirt and sneakers, and ran up the hill to my planting beds.

The mache was still there. Jade-green whorls of spoon-shaped leaves, beautiful against the straw mulch.

I'd done it.

There was no reason to be nervous.

I went back to the house. It was still super early, so I paced around and drank a cup of coffee. Then another cup. And a third.

My hands began to get a bit sweaty from the coffee and my nerves. I kept checking the window to see if the inspector had come, and I carried the printouts I'd made of all my forms everywhere with me so that by 11:00 there was a rumpled bend along one edge where I'd been gripping them too hard with my damp hands.

Then, at long last, a car pulled into my drive.

I watched the inspector hop out of his car, and, when enough time had passed that I figured it wouldn't seem too much like pouncing, I went out to meet him, telling myself as I walked that I was ready.

I was ready.

I sized him up. He was short, receding hairline, thin moustache. White crew socks folded over above his boots. Physically fit. Really physically fit. Not a scrap of fat.

The moustache and the socks and the physique gave the guy a cop-ish kind of look that didn't do anything for my nerves.

"Libby Samson?" He put out his hand. "I'm Chip Hanford."

Great. He had a cop-ish kind of name, too. "Nice to meet you, Chip. What do you want to see first?"

We got started.

Mostly it was him asking questions. Which was fine, at first. He went over everything. Where I bought my seed, where I stored my equipment. What water would I use to wash my produce? Who had owned my land before me and how did they use it?

It was a lot of the same stuff that was on my application forms, but of course he needed to hear me say it, too.

Then he wanted to walk the perimeter of my property to check my maps. He wanted to see the adjacent properties. Organic farmers need to prevent contamination from neighboring land. Pesticide sprays can drift, for instance. But in my case, my property wasn't bordered by any-thing that might present a problem. There was Dean's forest, country roads, undeveloped land on the other side of the roads. Not even a lawn that somebody might treat with something prohibited.

I was feeling better by the minute.

"Okay. Let's take a look at your plot, then," Chip said.

"This way."

We walked back downhill to my growing beds.

And suddenly it occurred to me.

What if the little man appeared?

I'd always seen him around dusk. So no way would he suddenly pop up in the middle of the day, right?

I scanned the beds and the hedgerow.

No sign of any supernatural beings.

"That's all you have in cultivation right now?" Chip asked me.

"What? Oh, yes. Yes. That's all. I do plan to—"

I broke off mid-sentence.

The little man!

He was seated on a big stone in the hedgerow separating this field from the next one, clearly visible in the dappled shadows cast by the hedgerow bushes.

He was kicking his feet out like a child. Watching me.

"Are you okay?" Chip said.

I swallowed, hard. "Yes. Fine. I thought I saw a—"

Yeeks! Chip was looking over at the hedgerow.

"Oh, gone now!" I yipped. "It was a rabbit, I think! Those rabbits. Gotta keep an eye on—" My glasses had started to slide on my sweaty nose, and I pushed them back into place. "Wow, it's a hot one today, isn't it?"

"Yeah." He frowned. "Tell me, Ms. Samson. What are you doing for soil amendments?"

I nodded gratefully at the question, glad for the opportunity to re-focus. "Soil amendments. Yes. Since the land has been fallow for several years, nothing this year. I plan in the future to mostly use green manure. Rotate the beds, plant white clover when, um—."

A movement caught my eye.

The little man stood up on the stone.

He wasn't going to hop down and walk out of the hedgerow, toward us. Was he?

Please, no.

"Um, yes," I sputtered, trying to remember what I was saying. "Clover. So I guess that means I will be growing something besides mache, won't it? But you knew that already!" I laughed nervously.

The crease in Chip's brow deepened.

I glanced again toward the stone. The little man was sitting again. And had I left my watering can out? The one I'd used to sprinkle that horsetail brew on my planting beds?

Must be I had. There it was, next to the hedgerow.

And then, to my horror, I saw that Chip Hanford had followed my glance and was looking at the watering can as well. "I'm sorry," he said, looking back at me. "Did you say you own the property east of this plot?" He pulled my map back out of the folder he was carrying, stepped over the bed, and headed toward the watering can.

"I—yes, sir. Yes. That's my land as well," I stammered, following him, forcing myself to not look at the stone where the little man was seated.

And fortunately, Chip didn't seem to notice the little man.

Unfortunately, however, he seemed suddenly quite interested in the watering can.

Too interested. He picked it up and looked inside. "What's in the can?"

"Oh! That? I was just—"

The little man again had started kicking his feet again. "Go AWAY" I mouthed to him over Chip's shoulder, making a sideways waving gesture with my hand.

The little man just sat there.

I looked back at Chip, who was now tilting my watering can, studying its contents. He held it up and sniffed it. "Ms. Samson?" He swirled it again and stuck his face back toward the opening to smell it for the second time. "What is in this can?"

I should have been able to say something reassuring. Something that would put any of Chip Hanford's questions quickly to rest.

But I was so flustered by the little man that my mind went completely blank.

Chip gave me the kind of look a cop gives when he realizes he's stumbled on a hardened criminal. "Have you been applying the contents of this watering can to your planting beds?"

"Uh, yeah," I said, weakly. "It's, uh, an herbal infusion."

"Herbal infusion."

"A friend, uh, suggested it—as a soil amendment."

"I believe you said you weren't using any amendments this year."

"It's not a commercial preparation." I shifted my feet as I realized I was now making a bad blunder even worse.

That the little man might be the least of my problems at that particular moment.

Libby, you idiot. You idiot.

Chip lifted the can and sniffed at it again. "I see. What sort of herbs did you use to make this?"

"Horsetail. *Equisetum Arvense*. It's very high in silica. I'm, er, a biologist."

"I see."

I felt my breathing relax a little. I was on better footing here. The silica thing was true. Mentioning it was possibly even a stroke of brilliance. What soil didn't need more mineral content? "It's an experiment, really. But interesting, don't you think?"

"You prepared it yourself?"

"Yes! Yes. One peck boiled in five gallons of water. Then I cooled it and strained it and used the can here to—I gathered the horsetail from down the hill there, next to the road—"

"Next to the road?"

His tone had been sharp. Now it was even sharper. "Yes, yes, in the d—alongside the road."

"Ms. Samson. You are aware that roadside plants are often heavily contaminated with heavy metals? Lead? And also possibly petrochemical residues?"

Oh my god.

Of all the organic certification people in the world, I get this one.

Chip reached into his vest pocket and whipped out a little vial. I watched as he pulled the vial's cork out with his teeth and poured some of the infusion into the vial.

The liquid looked vile, to be honest. Greenish and murky.

He set the watering can back down and thrust the cork back into place. "We'll have to have this tested. At your expense."

"No problem. I'm sure it will be fine."

"Anything else you want to tell me, Ms. Samson?"

He had a very stern look on his face.

A "confess now or we'll see you in court" kind of look. I felt about ready to throw up.

I followed Chip back down toward my house. I didn't dare look over my shoulder to see if the little man was still there.

Twenty-Four

My disastrous on-site organic certification visit set back the certification process. But on the other hand, somehow my mache continued to come in beautifully. So I consoled myself with that. And when the day came for me to gather my first harvest, Susan was thrilled. "It's beautiful, Libby," she said to me.

We stood side by side, looking down into my chest cooler at my beautiful, bright greens, ice chips gleaming on the leaves.

I felt a wave of elation.

I'd worked so hard all morning. I'd had trouble getting to sleep the night before, no surprise. And I'd started harvesting right as the sun was coming up, moving down the rows, cutting the plants off at the ground with a knife, flicking away the occasional slug, doing a bit of cosmetic trimming if any leaves were yellowed or chewed, plunging them in ice water to keep them from wilting, and then transferring them to the cooler...

Then Paul called my cell a little after 6, right when I was ready to leave for Susan's. Which was sweet but my hands were full, and since when is he up that early on a Saturday? So I missed the call and then felt guilty and called him back.

He wanted to wish me luck. He'd actually set his alarm so he could call me before I left, to wish me luck and firm up our plans to meet in the city, later, for lunch. Doubly sweet of him. But by the time we finished going back and forth about where to meet, and what time, and then another drawn-out discussion about whether we could extend the lunch date to a dinner-and-overnight—tempting, but I had so much to do and I knew I'd be tired—it put me even further behind schedule.

Argh.

But I'd made it. Without getting a speeding ticket. Or into an accident.

"I've never seen organic mache heads that big before." Susan picked one of the heads up. "You must have some amazing soil."

I laughed, feeling a mix of pleasure and nervousness. "They do look nice, don't they? But the land's been fallow for so long. Or maybe it's because it was pasture before. I guess that probably explains it."

She helped me carry the cooler from the car to a spot in the shade near their barn while I did some quick math in my head. We were expecting to move about 20 pounds of my greens that day. Some would go to CSA members coming out to work in the afternoon. David would take the rest to Rochester's open-air market this morning, adding it to the greens and herbs he and Susan were selling. Of course, at the market David would have to mark my greens as "transitional," not organic, since I hadn't gotten certified yet. So I wouldn't be getting top dollar. But income was income.

We started transferring mache from my cooler to the one David would take to the market.

I noticed they'd grown tatsoi.

"So, how'd your on-site visit go?" Susan said.

"Pretty good, I think."

We lifted David's cooler into the truck bed, and Susan climbed in to push it toward the cab.

"Mache is getting really popular," Susan said. "I bet he sells out of your stuff."

"I've got more," I said, feeling a flush of pride.

Could this really be happening?

Was I actually doing it? My whole own-a-farm dream?

"We can't seem to grow it here," Susan was saying. "Mache. Just doesn't like the clay, I guess."

I started to say, "I've got clay, too," but stopped myself.

Susan and David had been doing this for over fifteen years. Obviously, I'd gotten lucky.

And if it wasn't entirely luck? I'd best keep that to myself.

For obvious reasons.

Too many people already knew my secret.

"C'mon, there's coffee inside," Susan said, and I breathed a quiet sigh of relief. As if I'd escaped a potential trap.

ψ ψ ψ

I met Paul at Jine's, a diner in Rochester's Park Avenue district.

He was sitting in a booth, hunched over a menu, but then he saw me and waved me over.

Ritual lip peck.

"So how'd it go?" he said. "Didja bring in a cool million or two?"

Okay. He was teasing me. Because of course I wasn't going to make a million. "Susan thinks they'll sell everything I harvested today," I said gamely. "I'm off to a great start, she says."

"Look out, Cascadian Farms."

More teasing. But hey. Maybe one day I would be as big as some giant organic mega-corporation. Or at least a well-known brand name.

We ordered our food.

I watched Paul strip the paper off a straw and plunge it into his cola.

He seemed a bit fidgety.

"So, Lib, there's something we've gotta talk about," he said. "We need to make a couple more little changes to *Skin Tones*."

So much for our celebratory lunch date. "Really? Not again?"

"It's very minor, Lib. We don't think it's peppy enough. Josh wants a bit more zing."

Paul reached under the booth for his briefcase, opened it up on the seat next to him and pulled out a print-out of the latest draft of *Skin Tones*. I suppressed a wince. The pages were all marked up. Things were crossed out. And not just words, entire sentences. No, make that entire paragraphs. And the margins were a tangle of handwriting. Paul's handwriting.

This is my job, I reminded myself. Paul is just passing along what my client needs from me. *Accept what he says. No getting defensive.* "Okay. Let's do it."

"It's not much, really! I know it looks bad, but it's very close, very close. We just want to spice it up a bit. The target audience isn't the same as before." He paused and tipped the page to read something he'd written. "Here, in this story about the divorced woman."

"Marla?"

"Yeah. Like, where she talks, here, about starting her life over. We need more—more pain. You know? Like, she's afraid, she thinks she might never get remarried, she's pushing 50, is life over for her?"

"She's not pushing 50. She's only 34."

"Right. Well, you get my point."

I felt my neck muscles tense. "The reality is that she's actually pretty happy, now. Her ex was an alcoholic. She's glad it's over."

"Mmmmm," he said absently. "And in this piece, about the peptide research." He looked at his notes again, frowning. "It needs to be punched up, you know? The transformative effect. Everything has to come back to that. So it's not entirely about the research, know what I mean? It's transformation. It's like, the phoenix rising from the ashes. We need that excitement, kind of archetypal—"

"It's not just research, it's transformation," I repeated. "I'm not sure I get what that means, exactly."

I wasn't doing a great job of being non-defensive.

And Paul was picking up on it. He glanced over, a flicker of concern in his eyes. "Sorry about all this, Libby," he said. "I really am. But Josh—but here—" He pointed to another note he'd written on the page. "Like with alchemists. Lead or gold? Lead or gold? Our women, our target market, they want gold. They need gold. We've got gold for them, Libby, we just need to communicate it."

The server plunked down our plates, and thankfully, Paul stuck the marked-up pages back into his briefcase and opened his burger roll and began dumping ketchup onto the meat.

I pulled a toothpick out of my turkey club.

This wasn't Paul's fault.

Why was I so quick to get irritated by Paul?

I took a breath.

Start over, Libby. Offer solutions.

"Well," I said, "We'd talked about getting better contacts. Maybe that would help? Half the phone numbers turn out to be fake, and when I do reach a real person, a lot of them say they haven't even used Dormet Vous products."

"Yeah, sorry about that," Paul mumbled through his mouthful of burger. "Josh said the customer database was killer. Tell you what. I'll talk to him about having an intern do some pre-screening for you." He nodded. "But enough of *Skin Tones* for now. We can talk about it on Monday. This is your big day. Are you sure you can't—"

His cell phone buzzed.

He looked down. "Josh. I gotta take this, Lib, sorry."

I sat, listening to half a conversation.

Does he love me?

I looked at my plate and pushed aside the potato chips.

Do I love him?

I couldn't help but notice the couple sitting at the table next to us. They seemed so animated. Leaning in toward each other, making so much eye contact.

And over there, that elderly pair in the corner. He'd flagged that server to come over and was pointing, now, at his wife's meal. He was making sure his wife was happy about something. The server was nodding and leaving to go get something from the kitchen. Extra mayonnaise maybe? Another pickle?

Something the wife needed to be happy.

I glanced back at Paul.

He seemed to relish his job these days. But how different his work was from the days we were in the lab, doing research. Working side-by-side.

He'd moved into a different world. A world that was increasingly foreign to me.

And I'd moved into a world that was increasingly foreign to him.

But did that really matter? Or, more to the point, was I going to let it matter?

I took a bite of sandwich and chewed, slowly, watching him talk on his cell.

We had a solid thing going, the two of us. If our worlds no longer overlapped, it didn't mean we couldn't make it work. I just needed to be thoughtful. Make adjustments. Try a bit harder to make sure we stayed connected.

I set my sandwich down as Paul finished his call.

"I was thinking," I said, reaching over the table and touching his hand. "It's been a long time since we had a real date night. Maybe the farm stuff can wait until tomorrow."

His face lit up. "So you'll stay in town?"

I nodded. "I need a break. Let's have some fun."

Twenty-Five

Fun turned into a late night. Dinner, movie, followed by nightcap at a bar on Monroe Ave.

And the next morning I realized that it would feel odd if I just rushed out the door, so I ended up sticking around. Which turned into going out for Sunday brunch.

It was early afternoon when I finally got home.

And it's not that I regretted one minute of my time with Paul. But by the time I turned onto my road, I was fretting. The forecast had called for morning showers, but there wasn't a cloud in the sky. Were my beet seedlings okay? I should have watered them before I left for the market yesterday morning. If they were dead, I'd never forgive myself. And I needed to dig out a new planting bed. I'd start a late crop of green beans. Yes. That way when my first crop was done, I'd have more to sell…at least I was almost home. I'd just have to push, is all, I'd check the beets and then get as much of everything else done, today, as I could…

I pulled into my driveway.

A strange car was parked next to Maisey's.

One of her friends, right?

But why was the driver sitting in the car?

I peered over, curious, as I pulled in and parked,

The door of the other car swung open. "Libby? Libby Samson?"

She looked to be in her early twenties. High forehead and pale wispy hair. Wearing flip flops and a gauzy boho top.

Great. Not a friend of Maisey's, after all. It was somebody selling something. On a Sunday, no less. "I'm Libby. Can I help you?" I said politely.

But instead of reaching into her car to grab a stack of brochures on replacement windows or solar panels, the woman gave a little hop and a big grin broke out on her face. "This is soooo exciting! I've been *dying* to meet you ever since I read about you!"

I frowned.

She'd read about me?

Skin Tones? I was listed as editor on the masthead. So: a *Skin Tones* reader? A *Skin Tones*…fan? A *Skin Tones* fan so enamored of my writing that she'd tracked me down to my *house*?

"I just couldn't believe when I realized where you lived and everything!" The woman hadn't stopped talking as I stood there, puzzled. "Right here in Dansville! It really is amazing! You just can't know what this means. I've always known there was something special about this place. This hill. Well, really, the whole area. You know they used to see aliens here, only that hasn't happened for years, now. But *fairies*!"

WHAT?

The woman's lips were still moving, but I could no longer hear what she was saying.

Not after that word, "fairies," sent its shock through my body.

"Wait! What did you just say?" My voice came out a half-hysterical squeak.

"When my step-brother moved in I told him—"

"No!" I waved my arms at her. "Back up! What did you say before that?"

She stopped her chitter chatter, finally, and her eyes got big.

"I don't know you," I said. "How do you know who I am?"

"Oh!" Nervous giggle. "I read about you online."

Online?

How would someone read about me and the fairies online?

Who would—

But I knew. The second the question started to form, I knew.

The kids.

Maisey and Tyler.

It had to be Maisey and Tyler.

I forgot, instantly, about the woman, and whirled, and ran up the path to the house.

"MAISEY! TYLER!" I hollered as I stormed through the kitchen.

Muffled thuds from the direction of Maisey's room.

I went to the foot of the stairs. *"Youtwogetdownhererightnow!"*

More thuds. Doorknob rattling.

Tyler slunk into view, fumbling with the button at the waist of his jeans as he stood at the top of the stairs. "I'm sorry, Aunt Libby, I'll never do it—"

"There is a woman out there, standing in the front yard," I said through gritted teeth, "who claims she read about me on the INTERNET."

Tyler's face was already flushed. Now it flushed a deeper shade of red.

"Did one of you post something about me on the Internet?"

Maisey had appeared, now, like a shadow behind Ty.

"Well?" I glared at them.

But they didn't need to answer. I could read it on their faces. I could tell by the way they exchanged a quick, guilty glance.

Busted.

And then the enormity of what they'd done hit me for real.

My secret.

My awful, awful secret.

And I'd thought I could trust them.

But I'd been wrong.

"Oh. My. God," I gasped, reaching out to the doorway to steady myself.

They started talking, then, both at once. "It was—it was just that—" Tyler stuttered while Maisey began gushing about how it was a mistake and they were so sorry and they'd deleted everything, and then Tyler shook his head and touched Maisey's arm and said, "It's all my fault, Aunt Libby. Don't blame Maisey. She had nothing to do with it."

But I didn't want to hear it. I didn't want to hear another word out of either of them. "You both promised to keep it a secret! Do you know what that even means, to make a promise?"

That shut them up.

They stood at the top of the stairs, looking utterly ashamed. As they should have been.

"I can't even—I can't even look at you right now." I felt, suddenly, like I might burst into tears. Or crumple to the floor.

Why, why, why had I told anyone about any of this?

I slumped against the wall.

Tyler, an alarmed look on his face, started down the steps. But I shook my head angrily, putting my hand up. I didn't want him touching me.

"You need to do something about that woman out there," I said. "Get rid of her. Tell her you made it all up."

They filed past me toward the door.

Neither one of them meeting my eye.

ψ ψ ψ

I went for a walk.

Walked up the hill, past my planting beds. Pausing only long enough to make sure my beet seedlings weren't dead.

So, fine. The Internet was a big place. Whatever the kids had done, it was fixable.

Right?

And given how upset I'd been, they'd get the message, finally, that a secret is a secret and a promise is a promise. And they'd get rid of that young woman.

A few clouds had moved in, and their shadows made great dark blotches that swept across the valley below.

I started back down toward the house.

Maisey was sitting on the front steps. "You okay?" she said in a little voice as I approached.

But I was still angry. "I don't want to talk about it," I said, stepping around her.

"We told that girl it was all made up," she said. "And Tyler—he's moved out."

I paused without turning, my hand on the door handle. "I didn't say he should move out."

"He thought it would be better that way. Do you—do you want me out, too?"

"Of course not. I didn't tell him to move out."

"He's really sorry," she said.

"He should be," I answered, and went inside.

Twenty-Six

I put the broken-promise incident out of my mind.

It was in the past, now. Done. Finished. Behind me.

And it was the time of year that is busiest for a market grower. I was up at sunrise every morning, tending to my growing beds.

And also getting used to my not-that-imaginary companions. Because the little man and the little woman seemed to be hanging around more, including during the day. And the more I got used to them, the more I started talking to them.

And they'd started directing my work. Like my weeding. Pulling weeds should be simple, right? Now that some of my other crops had come up—beans and carrots, fennel, beets—all I needed to do was yank out everything else.

But no. There I was, yanking weeds, and suddenly I noticed the little man walking up the hedgerow.

"Morning," I said.

Might as well be sociable, right?

"You shouldn't have pulled that one," he said.

Figures. "Why not?" I muttered.

The little man crossed the few feet between the hedgerow and the planting bed where I was working. "You know less than you think," he said.

I sighed. "Okay. Which ones should I leave?"

And would you believe it, for the next three hours he shadowed me as I worked. And I had to ask on every plant. I'd touch a weed—a baby dandelion, or thistle, or purslane plant—and ask, "This one?" and he'd either say, "Pull it" or "leave it."

It seemed to follow no pattern.

I gave up on trying to figure it out and just did what he said.

When I'd finished, the beds looked—well, they looked awful. Weedy. Or anyway, weedier than I would have liked.

"I'm really supposed to leave all that crap there?" I muttered.

"Soil balance," I heard him say, but when I looked up, he was gone.

He was big on soil balance, the little fairy dude.

Another morning, I noticed him sitting on one of my planting beds. "I was thinking I'd thin the carrots," I said to him.

He didn't answer.

I knelt and began to work. The carrot plants were on their fourth set of feathery leaves. I moved down the row, removing the smaller plants and keeping the bigger, stronger ones. Thinning them would ensure that each plant I kept would have enough room for the fat orange root it would eventually grow.

The seedlings I pulled from the ground gave off a pungent, almost minty scent, and the damp earth had the faint smell of earthworms.

And I'd almost forgotten about the little man when suddenly he spoke up. "A half-pound of copper roofing nails," he said.

"Excuse me?" I wiped the film of sweat off my forehead and pushed my glasses back into place with the back of my hand. "What am I supposed to do with roofing nails?"

"Bury them. One every few feet."

I stood up. Was I really supposed to follow this imaginary being's peculiar instructions?

I thought about the mache. How Susan had remarked at how large the heads were, how healthy they'd looked. How she and David had trouble growing it.

Was it the horsetail brew that had done that?

And speaking of horsetail brew, when was I going to hear back on the lab tests?

I pushed the thought away. Because there wasn't anything I could do about that, either. "Okay. How deep do I bury the nails?"

"Eight inches."

"In the beds, or between?"

He paused a moment, then answered, "Both."

I crouched down and pulled out another carrot seedling.

So, okay, obviously, this was now going to be my new normal. I'd be taking bizarre advice from an imaginary being. I discarded another of my culled carrot seedlings. "That horsetail stuff you told me to put on my beds."

He didn't say anything.

"Is it going to be okay? When they test it?"

Still no answer.

My back felt stiff, and I stood up to stretch and saw that Maisey was walking up the hill.

Things were still a little strained between us. I'd put the broken-promise incident behind me. I wasn't exactly angry anymore. But I was still unhappy. And Maisey knew it. She was still acting wary around me.

I watched her approach.

Her head turned from side to side as she got closer. She was looking for the little man. In fact, I was pretty sure she slipped away by herself, sometimes, and came up to the fields to look for them.

Would she see him?

I wasn't sure if I wanted the answer to be yes, or no. If I was the only person who could see them, it would be a bit of a relief. It meant, for instance, that I could relax if another organic certification inspector came to visit and started poking around the place.

On the other hand, if nobody else could see them, they'd never be real to anyone else. Just me. Which meant that I couldn't prove they existed. Or that I wasn't actually crazy.

"Hi," I said when Maisey was close enough to talk.

She had my cell phone and handed it to me. "You got a call," she said.

"Right." I checked the number. Car dealership. The car I'd bought to replace my crushed Toyota must be due for a service call. Oil change or something.

I noticed the little man in my peripheral vision. He was flicking the leaf of a milkweed that was growing on one of my beds. One of the weeds he'd told me to leave in place.

Could Maisey see that the leaf was moving? A slight breeze had picked up in the past hour. Maybe even if she noticed the leaf, she'd think it was the breeze?

I glanced surreptitiously in her direction. She made no sign that she'd noticed anything unusual.

"Thanks for letting me know," I said.

She took the phone back and started down the hill.

I was kidding myself that she'd brought my phone up to be nice. It was an excuse to look for the little man.

I moved down the planting bed. I had a few more carrot seedlings that needed to be thinned.

"Anything else?" I asked the little man.

He didn't answer. I saw him melt away into the dense growth of motherwort and goldenrod that had sprouted up along the western boundary of the field.

I straightened up and stretched my back again.

This was the part of the day that was hardest. The part of the day when I had to leave my beautiful beds, shut myself back indoors, and face *Skin Tones*. And *Skin Tones* was genuinely turning into a nightmare. Josh had decided that a revision wasn't enough. The entire last issue had to be tossed out.

I was now starting over from scratch.

Paul had promised that today I'd finally have that fresh list of customers for me to interview, but I wasn't looking forward to it.

Poring over hundreds of names with whatever sparse information was available about each. The cold calls to introduce myself, explain what I wanted, coax people to talk...

I gathered my hand tools, started down the hill, and picked my way through the hedgerow between my fields and my house.

There was a car in the driveway, again, and I felt an unwelcome wave of *deja vu*.

Wasn't that the hippy chick's car? What was she doing back at my house?

Twenty-Seven

Yes. It was the hippy chick. Only this time, instead of waiting for me in the driveway she was inside, in the living room, sitting cross-legged on the floor, having a lively conversation with Maisey.

And Tyler.

Well, it was a lively conversation until the door banged shut behind me, and I crossed the kitchen, and they looked up and saw me in the living room doorway. They exchanged glances. Maisey stood up from the couch. "Hey, Aunt Libby, you've met Alexa."

Alexa stood up as well and slipped her feet back into her flip flops. She was a fragile looking little thing with that pale forehead and feathery hair. But there was something else about her, too, that I couldn't put my finger on. She was extremely sure of herself.

Maybe it was just that she was three or four years older than Maisey and Tyler.

"Hi, Aunt Libby," she said, smiling.

"Ty's been staying at Alexa's place," Maisey said.

Ah. Okay. I'd known he'd found somewhere in town to crash after he'd moved out. Guess now I knew where.

"Nice to meet you, Alexa," I said.

And I excused myself. I had work to do.

I went up to my office and sat down at my computer and opened the spreadsheet of Dormet Vous customers.

But I found it hard to focus. I found myself listening to the voices downstairs. Quiet, at first, but then the pitch and tempo picked up.

I was just about to go back down and ask them to keep it down when I heard the front door and then the house became still.

I listened for a car motor. Nothing.

I stood up and went to the window. The three of them were walking on the road past the front of the house. Toward Dean's place.

Dean.

How long had it been since I'd seen Dean?

I sat back down, staring again at the spreadsheet.

I felt an uneasy twinge in my stomach.

It was this job, I told myself. I was anxious because I had to make these phone calls, and I really didn't want to.

I forced myself to pick up my phone and dial the first number on the list.

ψ ψ ψ

"Hey, Aunt Libby, are you busy?" Maisey asked later, after Alexa and Ty had left. "I was wondering. Would you like to watch a movie tonight? Tyler got it set up, this afternoon, so we can stream stuff. It's really cool, you'll like it. Wait till you see how many movies we can watch for free."

Hmmmm...

Something in Maisey's manner had changed.

She didn't seem as wary anymore.

And, just like that, my last bit of anger about the broken-promise thing dissolved and disappeared.

This was my friend's daughter. I was responsible for her. She was a good kid. And even good kids make mistakes.

"Okay," I said. "That sounds like fun. Shall we have cocoa?"

And as I spoke, I realized it did sound like fun. Working on my farm, only seeing Paul once a week or so? I'd moved here, in part, to get away from people. But maybe my plan had worked too well. I had no friends around. And I really should call Gina. Odd, come to think of it, that she still hadn't reached out to check with me about her daughter.

Must be she was really heads-down involved with that Hawaiian guy.

I poured some milk in a pan to warm it for the cocoa and some butter in another pan to melt. I loaded the hot air popcorn popper with kernels.

Maisey was in the living room, fussing with the remote.

"So," I called out to her over noise of the popcorn popper, "I saw you guys walking up the road. Were you, uh, going for a random walk? Or did you go see Dean?"

There. I'd said it perfectly. Very natural sounding.

"Oh. She knows him already," Maisey called back. "She's his sister, do you believe it?"

"Ow!"

"What?"

"Nothing. Just spilled the cocoa. I'm okay. It wasn't very hot." I stuck the heel of my thumb into my mouth and sucked it to tame the pain.

The popcorn finished popping and I dumped it onto a bowl.

"You need some ice for that?" Maisey joined me in the kitchen and handed me a dish rag to wipe up the cocoa that had spilled on the stove. "Actually, she's his half-sister."

"Is she?" I said, taking my hand out of my mouth and forcing my voice to sound super- casual. While thinking okay, that explained why they'd all gone to see him. "Small world," I added. "Want to put the butter on the popcorn?"

"Sure. Alexa is awfully nice. She told us all about Dean. You wouldn't believe the stories. And Alexa cuts hair. She's going to cut mine tomorrow."

All about Dean?

I poured the rest of the cocoa into our mugs. I was more careful this time. And the pink spot on my hand didn't hurt quite so much anymore.

We headed to the living room. "So, uh, how are you going to have it cut?" I asked as I set the popcorn bowl on the couch between us.

"I dunno. Maybe sort of a retro bob. Like Uma in Pulp Fiction."

I blew on my cocoa to give myself some space to choose my words. "So. You were saying. Alexa is Dean's half-sister."

Fortunately, it didn't take much to get Maisey going. "Yeah! Their mother is dead. Terrible story. Cancer. And Alexa's father is dead too, isn't that awful? He came back east because of it—"

"Who came back east? The father?"

"No! No, Alexa's father died when she was a baby. I meant Dean. When their mother got sick, he came back east."

"Ah."

"But that isn't even why he's so sad! His heart was broken by an Iranian princess. So I was right! He's been living in the woods ever since, Alexa says, only before this, he lived out west. He was a logger, so *that* explains where he got all those muscles."

I sipped my cocoa, which was a mistake. It was still scalding, and my eyes watered as the cocoa hit the roof of my mouth. "An Iranian princess?" I said in a husky, just-burned-my-mouth voice. "That's, uh— far-fetched, don't you think?"

"I know, right?" Maisey said, picking up the remote. "What happened was, they met in college and fell madly in love, but her parents had this arranged marriage thing all set, and when they found out about her and Dean, they took her away. The princess. Kidnapped her, basically. Took her to, like, Pakistan or someplace. And he never saw her again."

I grimaced. "Maisey, nice story. But I don't believe it for a minute. That sort of thing doesn't happen. Not in real life. And why would an Iranian princess be spirited off to Pakistan?"

"Alexa says he wouldn't even talk to anyone for like, 18 months. Then their mother got these headaches, and it turned out to be the brain cancer, and Alexa had to find him and tell him because he didn't have a phone or anything."

The adult in me stepped in and took firm control. "You didn't bring any of this up to Dean, I hope." Because suppose there was some truth to this tale? I felt suddenly…protective. Whatever Dean's reasons for living like he did, he sure didn't need a bunch of kids pestering him about his private affairs.

"Oh, no. We just, you know, listen to music. And he carves stuff for us. He carved Tyler a talisman thing. It was going to be a key ring, but Tyler wanted a talisman."

"Talisman?"

"It's a wolf. Kind of. Dean's great fun. You should go with us, sometime." She plumped up one of the throw pillows and settled back onto the couch.

I blew on my cocoa some more, then set it down on the coffee table.

No way was I going to drop in on Dean. Not that I would mind seeing him. But a social call? Even considering the idea made me feel funny. Awkward.

Iranian princesses indeed.

Time to change the subject. "So what movie are we going to watch?" I asked.

"You like romcoms, right?"

"Sure."

Maisey pointed the remote at the TV screen and began scrolling through a panel of movie titles.

An Iranian princess? I touched the blister on the roof of my mouth with my tongue. Alexa had the story wrong, of course. But maybe there were elements of truth. Maybe even the part about some young woman's parents intervening in a budding love affair.

Dean nursing a broken heart wasn't as far-fetched as me, talking to fairies.

"Hey, is that your computer beeping?" Maisey said suddenly, cocking her head.

I'd noticed it too. The chiming noise that meant I'd gotten an email. "I must have forgotten to turn it off."

Maisey was still scrolling through movies. "That Hugh Grant sure was gorgeous when he was young."

Good. Something we could bond on. "Yeah," I said, nodding in agreement. "Is there a Hugh Grant movie?"

"I bet we can find one!"

I smiled, but then I heard my computer chime again. A bit odd. I didn't usually get emails this time of day. "Hang on," I said. "That noise is going to bug me. I'm going upstairs to shut my PC down."

I didn't bother looking to see what the emails were about. Because either they were spam, which meant I'd have to deal with tweaking my spam filters, or they were work emails, which meant Josh had changed his mind, again, about *Skin Tones*. And no way was I going to deal with that.

Not now, when I was about to spend a nice evening bonding with my friend Gina's daughter.

The emails, I decided, would wait until tomorrow.

Twenty-Eight

It wasn't until the next day that I opened my Outlook to check those emails.

Yikes. There were over forty. And although I didn't recognize the addresses, they didn't look like spam.

I leaned in, scrolling, and that's when I saw it.

Dozens of them had "fairies" in the subject line.

I opened one.

i just had to email u. ur story is amzing. i would so luv to meet u sometime. its peeps like u who will save gaia from total destruct. luv, sandy.

What the hell?

I opened another. And another.

I let out a little moan.

Were these all because Tyler had posted something about me online?

They had to be.

But he'd said he would delete it.

He wouldn't have posted something else, would he?

I opened another email. It was pretty nasty. Accusing me of—of—I wasn't quite sure. Satanism? Being a charlatan? Both at once, I supposed. Might as well cover all your bases when emailing anonymous insults.

I heard Maisey coming up the stairs. "Maisey, can I see you for a minute?"

"Yeah?" she answered cautiously. She could tell from the tone of my voice that I was on the edge, again.

"Look at this." I brought up the first email again and Maisey read it over her shoulder.

"Has Tyler posted something again about the fairy thing?"

"No! No, of course not!"

I swiveled around to look at the girl's face. She looked sincere. Upset. But sincere.

"He didn't post about it ever," Maisey continued. "Not really. Not on purpose. It was in the comments."

Maisey wasn't a liar. But something didn't make sense.

I told myself to speak calmly. "Okay. But I don't understand, then, how these people have my email address." I minimized the message and pointed at my inbox queue. "Look. Four more new ones just came in." I did a double take. "No. Make that seven. Eight."

"I have no idea how this could be happening, Aunt Libby. I swear!"

I started deleting the emails when it hit me.

Dormet Vous posted *Skin Tones* up on their website.

And I was listed as editorial contact.

And sure enough, a quick Google connected the dots. My email address was listed as the *Skin Tones* contact.

Maisey was still standing behind me, watching my screen. "Uh, Aunt Libby? Go back to Google real quick." Her voice sounded funny.

But I'd noticed it too. When I'd searched my name, it had come up more than once.

I clicked the second link. It was a website titled something like Psychoparanormalnews.

I started reading. *Exciting news, gals and guys, a woman by the name of Libby Samson has made contact with the Little Folk in Upstate New York...*

I groaned aloud as I scrolled back to the top of the page. The article was bylined by someone calling themselves "Heavenly Starlight."

"Aunt Libby," Maisey said, her voice just about a whisper. "You have to believe me. Tyler didn't mean to—"

I clicked on the website's home page. I was looking for a contact. Someone without a fake name, someone I could hire a lawyer to hunt down. The lawyer I was going to hire, if I had to, to issue a cease and desist letter to this Heavenly Starlight person.

"Ty posts a lot about supernatural stuff, you know?" Maisey was saying. "So his readers—and all he did was—he wrote about finding this new hotspot, you know, your farm, only he didn't reveal your name or anything, I swear. But then in the comments these people got going, and you know some of them just can't let it go—"

Ugh. I could not find a contact listed on that stupid site…

I pushed back from the desk. And, oh crap. Maisey was crying.

And I felt, suddenly, horrible. Evil, even. Because of course, this whole thing had probably been really hard on the girl.

And I hadn't reacted rationally. I'd fallen apart. I'd made her boyfriend so uncomfortable he'd moved out.

I needed to do better. I needed to be a better person.

I reached out and touched Maisey's shoulder.

That's all it took. She collapsed into my arms. "I'm so sorry," she sobbed. "We didn't mean to make you mad!"

"Shhh. It's okay. Don't worry about it." I patted her back like a mother pats a six-year-old with a skinned knee. "It's not that big a deal. Really. It'll be okay."

My computer chimed.

It chimed again.

Maisey stepped away as I turned and opened Outlook again.

Five new emails from people I didn't know.

I didn't read them. Just deleted them.

It would go away. All I had to do was ignore it.

Ignore it, except for Heavenly Starlight, who would soon be hearing from my lawyer.

Assuming I could afford a lawyer.

Maisey was watching me. Her eyes red. So full of remorse.

"It's okay," I said. "Really. I'll deal with it. It'll be fine." I stood up and pushed away from the desk. "I need to run to the hardware store. Want to come?"

Run to the hardware store to buy a half pound of copper roofing nails because a supernatural being told me to bury them on my property.

And okay, so a bunch of people had read a comment on a website somewhere.

What was the worst that could happen?

Twenty-Nine

"Whoa, Aunt Libby, you are totally *viral*."

"Thanks," I said dryly.

Tyler had been maneuvering around the 'net for a good 30 minutes by then, and I'd finally given up watching. I'd moved to the love seat against the far wall of my office.

Maisey was still watching, though, draped over Tyler's shoulder.

"He means that in a good way, Aunt Libby!" Maisey turned toward me, an anxious look on her face. "He means you've spread all over."

I rolled my eyes. "I know what it means, Maise. I'm not *that* old."

"Well, you're not really into computers and stuff," Maisey said.

Alexa giggled and I shot her a look to let her know I didn't appreciate being made fun of at that particular moment.

Yeah, Alexa was there, too. Sitting on the rug, legs wrapped around each other under her skirt.

"How many mentions have you found so far?" I asked, turning my attention back to Tyler.

"That's two more."

So it brought the total to about twenty, then. Twenty different websites and forums and reddit threads proclaiming that Libby Samson was *the* psychic phenomenon of the new millennium.

Needless to say, I'd abandoned the idea of legal action. At least for now. What was I going to do? Pay a lawyer two hundred an hour to write "cease and desist" letters to twenty fifteen-year-old

Instagrammers and Tweeters? Most of whom were posting under pseudonyms?

And anyway, Tyler had volunteered to jump in where he could and contact people and try to get them to quit re-posting about it.

Although I'd also noticed that the more sites he uncovered, the less confident he sounded about that particular plan. "It's definitely viral," he murmured now, as if reading my thoughts. "It's all over the place."

"What are their names?" Alexa asked.

"Their names?" I thought she meant the names of the Tweeters who were spreading my virus.

"When they appear to you, what do you call them?"

Ah. She meant the fairies. "I don't call them anything. I'm not sure they have names."

Alexa's eyes fixed on me, gleaming with interest. "Have you ever asked them?"

I sighed. I couldn't blame Alexa. I'd be curious, too. After all, this wasn't about fairies, was it? It was about whether humans are really bound by the mundane, the laws of physics, the plain Jane everyday-ness that for most people passes for life. Which made me living proof, to this little slip of an orphan, that there was something more out there than rocks and dirt, and the endless grind of the seasons always taking, taking, taking.

On the other hand, that wasn't a role I'd asked for. I was a biologist. A biologist turned farmer. I shook my head. "No. I've never asked them."

"You should." Alexa leaned forward. "Can I go with you, sometime? When you meet with them?"

"I've already asked," Maisey cut in. "She won't let you."

I looked over at her, curious. She'd seemed a bit funny around Alexa today.

I guess it was natural for Maisey to make darn sure that if anyone went along to see the fairies, it was going to be Maisey. She'd been here first, after all.

"I don't actually 'meet' with them, anyway," I said to Alexa. "I go up there and work, and if there's something I need to do, something they can help me with, they show up. That's all."

"Well, could we go with you? We could help you work," Alexa pressed hopefully.

I shifted in her seat. "It wouldn't matter. I don't think you can see them."

Maisey and Alexa both gasped.

"Really?" said Alexa, sounding excited.

"Really?" Maisey said, sounding disappointed.

So I told them about the time Maisey had given me the phone message.

"He was *right there*?" Maisey said.

"He was."

"Wow," Alexa said.

Tyler swiveled around in my office chair to face me. "You could, like, give workshops on how to see them," he said.

"Oh, Ty, that is a *great* idea!" Alexa beamed first at Tyler, then at me. "It would be awesome, and think how great for mass consciousness and everything!"

"Forget it. There's no way. And I don't know how to see them. I just do."

"You should ask them!" Alexa said.

"Ask them what?"

"How to help people see them. And you should ask them their names," she added quickly.

I stood up. Enough was enough. "It's not like that."

I paused a moment. What I wanted to say was "It's not the relationship I want to have with them."

But there was no point in going into it any further. They wouldn't understand.

I wish I'd never seen the fairies in the first place.

The thought of turning them—and me—into a public spectacle?

Nightmare.

I shooed them out of my office. "Look, I have to get some work done. Thanks for what you're doing, Ty, but you have to finish up on your phone."

Thirty

I really needed to get that doorbell fixed.

That's what I was thinking to myself when I scrambled down the stairs to see who was banging on my door at 8:30 on a Saturday night.

The stoop light was on. Maisey was out somewhere with Tyler and, probably, Alexa. Seemed like the three of them were always together lately.

I opened the door. A couple of boomers were standing on my stoop. He was normal-looking enough. Khaki shorts and closely trimmed graying beard, Imagine World Peace baseball cap. But she was tall. Really, really tall. And she was wrapped in—was that a cape? A purple silky cape with stars embroidered on it?

"Can I help you?"

"We're so sorry to bother you," the woman said. "Are you Libby Samson? We're looking for Libby Samson, the woman who talks to the little people."

Oh, great. The emails were one thing. The emails that, by the way, were increasing in volume by the day. But in-person visits?

"Sorry," I said, forcing myself to remember my manners. "I'm busy right now."

"Oh, Libby!" The woman stepped toward me.

I reacted like any normal person would. I took a step backward.

Big mistake. The next moment the boomers were both inside my house, looking around eagerly like they expected fairies in cages hanging from the ceiling. Or sitting around little rough-hewn tables in my kitchen, drinking mead out of miniature goblets.

"I'm so pleased we found you," the woman exclaimed as she scanned the room. "We've come all the way from Vermont. I told Danny we could find you!"

"She's an intuitive," Danny said. "Gifted."

"You have a charming home. Charming."

I raised an eyebrow. I'm not the neatest person in the world. I was hosting a teenager who is also not the neatest. And a good share of my furniture had come from the Goodwill. The overall effect was not exactly what I'd call charming.

"Look," I said. "I don't mean to be rude—"

"May we sit down? We won't stay long. We have a hotel in town. We came so far."

"It would have been a seven-hour drive," Danny said, nodding. "Then we hit awful traffic outside Albany. Huge accident."

"Huge. I had to purify the scene." The woman looked at Danny. "Danny wouldn't let me get out, though. I had to do it through the window. Sometimes emergency service personnel don't understand."

"Jade doesn't like being told what to do," Danny said.

What was your first clue. I sighed. Maybe if I just humored the two for a few minutes, their curiosity would be satisfied and they'd leave. "In here," I gestured toward the living room.

They sat on the couch, and Jade tossed the cape back from her shoulders and surveyed the room. "Ah, you read mass market paperbacks." She smiled. "Interesting. Okay in small doses but do be careful. A steady diet can lower your vibrations. Of course, I can help you with that."

"It's part of The Work," Danny added.

"And needless to say, you'd get the friends and family rate." Jade shot me an exaggerated wink, then looked around the room again. "Oh, would you mind? I'm feeling a bit dry. Do you have good water here? Are you on a well? The water in town will be treated, I'm sure. Toxic. You're on a well, right?"

It crossed my mind that these two creatures were stranger than little men popping up in a field in the dark. And that there was something off about this Jade person in particular. She seemed sincere, in a way, and yet…

I went to the kitchen and returned with two glasses of water. Because who was I to judge? Wasn't I the person who had dumped a dicey tea brewed from *Equisetum Arvense* on my planting beds because magical beings told me it would correct a crystalline alignment?

Jade sniffed her water with a thoughtful look, took a cautious sip, then nodded. "It's fine, hon," she said to Danny.

"Anyway," he said, "we know it's late—"

"Yes, it's late," I broke in quickly. "And I'm sorry to disappoint, but whatever you've read online? It's not—"

"Oh, that's fine. We can come back tomorrow, when everyone's rested," Jade said. "We just wanted to introduce ourselves, really."

Tomorrow?

"We've just gotten back from Findhorn," Danny said.

He and Jade started nodding vigorously.

Findhorn.

A week ago, the name would have meant nothing to me. But I was quickly becoming an expert on modern sightings of the little people. With Tyler's help. I now knew that Findhorn was a community on the coast of Scotland. In the 1960s, some people living there had communicated regularly with fairies. So the stories went.

"There are so many possibilities," Jade was saying. "It's rare to find an experience like yours that comes across as so authentic. Especially in the New World."

"Jade is really good at picking up on energies," Danny chimed in. "Sometimes it even affects her physically."

"I've been led here, Libby. I'm here to help you."

Help me? I stood up. "Thanks for your offer," I said, "but I'm not really looking for help. I'm also very busy tomorrow."

Danny had noticed me stand up and started to stand, too, but then he sat back down. Because Jade was oblivious. She'd produced an enormous carpet bag from inside her cape and was bent over it, rooting around. "So I'm writing a book," she said, "and I have my tape recorder here, somewhere. We'll help you tell your story, on your terms. Ah, here it is." She started unwrapping a microcassette.

What?

"I really can't do this right now," I said.

Jade finally noticed that I was standing. "Oh," she said. "It is late."

Good, getting the message, finally. I nodded.

"So what time tomorrow works for you?"

Argh! That's not the message!

And then it hit me. If I wanted to get through to them, I'd need to use their lingo, not mine. "Look," I said. "I appreciate your offer. I really do. But, uh, I have to check, first, if I'm going to involve anyone else in The Work. And there are, ah, certain protocols that they've given me. Before I bring on helpers."

Jade's face went blank when I started talking, but then she nodded. "Of course, dear! Of course. You'll need to rebalance, won't you? And integrate our energies. I understand completely."

Yes! The momentum was now clearly in my favor, and I went with it. "Exactly. We're right in the middle of a very delicate, ah, rebalancing right now. And over the next week, well, it's a delicate time."

It wasn't a total lie. Burying those copper roofing nails, like the little man had instructed? It had something to do with rebalancing, right?

I pulled out my cell to check the time. It was after 9:00. "It was really wonderful to meet you. I'm so glad you understand. And I have some critical preparations I need to, uh, finish tonight."

Also not a lie. If I didn't make progress on my *Skin Tones* feature, it would be hanging over my head all day tomorrow.

"Oh, my dear! We do understand. Completely," Jade said. "Dan, there is that amazing psychic we'd hoped to see out by Lily Dale. Let's get to our hotel and try to reach her again. You'll have to meet her, Libby, she channels animal spirits. Horses, mostly. The stories they have! Horrible. I'm glad you aren't keeping animals here. Oh, and we'll do our essences." She turned to me again. "Are you doing essences?"

"Essences?"

"You should, dear. The little people will tell you how, I'm sure. They're probably preparing to tell you."

I nodded and smiled brightly. "Yes, essences. Of course."

"Come on, Danny." Jade got up from the couch and fastened the button at the neck of her cape.

I escorted them to the door and watched the rear lights of their Prius as they rolled slowly down my driveway.

Maisey's car was pulling up as they were leaving. She stopped and waited on the road to let them pass.

"Who was that?" she said a moment later.

"Jade and Danny. Here to talk about fairies."

"Oh. Aunt Libby," she said. "I'm so sorry."

"It's okay." I wished I hadn't come down on her and Tyler so hard. Especially Tyler. "At least most of these people don't know where I live."

"Yeah. Aunt Libby, about that."

I was setting Danny and Jade's glasses down in the sink, but something in Maisey's voice made me turn to look at her.

"Tyler was online today, and someone's organized a meet-up."

"What? What do you mean, a meet-up?"

"In Dansville. You know, so people who—people who are into all this can, like, get together and stuff."

My brain tried to process what that meant. Also, my brain reminded me that the last thing I wanted to do was lose my temper at Maisey again. The girl felt guilty enough already.

I drew a breath. "Well, they'll be in Dansville, right? They don't know where I live."

Maisey nodded in agreement. "That's what we were saying."

Something in my manner must have reassured her, because she turned and began unloading groceries onto the counter. "Oh, and Mom called me today. She said she tried to call you and you didn't pick up."

"Aw, darn it. How's she doing?"

"She's flying back."

Oh, really? "What happened?"

"Nothing bad, I don't think," Maisey said. "But she says for you to call her back."

I felt a smile curve my lips. Maybe my old friend Gina and I would finally be able to reconnect. "So where's she headed? Back to Washington?"

"No, actually." Maisey shook her head. "She wants to come here. She's flying into Rochester, and I'm supposed to pick her up and everything."

Oh. Okay. Well, that was Gina. She'd never met an impulse that she didn't think was worth indulging. And hadn't I just been mooning about feeling a bit lonely? "Did she tell you anything else?"

Maisey shook her head. "Nope. Just that she needs to talk to you."

And okay, I let an unfriendly thought cross my mind.

I hope she isn't going to ask me, again, for a loan. Because Gina was a marvelous person in many ways, but she was also the sort of person who tended to go on grand adventures that ended in semi-catastrophe, after which she'd come running to her friends and family asking them to please help her undo the damage. And for some reason she'd gotten it into her head that my divorce settlement was considerably larger than it actually was. It seemed, in fact, that in Gina's mind the settlement was in the multi-millions.

She'd been reading too many tabloid headlines. Wallace had blurred into a Jeff Bezos or somebody, some rich celebrity ex.

I noticed that Maisey had stopped putting groceries away, and instead was leaning against the counter with a funny look on her face. Kind of tired and blank. And it occurred to me that it was kind of early, on a Saturday night, for the teenager to be home. "Hey," I said cautiously. "Looks like you decided to make it an early night?"

"Yeah. Tyler said he wasn't feeling very good. I guess he and Alexa kind of tied one on last night."

"Oh." I searched her face. "I thought Tyler didn't drink?"

"He didn't. He doesn't." She turned and put a couple of yogurts in the refrigerator and stuffed the emptied grocery bag in the box I kept near the door.

"Do you want to watch a movie?" I said.

"Nah, Aunt Libby. I don't think so. Not tonight. I think I'll have a vape and go to bed. I'm kinda tired."

"Okay."

"Don't worry about this meet-up thing, Aunt Libby," Maisey said from the stairs. "Tyler posted, saying it was called off, so nobody will show up, anyhow."

Thirty-One

Right.

So, I'm sure Tyler tried to call it off.

The "meet-up."

Unfortunately, it didn't work.

Also, unfortunately, instead of "meeting up" in some random place in Dansville, word somehow got out that the place to be was my property.

Specifically, my front yard. Which, a few days later, was slowly filling up with tents.

"How many are there?" I asked.

"Twelve," Maisey said. "One of them is pretty big, though. I think there might be, like, eight people sleeping in it. Oh, they've got the fire going again."

We were in the living room, and Maisey was lifting the corner of the bedspread we'd duct-taped over the windows. We'd done that two nights ago, after we noticed someone standing outside, cupping his hands against the glass to look in around the edge of the shades.

Because of the bedspread, the room was dim and stuffy as the two of us sat drinking our morning coffee.

"Got to hand it to them," I said. "Sticking it out in this rain."

Maisey nodded.

The downspout on the northeast corner of the house must have fallen apart again. I could hear the staccato clank as water from the gutter struck it, where it had come to rest next to the foundation. Which meant water would be running into my basement pretty soon. And normally all I'd have to do was throw on my plastic poncho and grab a ladder and reassemble the spout. But now, instead, I was in hiding. In my own home.

Maisey was scrolling through her cell's sent text messages. Now she dialed a number. Held the phone to her ear a moment, then shut it.

"Ty's still not picking up?"

Maisey shook her head quickly.

I tried to read her face. Maisey hadn't confided in me. But I was beginning to suspect something might be going on with her and Tyler.

She peeked around the bedspread again. "Dean says you should call the cops. Or get a dog." She looked at me hopefully.

"I don't want a dog." I tilted my coffee mug and looked inside. "And I'm not calling the cops." Because if I called the police, the whole thing might hit the papers. And if it hit the papers, Paul would find out. And the last thing I needed was to have my boyfriend find out from the newspaper that I was Internet-famous because I talked to supernatural beings. "So you guys have been to see Dean again?"

"I went."

"Oh. You went there alone?"

"We've gotten kind of close," Maisey said, then added quickly, "but don't worry, I think he likes you. In *that* way."

I laughed a nervous little "heh" and stood up. "I seriously doubt that, Maisey. I'm going to fix some breakfast. Want some eggs?"

"Nah. Is there any more coffee?"

I crouched a bit as I moved into the kitchen. The kitchen windows weren't covered, and I felt funny about all those strangers outside.

"Don't you like Dean?" Maisey had followed me.

I pulled an egg box from the fridge. "Of course I do."

"He's over that Iranian."

"The princess?"

"Turns out she wasn't exactly a princess. Dean says Alexa exaggerates sometimes." Maisey made a face. "Don't you like Dean?"

"I just said I did."

"Why don't you invite him over?"

"Why would I do that? I have a boyfriend, Maisey."

"Paul." She made a face again.

"There's nothing wrong with Paul. When I was going through the divorce—"

I broke off, setting the carton of eggs on the counter. When I was going through the divorce, Paul had been my rock. He'd been kind, and understanding, and supportive…

And I'd admired Paul even before we started dating. Admired his dedication. He'd been a damned good biologist, too. For some people, lab work is all in the method. Paul was careful, of course, he wasn't sloppy, but he had a knack for anticipating where research was going to lead. He'd get into the zone. Yet if the results weren't there, it never bothered him.

I'd admired that. A lot.

"Only the rest of the story was still true," Maisey interrupted my musing. "Other than the princess part."

I cracked an egg into a dish. "Maybe you shouldn't be prying into Dean's private life."

"Oh, we talk about everything. He says he's been living alone for so long, he forgot how nice it was to talk."

I remembered the night we'd drunk the wine together. How easy he'd been to talk to.

Maisey was dialing her cell again. I glanced over and saw the girl's mouth tighten before she gave up and stuck the phone back into the pocket of her shorts.

"Maisey," I said. "Why don't you just go into town?"

"But the campers. If they see me leave, they'll want to know what I'm doing. And then they might come to the house and bug you, too, right?"

"They already bug me." I gave a wry smile. "Look, Maisey, this isn't fair to you. Ty probably wants to see you."

"Are you sure you're okay with me leaving?"

She'd been holed up with me for three days. "Yup. I'm sure."

Maisey set down her mug. "Okay."

"When's your mom's flight getting in?"

"5:45."

"So we'll see you here for dinner then, seven-ish. Tyler, too."

I watched through the window as Maisey went to her car. And sure enough, as soon as they noticed her, a couple of the campers trotted over. I couldn't hear what they were saying, but Maisey was shaking her head. Telling them I wasn't home, maybe?

A couple of them thrust notes into her hand. That's what they'd started to do, now that they'd realized I wouldn't talk to them. They'd corner poor Maisey and ask her questions or give her notes to pass along to me.

The notes were mostly the same kind of messages I was getting in the emails. Some were questions directed at the little people themselves. "Why have you come?" "What is your message to mankind about our destruction of the environment?" Others were addressed to me. "I need to talk to them. Please arrange it, please." "Do you meditate? Is there a practice I can do so I can talk to fairies, too?"

And of course, a few requests for gardening advice. "My delphiniums keep turning yellow and dropping their leaves."

Or, most poignant at all, the ones from people who were hurt or sick. Asking for medical advice. Asking to be healed. Asking for help finding love.

Maisey got into her car and the little clump of campers turned and looked back toward the house. I thought for a minute they might come up and bang on the door again—they'd done that, too—but instead they straggled back toward their tents.

The rain was falling again, heavier now.

It was probably pretty damp and cold and miserable to sleep in a tent in all that rain. It almost made me feel a bit sorry for them. But then again, if they got damp and cold and miserable enough, maybe they'd all go away.

Thirty-Two

The rain let up some that evening, and as the sun began to lower, mist formed in the valley below the farm.

I heard Maisey's car, finally, and stood in the front doorway and watched as she and Gina got out.

Gina. One of my oldest friends. A person I admired for the peculiar reason of being absolutely nothing like me. So unlike me that sometimes I felt like, after Gina was created, there were enough unused parts left over to create one other person—and that person was Libby Samson.

I watched as a bunch of campers flocked over to the car. And then, to my amazement, Gina said something to them, kind of waving her arms in an animated way as she spoke, and a moment later they let Gina pass through, Maisey and Tyler trailing behind.

Amazing.

I opened the door as they climbed the steps to the stoop.

"I am *totally* pissed off at you," Gina cried out dramatically, and then broke into her huge grin and grabbed me in a bear hug. "Why didn't you tell me what was going on?" She bent her body back and forth at her waist, which—because she was holding me so tight—made my body bend too, like we were dancing.

"I've been busy!" I protested. "And it's not like you were exactly answering your phone when I called you back."

She set me loose and took a step back. "Well! Thank you for looking after my baby girl. You're so adorable, looking after my baby girl like that!"

I took her duffel bag. "How was your flight?"

"The airplane cabin was freezing cold. How long is this rain here for?"

"It's supposed to be nice tomorrow."

Gina wrinkled her nose. "You don't know nice. You should try Hawaii."

"Something smells good, Aunt Libby," Tyler said.

I smiled at him and then at Gina. "Bean casserole." Gina didn't eat meat. Or anyway, she didn't the last I knew. "Tyler, would you please carry Gina's duffel up to Maisey's bedroom? I hope you don't mind sharing Maisey's air mattress, Gina."

"Sounds divine," Gina said. "I'm exhausted."

ψ ψ ψ

Gina and Maisey were already up the next morning when I came downstairs. They were in the living room, on the couch, and Maisey was combing out Gina's hair. Which was long and sleek and blond. Like I said. Frizzy-haired Libby got all the parts left over when they made Gina.

"Maisey and I have been chatting about this," Gina said, tipping her head at the covered windows so I'd know she meant the campers. "Why are you hiding from them?"

"It's all part of the plan," I said. "If we avoid them—"

"They'll lose interest and go away," Gina finished my sentence. "That's possible, I suppose. But doubtful." She shot me a teasing side-eye. "You're still a total introvert, Libby."

I sighed. "What else is new? If you have a better idea, I'm all ears."

"How about this? I'll organize them," Gina said. "It's just a matter of organization. Maisey and her friends can help."

Maisey glanced at me. "I don't think Aunt Libby wants them organized, Mom." She moved, now, to the back of the couch, and started splitting her mother's hair into thirds, getting ready to re-braid it.

"If you want to do something for me, go out there and tell them to leave," I said.

"You can't fight it, Libby," Gina said. "Don't you see? It's a shift in consciousness. It's a movement."

"How can it be a movement? I don't even talk to them."

Gina couldn't move her head without pulling her hair out of Maisey's hands, so she just slid her eyes toward me again with a "you just don't get it" look. But then she changed the subject. "I need you to ask your contacts about our pineapples."

"My contacts?"

"Your little people. They give you advice about your farm, isn't that right? That's what Maisey said."

"Well sure, but I don't know—"

"It'll be fine!" Gina smiled. "You'll see."

"This isn't the Oracle of Delphi," I muttered. "Where do people get the idea that I can get answers to all their questions? They probably don't even know what a pineapple is."

"Hmmmm," Gina said. "Well, if not, they can just contact the energies in Hawaii."

She sounded just like that Jade woman. Which made sense. They were both from that same world, that world where we scientists don't belong. The world of energies and crystals, and where simply believing something hard enough can make it happen.

I tried for another moment to come up with a logical response to Gina's suggestion, but came up empty. "I need coffee. Anyone else need coffee?"

ॐ ॐ ॐ

An introvert.

Gina was right, of course. I was an introvert. Always had been. The kind of person who, as a kid, sat in the middle of the classroom. Never the front, where I might get called on too much by the teacher, and certainly not the back, where the clowns and troublemakers tended to congregate.

The middle. Where—hopefully—nobody would notice me.

And then my freshman year in college, I was the student who spent all her time studying. My roommates thought I was weird, because I never wanted to go to the parties or try to get into the bars.

If I hadn't met Gina, I probably would have spent the next three years holed up in the library or my dorm room. But then we met and unlike most of the extroverts I'd encountered, she actually seemed to like me. And she adopted me. She wouldn't take "no" for an answer when she invited me to go out somewhere. And she was such a fascinating person. As a single mom, she'd started college late, so she was older than me and my peers. And she seemed to know everybody. And if she didn't, she'd be friends with them anyway in about five minutes. And she wasn't afraid to dress in ways that called attention to herself, her hands covered with rings, her bright lipstick, her tops cut low to show off her cleavage.

It was Gina who introduced me to Wallace. They were friends. And he was very much like her in a lot of ways, which I enjoyed, at first. He seemed to balance me. And by then I'd had some practice being around Gina, so I wasn't as uncomfortable as I would have been. I didn't mind things like eating out every night instead of cooking at home. And not just eating out but sitting at the bar so Wallace could chat with people, chat with the bartender, meet people.

Of course, he was a salesman, so everyone he met was someone who, one day, might need a car.

And I told myself he was exciting, and I was proud of him. And it was fine, at first. But then it started to catch up to me. It would tire me out, being around other people all the time. He'd invite people to our house night after night the first couple years we were married, until I finally begged him to stop.

And then I started begging off going out to eat. "You go, honey," I'd say. "I'm not hungry. I'll have crackers and cheese or something."

I wanted to stay in at night, once in a while. Curl up with a book, sit in a room that was still and peaceful with a book and my thoughts...

I was reverting, more and more, to my default self.

I suppose it was inevitable that we began to come apart.

And yet I refused, for so long, to face the truth about him. Because I knew if I faced the truth I'd have to leave, and leaving Wallace felt like stepping off a cliff into...what?

I had no idea.

Thirty-Three

The campers were interfering with my ability to work my farm.

My fault, I suppose. I was letting it get to me. The thought of them out there, watching for me, lying in wait for their new guru to emerge from the house and answer all their questions about the universe…

I didn't want to go outside. I didn't want to leave my house. I wanted to hide.

So that's what I did. I hid. Worked on *Skin Tones*, dusted, re-organized my linen closet. All while fretting about my crops. I needed to weed. I needed to see how many carrots I'd be able to harvest next weekend. I needed to thin the beets.

I needed to bury a half-pound of copper roofing nails.

"Are you actually sorting your junk drawer?" Gina had come up behind me in the kitchen and I now had the feeling that she'd been watching me for longer than I'd realized.

"Maybe," I answered as I finished rewinding a little ball of twine. I tucked it into the front corner of the drawer.

"Have you seen my cell phone charger? I thought I left it on the end table by the couch, but it's not there."

Things go missing in this house.

"Did you check with Maisey?" I said. "Maybe she borrowed it."

"I asked. She hasn't seen it, either."

The things that go missing in this house always turn back up.

"Well, you must have done something with it." I pretended to be deeply interested in whether I should store my boxed set of miniature screwdrivers near the front of the drawer or the back. "It'll turn up."

They're playing with us.

Gina heaved a dramatic sigh and left me to my sorting.

A few minutes later, she walked through the kitchen again and went outside.

I went up to my office and lifted a slat of the window blinds. She was out there, with the campers. Standing by the tents, gesturing as she talked, her Indian-print skirt rippling in the breeze. She'd made friends with them. Friends! How could it be so easy for some people to make friends? And with complete strangers, no less?

And oh, look, now Maisey and Tyler were out there, too, ambling over toward the group.

Which meant—

This is your chance, Libby!

I wasn't really dressed for outdoor work.

But I didn't have time to change.

And if I was going to slip out without being seen, I couldn't use either of the house's doors. I'd have to go through a window. The dining room window, on the back of the house.

Which turned out to be stuck. Because when your house is a very old farmhouse, that's what happens. Windows get stuck.

I ran down to the basement for a putty knife.

Fortunately, the putty knife had not gone missing.

I made a quick stop in the living room to peek out the window—Gina and crew were still out there, good!—and then began chipping at the paint gluing the dining room sash to the frame.

My window frame soon looked like it had been attacked by tiny, evil beavers.

But at long last, when I pushed at the sash again, it moved. Very grudgingly. But it moved. An inch…another inch…another…

I stood back and eyeballed the space between the sill and the sash. Was it open wide enough for me to squish through?

I reached through the gap and wrestled the screen out of the way.

And then I eyeballed the four-foot drop from the window to the ground.

Argh.

So, okay. I could try going through headfirst…

I imagined myself losing my balance and diving head-first into the ground, resulting in grievous injury if not paralysis.

Scratch that.

Okay, option two: go through feet first.

I now imagined myself getting stuck part-way, legs dangling out the window, and how that photo would look on Facebook. Woman Who Talks to Fairies Gets Wedged in Window.

The sun was getting so high in the sky. This was taking far too long!

I dragged a chair over to the window, climbed up on it, faced my backside toward the great outdoors, and hoisted my legs one at a time onto the sill.

I shifted my weight backwards. The metal frame of the screens dug into my shins and I suppressed a yelp of pain.

I wriggled a bit further out of the window until my butt squeezed through—barely.

I wriggled a bit further.

My hands began to sweat as I realized I was reaching the point of no return. And that there was nothing under my legs but air.

My arms ached.

One last push…

The window sash caught my shirt, pulling it up toward my shoulders so now I could no longer see the ground, and I felt the air cool against my naked skin (this photo plastered on Facebook was going to be a doozy) and then I let go and dropped to the ground.

I did not nail my landing.

On the contrary, it was more like the ground hit me. So, of course, I lost my balance and flopped onto my side.

I laid there for a minute, noticing how, this time of year, the ground was dried out and hard as rock.

I moved my legs.

Nothing seemed to be broken.

I stood up. Ouch. My right hip hurt. But I ignored the pain and broke into a run, darting to my shed to grab my gloves and canvas bag of hand tools. And the little brown paper bag of roofing nails.

I dashed to the sapling grove.

Made it.

I reached the low end of my first field.

A crow cawed from a tree in Dean's forest.

I picked up my pace again. I could see the beds from here and everything looked okay, so far. I could see my crops, they looked big, green, beautiful...

And then I got a little closer and stopped short. The campers had been there. Their footprints were everywhere. Including on the beds. Idiots. They'd actually stepped on some of my plants. Idiots.

Oh, and look over there! They'd built a little stone alter, using stones from the wall in the hedgerow. There was a quartz crystal the size of a golf ball on top of it, and a bunch of burnt incense butts, and some wilted wildflowers.

Cute.

"The soil acidity has drifted slightly."

I sucked in my breath. The little man!

I'd had no idea how happy I would be to hear that impossible voice.

I looked around, looking for him. The air was humid, and the sun was high and bright, so at first the glare obscured him. But then, finally, I saw him, seated on that same stone he'd sat on the day Chip Hanford had done his on-site.

"Does it need to be corrected?" I asked happily.

"Perhaps. The rain helped."

"I was thinking I might weed around the Brussels sprouts."

Brussels sprouts had been the little man's suggestion. And they're in the cabbage family, like tatsoi, so of course I'd figured they'd get slaughtered by flea beetles, too, but the little man had told me not to worry. And sure enough, they were fine. A few holes in the plants' baby leaves here and there, but nothing major. The flea beetles that had descended rapaciously on my tatsoi had apparently moved on.

And the Brussels sprouts would be amazing come fall. I planned to harvest them by cutting off the whole stalk. People love buying them that way, the whole stalk with the sprouts still attached.

"Clear the weeds to about four inches back from the plants," the little man said. "Leave everything else."

"Okay." I felt so happy.

I knelt and pulled a dandelion, then glanced back at the little man and pointed toward the altar. "I see you've had some company."

He didn't answer.

"They can't see you, right?"

"Why don't you ask them?" he answered.

Oh, no!

I stood up and looked behind me. Campers were rushing toward me. Dozens of them. Only it looked to me more like hundreds.

Gina was with them. Striding out in front, her skirt flapping around her legs, purposeful and triumphant, striding up the hill like Attila the Hippy.

Thirty-Four

So much for thinking I could handle this by sneaking out of my house when nobody was looking.

And boy, was I glad I was weeding and not burying roofing nails...

The campers were now halfway up the field.

I cannot let these idiots trample my beds.

"Hey!" I yipped, waving my arms. "Do NOT walk on the planting beds!" I bounded forward to head them off. "Halt!" I yelled, ridiculously, spinning my arms through the air like a drunken windmill.

It worked. Probably by frightening them. They slowed down. They clumped. They looked back and forth, first at me, and then at Gina.

It was, in retrospect, a huge milestone for a lifelong introvert.

"Are you holding a session?" Gina said as the clump of campers edged closer.

But my burst of courage had burned out instantly and was gone. "What?" I muttered. "A what? I'm—I'm weeding."

"Can we help?" someone in the pack piped up.

"Yeah, we'll help!"

The pack was now crowding into a circle around me, and they started peppering me with questions. "Have you seen the little people today?" "How about Pan, have you ever seen Pan?" "Do they appear in visual form or are you just linking up with their energies?" "I told Machaelle Small Wright she should contact you. Did she ever contact you?"

My head swiveled back and forth as I tried to process all those the words hitting me all at once. "Uh, uh—g-guys?" I gurgled. "I don't—I can't—"

I turned my eyes on Gina. *Bail me out here, please?*

And, phew. She smiled and nodded, and then turned to the campers and held up a hand.

They instantly fell silent.

"Guys," she said, "we all have a ton of questions, I know. But Libby, here, is feeling a little overwhelmed. So, rather than come at her all at once like this, let's try something different."

They stood quietly, waiting.

She was soooo good at this.

"We'll put our questions in writing." She winked at me, then turned back to the campers. "We'll schedule a time to meet, and Libby can pick which questions to answer. How's that?"

I suppressed a groan. This wasn't exactly the assist I was hoping for. But it was too late. The campers were murmuring their approval and nodding at Gina and nodding at me. But at least the circle started, then, to break up and move away. So I didn't have all those eyes staring at me anymore.

Gina stood next to me as one clump of campers start back down the hill, while a few others headed across the field toward the little altar, breaking off stalks of the wildflowers—lavender geranium, white campion—that were growing along the edge of the field.

"Gina," I whispered anxiously when everyone else was out of earshot. "Don't let them walk on my beds. They've been walking on my beds."

"Hey, guys, watch where you're walking," she called out. "Don't step on Libby's plants."

The campers by the alter turned and gave us a thumbs up.

I let out a sigh. "I can't stand this." I pushed my glasses up onto my forehead and pressed my fingers against my eyes. "You can't believe how awful this is, for me. I want my life back."

Gina patted me on the shoulder. "It'll be okay. We can turn this around."

A bird flew in and out of the tree line bordering Dean's property, as if it was weaving something into the trees. "What do you mean? Can you get these people to leave?" I turned to my friend, hoping against hope.

But she shook her head. "Not exactly. It's too late for that, I'm afraid. But I was thinking. You could use another source of income, right?"

"Maybe?" I said cautiously.

"And if life gives you lemons, set up a lemonade stand. Right? So here's my idea. We'll have Tyler put up a website. You can hold workshops. You're basically famous. You could hold workshops. You could charge for them."

"I don't want to hold workshops," I said in a tiny little introvert voice.

She sighed. "You just said you need the income."

"Well, yes. But—"

"I'll help you, Libby." She patted my shoulder. "Leave it to me. It'll be fine."

"Hey, guess what!" The knot of campers who'd gone to check the alter were heading back toward us, again. "The pita chips are gone! Libby, did they say anything about us leaving them food? Do they like pita chips?"

Pita chips?

Really?

And maybe I was finally getting used to a bunch of strangers asking me inane questions. Or—more likely—I finally lost it. "Of course not! Why would they like pita chips? They like—they like—" I paused, and then said the next thing that came into my head. "Thai food."

Gina shot me a look.

"In fact, they like take-out Thai food!" My voice was now rising a bit. "They like Masuman chicken!"

"Libby?" Gina murmured.

Hysterical. I was getting hysterical. "So any time you guys want to send out for Masuman chicken, have at it, and I'll see the little people get it."

Okay. So everyone was staring at me again. But do you blame me? And I guess I had Thai food on the brain. Because how long had it been since I'd had my favorite dish in the world? Masuman chicken?

Paul was flying out tomorrow to a trade show. He was awfully busy. But it had been ages, now, since our last date night. Maybe if I called him and begged sweetly, he'd agree to take a break from preparing his presentation. Maybe he'd meet me for Thai...

"I could go pick up the order." The camper's words interrupted my dinner-date mini-fantasy, and I did a double take.

They were actually talking about doing it? These goofy campers hadn't realized I was kidding? They were actually planning to go buy Thai food—for the *fairies*?

A giggle started to form in my belly, and I clamped down, hard, to keep it from erupting.

"We'll take up a collection to pay for it," a camper was saying now. "Can we go with you?" said another, addressing me, this time. "When you offer the chicken to the fairies?"

I felt Gina's hand come to rest, suddenly, on my shoulder. "You're losing it," she said, bending toward me and murmuring into my ear. "You really want them to bring you Masuman chicken? But it's for you, right? Not the fairies?"

The giggle inside me died, and my knees felt funny. "I'm—um—"

"Hey! Whose dog is that?"

Bo!

Saved by Bo.

The dog bounded out of the woods toward us and bounded over, pressing his heavy body against me to be petted.

I stroked his head.

Bo...

I looked up. Looked out toward the trees.

Dean was over there, somewhere...

Must be nice to be able to hide.

The dog shuffled away to greet the campers.

"Libby?" Gina touched my shoulder again. "What shall I tell them? About the Thai food?"

I opened my mouth to tell her not to bother. To explain that I'd been joking. That the Thai food thing was Libby Samson's bad idea of a joke.

But she was still talking. "I mean, if you really want take-out, they'll do it for you. They want to support you. That's what I'm trying to tell you. They'll spend money just to be around you, Libby."

Dean was awfully good at hiding. No matter how hard I looked, I couldn't see him.

I realized Gina was waiting for me to answer, and I turned, re-focusing my eyes on her face. She meant what she'd just said, I guess. Her eyes were calm. Sincere.

So, okay. They wanted to support me. Whatever that meant. Let them support me. "Right," I said. "Fine. I'll take one order of Masuman chicken, and one beef dish. Something spicy. And two spring rolls."

"Okay. I'll tell them." Gina smiled. "It's okay to accept support from people, Libby. Really."

I nodded absently as I watched her walk over to the campers.

I half-listened as they made arrangements to buy me dinner.

I'd call Paul. I'd ask him to meet me somewhere, halfway between my place and the city. We'd have a picnic. We'd sit on a park bench and eat Thai food from the take-out boxes.

He'd have time for that, right?

I gave my body an uneasy little shake. Thinking about Paul reminded me that I still hadn't told him anything. About any of this.

He'd flip out if he had any idea what was going on at my house.

I had to get rid of these people, somehow. I had to get my life back.

ψ ψ ψ

The last of the campers that had followed me up the hill finally realized that, no, I wasn't going to call up a ring of dancing fairies and invite everyone to step up for selfies.

I went back to my weeding.

I looked over my shoulder to double-check that the campers had really left, and began surreptitiously tucking roofing nails into the soil, here and there, as I worked my way down the bed.

But then I noticed Bo again, loping down the edge of my property.

Was Dean still there? I walked over, peering into the trees. "Dean?"

I saw a movement.

It was him. Standing next to a thick-trunked oak about twenty feet in from the stone wall.

"You need to get rid of those people, Libby," he said.

I shrugged. "If only it were that easy."

"It's very easy. Just tell them to get the hell off your property."

"Some of them leave, but then others show up." I sighed. "My friend Gina thinks I should just go with it. Charge admission."

His turn to shrug. "It's your life," he said. "It would drive me crazy, though."

"Oh, it's driving me crazy."

He looked away. "Well. I'll leave you to your work. C'mere, Bo."

"Wait. Dean?"

He turned back around.

That Thai food.

And how likely was it that Paul could make the time, this evening, to meet me for my Thai take-out picnic? Not very.

"Can you come by the house later? For dinner? I—I owe you a dinner, still." I spoke quickly, getting the words out before I could second-guess myself and change my mind.

Because okay. I found Dean attractive. And he'd once kissed me.

Inviting him to my house? Maybe not the smartest move in the world.

But how I hated being cooped up all the time. How lonely it made me feel to be trapped in my own house...

I swallowed as I realized how much I hoped he'd say "yes."

But he didn't say yes. Of course he didn't. "I don't think that's a very good idea, Libby. I mean, thanks for the offer, but to be honest? Your place is a circus. I don't want anything to do with it."

Of course he didn't.

I suppose I looked crushed. I certainly felt crushed. Because instead of walking away, he paused. "How about this, instead. If you think you can get away without them following you, why don't you come over to my place?"

I felt a little surge of hope.

"I couldn't go by the road," I said. "I'd have to come this way. Through the woods. And I'd probably better wait till after dark."

He nodded. "I'll meet you right here."

My surge of hope turned into a flutter of happiness. "It's a deal. But I'm bringing the food. Is Thai okay?"

His eyebrows shot up in surprise. "You cook Thai?"

"No." I felt the giggles start to bubble up again. "It's, uh—one of my devotees is making an offering."

"You're kidding me." He laughed.

I'd never heard him laugh before. It was a nice laugh.

"So I'll be here at—" I broke off, thinking. The days were long. The sun wasn't setting until well after eight. "Say about ten o'clock?"

"Sounds good."

I watched him melt back into the forest.

It wasn't a date. It was a friendly get together with a neighbor who'd been very kind to me.

I was reciprocating. That's all.

Thirty-Five

I spent the rest of the day pacing, doing a little housework, trying not to count the minutes until I could leave for Dean's.

I tried to figure out how I'd slip out without Gina and Maisey noticing, then breathed a sigh of relief when they told me they were going into town to hang out with Tyler.

"Why don't you come along?" Gina said, but I reminded her I was expecting my order of Thai food.

I called Paul called and wished him good luck on his trip.

Finally it was 9:00 and there was a knock on my door, and a camper was standing on my stoop, white plastic bag in hand. A woman with a broad, hopeful face.

"Thanks," I said, taking the bag.

She looked at me expectantly. "What are you going to do now? Is it true fairies eat Thai food? Are you going to present it to them at our alter?"

Great. Must be Gina hadn't explained that the Thai food was for me, not the fairies.

"It's, uh—complicated," I said. "But, uh—thanks for your help."

I started to close the door.

"Wait," the camper said. "When are you taking it to them? Every-one is asking!"

I noticed that "everyone" had started to gather behind her, moving into the pool of light at the foot of my front steps.

I swallowed, hard.

And then I did it. I told a little lie. "Uh, everyone? I need to, uh, line up some energies here, or the fairies won't—they won't—so I need a bit of space and quiet. So if you wouldn't mind—and then later I'll—"

Lame.

But it seemed to work.

"Hear that, guys?" one of them said. "We need to keep our distance. We'll keep at a distance, okay, ma'am?"

I wondered what that meant, exactly.

But the campers began to move off.

I shut the door.

I shut off the porch light.

I went to the living room and lifted a corner of the bedspread. The campers that had gathered at my door were walking across the yard, rejoining the circle by the campfire.

I shut off the light in the kitchen.

I went upstairs and fetched a backpack from my closet and checked the time. I needed to be patient. I needed to make sure they were all settled, enjoying their joints and beer.

I peeked through the living room window again. One of the campers had brought out a guitar, and I could hear the strumming, faintly, through the window.

I tiptoed to the dining room and pushed the sash open.

Thankfully, it didn't stick this time.

I dropped the backpack with the takeout boxes inside out the window and, a couple seconds later dropped down onto the ground next to it.

I didn't fall, this time. I was getting better at this. A little more practice, and I'd be a bona fide ninja.

ψ ψ ψ

The moon was up, but it was barely larger than a sliver.

I leaned up against the side of my house, hugging the backpack to my chest, waiting for my eyes to adjust.

I could smell coconut and curry. And I was ravenous. When had I eaten last?

The sounds of the guitar were clearer, now. The campers' voices rose once in a while as the conversation became animated. I heard a burst of laughter.

I stepped away from the house and strode across the lawn.

I didn't dare use a flashlight, and I knew the hedgerow between my lawn and the first field would be tricky in the dark, so I slung the backpack over my shoulders and used my feet to feel my way, to keep myself on the footpath.

At last I reached the first field.

So dark! The field was a shadow overlain with shadows, and the woods to my right were beyond shadows. They were pitch black.

I reached the ditch.

Was the little man around?

I couldn't tell for sure. But it didn't feel like he was around.

And when had I learned to feel when he was around?

I crossed the ditch and stopped. Field crickets chirped. From way down in the valley, I could hear the faint hum of the traffic on route 390.

I started walking again.

And then a voice came out through the darkness.

It wasn't the little man.

"Hey! I think I saw something move."

I froze, my heart thudding.

Shit. They had staked out my field? They had actually staked out my field?

I dropped into a crouch.

A flashlight beam switched on and began playing over the ground in front of me.

"Hey, is somebody there? Lisa? Is that you?"

"Maybe it's one of the fairies," said the other voice.

"Yeah, well if it is, you hold the torch, cuz I'm gonna catch it."

"Just don't spill your beer!"

The light danced over the hedgerow to my left.

It was my chance. Maybe my only chance. Keeping myself as low as I could, I made a break in the opposite direction of the flashlight beam.

I needed to make it to the stone wall. To the edge of Dean's property. If I could do that, I would be safe. I could hide myself in the trees like Dean did, and somehow find my way to the spot where he was waiting.

By some miracle, I didn't trip.

By some miracle, they didn't hear me.

I climbed over the wall and stood behind a tree, catching my breath. Listening.

"I gotta pee." "Not on the gardens, man." "I wouldn't do that. What do you think I am, a rude pisser?" "You've walked on them, like, fifty times. Fairies gonna put a hex on you." "I told you to turn on the light." "That would kind of defeat the purpose of the stake-out, wouldn't it, doofus?"

Doofus didn't answer, presumably because he was now relieving himself.

I began moving deeper into the forest, even more careful, now, to test the ground under my feet before I stepped. If I snapped a branch by accident, they'd hear me. And if they heard me?

It would have been easier before the ice storm. The ground was littered with branches.

But I was making headway.

I started to relax a bit, started to move a bit faster.

Mistake. A branch hooked my left ankle and I started to go down, only catching myself at the last minute by grabbing ahold of a nearby tree trunk, and, *gross, gross,* my fingers touched something slimy and I yanked my hand away, *gross, gross.*

I pulled a tissue from my pocket to wipe away whatever-it-was, feeling my heart pound in my chest.

I re-straightened my glasses.

I listened.

Good. They were talking, again. Something about one of the other campers, was she hot or not.

So they hadn't heard me fall.

I took another step, and another, angling uphill as I walked. Slowly, slowly...

Just do NOT trip again, Libby, whatever you do...

I had no idea how close I was to the spot where I was supposed to meet Dean.

I pulled off my backpack and leaned against a tree.

I wasn't in awful shape. But oh, man, between wrestling with stuck windows and then falling out of them and running in a crouch across fields and picking my way through that tangle of fallen branches—

Then suddenly, the thing I most wanted to hear. Dean's voice. Surprisingly close by. And sounding so deep and reassuring in the darkness. "I see you made it."

I peered into the darkness.

I could make out his silhouette.

I suppressed the urge to lunge forward and grab him in an enormous and grateful hug.

"They've posted look-outs," I said in a low voice.

"So I noticed."

"Are we going to cut through the woods? In the dark?"

"We're sure not going down to the road," Dean answered. "Want me to carry that?"

I handed him the backpack, and he turned and began walking into the woods.

A branch hit my face.

I fell back a half-step, staring into the black. "Dean," I whispered. "I can't see you anymore."

"Right here." I heard the faint rustle of forest litter as he came back toward me.

I put my hand out and rested it on his shoulder.

And that's how we made our way through the shadows to his cabin. Me, with my hand on Dean's shoulder. To keep from getting lost.

Thirty-Six

"The food's probably cold," I said as Dean unpacked the boxes.

Bo was watching, too. I could understand why. Cold or not, the food smelled divine. And fortunately it didn't take too long to re-heat.

🌱 🌱 🌱

"I got some good news the other day," I said a little while later.

We'd finished our meal and were sitting on opposite ends of the couch. Dean had opened a bottle of Riesling, which had gone nicely with the Thai food and tasted pretty good afterward, too.

"I got the results of some lab work they asked me to do to get my organic certification." I couldn't help but smile. "It's all good. I'm cleared to be certified."

"No kidding. Congratulations."

I took a sip of wine, trying not to smile too much. It was such a relief that they hadn't found anything prohibited in my horsetail brew.

Were things finally going to break my way?

"I have something to tell you, too," Dean said. "It's why I came over, today."

I looked at him, curiously.

He'd lit one of the oil lamps. It cast a dim, warm light over the room from its spot on the bookshelf. It was like sitting in an old painting. An old, quiet, peaceful painting, with a handsome bearded man looking down, thoughtfully, into his glass of wine...

"I think Bo can tell when your little people are around," he said.

My heart jumped.

Had I heard that right?

"Really?" I said.

He nodded.

"What makes you think so?" My voice sounded quavery as I spoke.

"It's how he acts. He seems to avoid certain spots."

"On my land, you mean?"

Dean nodded again. "It's hard to tell in the woods, so I don't know, maybe he does it around here, too. But over on your property, yeah, that's where I've noticed it."

I looked down at Bo. The dog had given up hope on any Thai handouts and was dozing at my feet.

"You were talking to one of them today, right?" Dean said. "Because Bo circled way around when he headed toward you. As if he was avoiding something."

I felt tears start in my eyes.

"And sometimes when we've been over that way, when you aren't there, he'll start off toward something, a rabbit or something else that's caught his eye, and then he'll kind of slow down all of a sudden and—I don't know how else to explain it. He circles."

"Wow," I said. "Wow." I took off my glasses and wiped my eyes with the back of my sleeve.

Why was this making me cry?

I knew the answer. It meant I wasn't a crackpot. It meant that I wasn't completely alone. I bent over and stroked the dog. "Bo," I whispered. "Is it true? Do you see them, too?"

I looked back at Dean. "I'm—wow. You can't know how glad this makes me."

"You're crying."

"Kind of. But they're happy tears. I think. I hope." I paused. "I'm under a bit of stress."

He nodded. "They've been digging latrines on my property."

Oh, no. "I'm so sorry. They've asked me a couple times if they could use my bathroom, but I've told them no. I figured they were going into town."

"You need to tell them to leave," Dean said. "You know that, right?"

I felt myself stiffen. Hadn't we already covered this topic a few hours ago? "That's easier said than done."

"There are ways."

"Like call the cops?" A touch of bitterness crept into my voice. "I can't do anything that will call more attention to this. I don't—the publicity—"

Paul. I can't let Paul find out like that.

"Calling the police is one option," Dean said. "There are others. More wine?"

"No, thanks." I'd felt such a stir of relief when I'd learned that Bo—maybe—could detect the little people. And now it was gone, replaced by the familiar knot in my stomach. "I should probably be getting back. Gina and Maisey will be home soon."

"They're not home?"

"They're with Tyler. Probably at Alexa's."

I'd been sitting with my right leg tucked under me, and it had fallen asleep. Now I untucked it and turned so that I was no longer half-facing Dean.

"You know she's my sister," he said.

"Yeah. Maisey told me."

"She's pretty fascinated by your experience," he said.

I nodded. "No kidding. And not just her. It's everyone. Maisey, Tyler. Maisey's mom, Gina."

I was thinking about what Gina had said earlier. About putting up a website. Holding workshops. Turning it into a business.

I didn't say any of that aloud. But Dean read my thoughts. "So are you going to do it? Charge admission? Give up on the farm idea?"

I stiffened. What could I say? There didn't seem to be any easy answers. Maybe Gina had a point. Plus, I'd come over to get away from the circus, as he'd called it. Not to have a conversation about it. Especially a conversation like this one.

But instead of letting it go, he pushed me.

"You need to stand up for yourself, Libby."

Okay. Nobody appreciates being lectured. And what business was it of his, if I decided to join Gina's scheme, do workshops, make a little money from this debacle?

And who was he to tell me I should stand up for myself? What did he know?

Because I might be an introvert. But "introvert" isn't the same as "weak."

"Stand up for myself?" I said without thinking. "You're one to talk."

"Excuse me?" Dean said.

I froze.

Had I really said that? Out loud?

Because of course I'd never forgotten the story Maisey had told me about the Iranian princess. And it was quite the dramatic story. Because here was this man, holed up in his lonely cabin in the woods, and why? Because when it was his turn to stand up for something, he hadn't. He'd given up. He'd given up his princess.

He'd run away. He'd run into the woods.

To hide.

"What do you mean by that?" Dean was saying, and now there was a cool note in his voice. "That I'm the one to talk?"

And I should have found a way to let it drop. I should have changed the subject. Something.

But instead, I kept going. "I know your story, Dean. Maisey told me. About how you were going to be married, and it didn't work out, and that's how you ended up—"

I broke off.

I suddenly had one of those awful moments when you realize that you crossed a line. That you've done awful damage.

More damage than you'd realized could be done.

And now, it was too late. This intensely private man now knew that people were discussing his past, sharing stories about his past, rumors.

And that I was joining in.

"I'm sorry, Dean," I muttered. "It's none of my business. I shouldn't have—Maisey shouldn't have—"

He didn't answer.

He didn't look at me.

I stood up and set my unfinished wine on the end table.

Bo raised his head expectantly.

"I should be going," I said, my eyes cast down toward the floor.

Dean didn't say a word the whole walk back, as he led me back through the woods. Not a word.

I hardly even knew the guy. But he'd been decent to me. More than once.

And I'd found a pretty crappy way to repay him.

Thirty-Seven

I woke up the next morning feeling awful.

And it wasn't the bruise on my hip. Or even the headache.

It was what I'd said to Dean.

I told myself that what was done, was done. That I had other things to think about. Other priorities. Like how Al Butterman had warned that if I didn't keep my fallow land mown, it would start sprouting a new forest. And he was right. I'd noticed young saplings starting to poke up through the weeds. Ash trees, mostly, but a few maples.

And pretty soon it would be time to till more land, to start to prep for next spring.

I needed that tractor.

I brewed a cup of coffee and took it up to my office and opened my spreadsheet. But I was only going through the motions. My savings account was nearly empty and the income from my *Skin Tones* gig and first years' crops was barely enough to cover my monthly expenses.

If I was going to get a tractor—even a little second-hand tractor—I'd need to finance it. I'd need to go deeper into debt.

But what choice did I have?

And why had I said those awful things to Dean?

I heard the front door slam. And voices. Gina, sounded like, and that was Tyler…

I closed the spreadsheet and walked to the window.

There were more tents than ever on my yard. And if I pressed my face against the glass, I could see parked cars stretched down the road a quarter mile from my driveway, in both directions, on both sides of the road. Which, I knew, sported license plates from all over. Connecticut. Maine. Oregon. California. Kentucky. Texas.

A circus.

Dean was right.

I needed to stop thinking about Dean.

I needed to wash last night's dishes and get outside and get some work done. And the campers were getting wise to me, so I'd have company. I'd have people following me and pestering me with questions and taking pictures with their phones.

☙ ☙ ☙

"Hey, Libby!" Gina called from the living room when she heard me come downstairs. "Is that you? Do you have a few minutes? We need to review some of these questions from your guests."

I stopped at the living room doorway and looked in. Gina, Alexa, and Maisey were on the couch. Tyler was sitting cross-legged on the floor in front of Alexa, holding a stack of index cards.

"I'm sort of busy," I muttered. "Also, technically those people aren't my guests, because, as you may have noticed, I didn't exactly invite them."

"Don't worry. We'll do the heavy lifting." Gina smiled encouragingly and gestured at me to come into the room. "Alexa brought her tablet. She's gonna take notes. And later, I'll help you prepare your talk."

My talk?

"What's the first question, Ty?" Gina said. "Libby, you can sit over there." She gestured now to the overstuffed chair opposite the couch.

I sighed and gave in and took a seat.

"First one," Tyler said, reading off a card. "Dear Fairy Lady."

Fairy Lady? Great.

"My question is," Tyler continued, "All the natural world became what it is, today, by evolving. Did fairies evolve, and what did they evolve from? Thank you for answering my question.'"

"What?" My jaw dropped. "How'm I supposed to answer a question like that?"

"I wonder what they *did* evolve from," Alexa said dreamily.

"Well, we have to say something." Gina looked at me, and then at Tyler, and then back at me again, a slight crease forming between her eyebrows. "Let's see. Alexa, you ready? What's the questioner's name, Tyler?"

"Tom."

"Okay, Alexa." Gina settled back against the couch and her brow smoothed. "Write this. 'Dear Tom. Fairies and humans do, in fact, share a common ancestor—'"

"You can't say that!" I straightened up in my seat. "They're—like archetypes. Archetypes don't evolve!"

"You can't say 'archetypes' either." Gina shook her head. "Nobody knows what an archetype is. Did you get what I said, Alexa?"

Alexa nodded, her fingers poised above her screen.

"'However,'" Gina re-started her dictation, "as you... Hmmmm. Scratch that." She thought it over for a second. "Okay, write it this way. The human and fairy lines split about three million years ago...'"

I stared.

"'...when humans embraced violence and a doctrine of subjugating nature, while the fairies retained their kinship with all living things.' There, is that enough, do you think?"

She was asking Alexa. Not me.

"Wow, that's pretty good, you guys," Tyler said, smiling. The traitor.

"Gina," I said. "You can't just make stuff up."

She raised an eyebrow at me. "This is coming from the woman who claimed fairies eat Masuman chicken."

My face reddened. She had me, there.

I slumped back into my seat.

"Next question, Ty," Gina said.

ψ ψ ψ

I'd stopped listening.

It's not like they really needed my help.

My mind began to drift. I should just shop for that tractor. I should go tomorrow. If I could find a good second-hand tractor tomorrow, and get financing, they could deliver it this week. And I could mow...and wow, I just realized that Maisey had gotten a new haircut. Had Alexa done it? A bob. Looked cute on her...but what about the way she was sitting there, her feet on the couch, her chin resting on her knees?

Odd. She wasn't joining in with the others.

And her eyes were unfocused, distant.

Something was wrong. And whatever it was, it had nothing to do with letters about fairies.

"Hey, Maisey, I like your haircut," I said.

She looked up. "Thanks, Aunt Libby."

But that's all she said, and then the faraway look on her face came back again.

ψ ψ ψ

Gina was saying something about energetic vortices when I heard a cell phone buzz.

Nobody reacted to the buzz. Which meant it must be my phone. And where had I left it? On the kitchen counter—I'd dropped it there with my keys when I'd come in.

I jumped up. "Be right back," I said, running to the kitchen.

I got there in time to catch the call.

It was Paul.

"Hey!" I said.

"Hey, babe!" he said back. "Want some company?"

197

Wait, what? Company?

"Can you hear me okay?" he was saying. "I'm on speaker. I'm—let's see. Just passed the Avon exit. See you in, what, about twenty minutes?"

I looked wildly around the room. Paul? Here? Today?

"Um, Paul? Paul? The place—I wasn't expecting—it's a mess. I'm kind of—"

This was the one I really, really hadn't planned for. I mean, I'd lived here for months, and he'd only visited me once that whole time. And now he was making the 40-odd-mile drive. With no warning. On a Sunday morning?

"I don't mind a mess," Paul said. "And it's way past my turn to visit."

Damn damn damn.

I hung up the phone and ran back to the living room. "Guys, it's—I've got an emergency. Paul's coming—Paul's on his way—he'll be here in fifteen and—"

They looked at me. They weren't comprehending.

"Gina," I pleaded. "This meeting, or whatever it is, is over. I've got to—Paul doesn't know about all these campers, here, and—"

Gina finally understood and she jumped up. "I see, Libby," she said, nodding. "I get it. He's in for a little shock. Kids, you'd better head to Alexa's for a bit. We'll reconvene later."

"Sure thing," Tyler said.

☙ ☙ ☙

I felt like puking.

But I didn't have time to puke.

I went into full-bore clean-up mode. I guess it was a defensive thing. Like, if the interior of my house was in perfect order, the freak show sprawling across my yard and spilling down the road wouldn't seem so bad.

So I ran around like a maniac. I yanked the bedding off the windows and folded it and ran upstairs and stuffed it in my closet. I plumped the throw pillows. Wiped the crumbs off the coffee table.

Then I darted to the kitchen to wash the dishes that had piled up in the sink.

Gina, to my relief, pitched in. She swept the floor and carried the food scraps out to the compost pile, and started drying dishes as I stuck them in the drainboard.

I heard Paul's car.

And in retrospect, I should have run out and met him in the driveway. I should have jumped into the passenger seat and ordered him to drive. I should have gotten him away from there to talk.

But he was already out of his car.

And—could it get any worse?—a couple of the campers were strolling up to him. "Hey," I heard one of them say from where I stood on the stoop. "You're not allowed to park in the driveway. You need to park on the side of the road."

"The fuck?" Paul answered, looking around him as he walked toward the house.

He noticed me standing by the door. "Libby. What the fuck is going on, here?"

"I, uh—I was trying to find a time to tell you," I said. Sounding as lame as I felt.

"Tell me what?" he said sharply as he climbed the steps. "That you're running a *campground*? Do you have a *permit* for all that?"

I shut the door behind him as he stepped inside. "No! I mean, no, I haven't opened a campground. It's not—I didn't invite them."

"They came because Libby talks to fairies."

Gina. From where she was standing near the sink, drying the last of the dishes.

I felt a sickening sensation, as if the floor had disappeared out from under my feet.

Paul was now staring at Gina. "Libby. Who is this?"

"Gina. I've told you about my friend, Gina."

He looked back at me. "What the fuck did Gina just say? Just now?"

"Oh wow," Gina breathed. "Paul doesn't know about the fairies, either?"

I shook my head miserably. "Hey Gina, we need a little private time," I whispered. "Paul, let's go up to my office, okay?"

⚜ ⚜ ⚜

I sat on my office chair, but then I stood up again. I was too nervous to stay settled. And I told him. Well, the abbreviated version, at least. Starting with the night the little man had popped up out of the ditch, and the warning to move my car, and then about how I'd started taking his advice on the care of my crops. And that the advice seemed, as far as I could tell, to be helpful.

"I didn't mean to keep it from you," I said. "But I never expected it would get out of control like this."

He was looking at me funny. Like I was from another galaxy far, far away.

"I didn't ask for this, Paul. I don't know why it happened—"

"Libby!" He shook his head. "Have you talked to your *doctor* about this?"

Ugh. My worst fear, realized. Paul thought I was nuts. "No," I said. "I haven't really talked to anyone. Except—"

Except Gina, and Maisey, and Tyler, and Alexa, and several dozen weirdos camping in my yard.

And Dean...

"Well, an appointment with your GP would be an excellent place to start," Paul snorted.

My shoulders sagged. I couldn't tell a doctor about this. Not my doctor. He was the sort of doc who thought taking Vitamin C was radical. There was just no way I could waltz into his office and start talking about magical beings.

"And by the way, what about them?" Paul jerked his thumb in the direction of my front yard. AKA the tent village. "Do they talk to fairies, too?"

"I was about to get to that. Word got out. On the Internet. They are—fans. Kind of."

"Jesus."

"It will blow over. It's not like I encourage it, Paul. I don't encourage them, believe me."

"Do you realize what could happen?"

What could happen? A sudden feeling of dread rose in my throat. Could I be in trouble with the law for running an unauthorized campground? Could my property be seized?

Or was he talking about my health? Maybe I had a brain tumor? Maybe it would be like in the movie Phenomenon, when John Travolta developed those bizarre mental powers? He'd died in that movie. Was I going to die?

"What?" I whispered. "What could happen?"

"Josh could find out."

Huh?

"He could find out that *Skin Tones* is being edited by—by a New Age freak case space cadet."

Really? Paul was most worried about what his *boss* might think?

"How's he going to find out, Paul?" I muttered.

But as soon as the words left my lips, I knew the answer to my question.

He'd find out the way the rest of the universe had found out. He'd read about me on the Internet.

Paul stood up. "Look. I have to get out of here. I need to think this over."

"I'll fix it, Paul. I swear, I'll get it sorted out."

He eyed me again for a second, opened his mouth, shut it, then opened it a second time. "I'm sorry, Libby. I'm not being very sympathetic here. But you have to understand. Dormet's image is very important."

My entire body went cold. I needed that gig. I needed *Skin Tones*. If I didn't have *Skin Tones*, I wouldn't be able to meet my mortgage payments.

I'd lose my farm.

"I'll do whatever needs to be done, Paul. I promise. I understand what you're trying to say."

"You'll talk to your doctor?"

"Yes!" I nodded vigorously. "And also, we can, you know, take my name off the newsletter masthead. That way—"

He waved my suggestion away. "We're getting ahead of ourselves here. You need a full physical. Probably an MRI or something. And you need to get rid of these freaks on your property. That much I can tell you."

I nodded. Wondering, as I nodded, how the hell I was going to do that.

I walked with him to the door.

He kissed me.

"I'll phone you later," he said, and I watched him scowl in the direction of the campers and shake his head as he walked to his car.

"Wow. That's one up-tight boyfriend you got there."

I jumped. I'd forgotten Gina was there.

"He makes ol' Wallace look like a prince."

And then she saw my face. "Aw, no, Libby. Are you *crying* over that asshole?"

"He's not an asshole," I blubbered as she folded me into a hug. "He's Paul."

"Mmm hmm," she said. "He's Paul."

Thirty-Eight

I had no real reason to ignore Paul's "see a doctor" advice.

No rational reason, anyway. And if I was perfectly honest with myself? If it had been Paul, not me, who'd suddenly started seeing supernatural humanoid entities?

I'd have had the same reaction.

Still, I wished he wasn't pushing it so hard.

But he was. He phoned me the next morning to push, in fact. From work.

At least he'd cooled off enough, by then, to listen to my argument that maybe my GP wasn't the right doctor. "Good point," he said. "A specialist would be better."

And then he called back, twenty minutes later, with the names and phone numbers of three shrinks. "A psychiatrist is your best bet," he said. "Since they're medical doctors, they can order up lab work. Or meds if you need them."

Meds.

I hung up.

He texted me the links a moment later, and I sat, looking at my phone.

I'm not crazy. I'm not crazy.

I remembered what Dean had told me. *Bo sees them, too.*

"Have you seen my vape pen?"

I looked up. Maisey, still in PJs, was standing in the doorway to my office.

"Uh oh," I said.

"What do you mean, 'uh oh'?"

I sighed. I was getting tired of acting like all the strangeness around me was some kind of big secret. "Maisey," I said flatly. "Haven't you noticed that things in this house have a way of disappearing? And then showing up again a few hours later?"

"Whoa," she breathed. "The fairies? They took my vape pen?"

"I have no idea, really. All I'm saying is that things around this house go missing. And then turn back up."

Our eyes locked. And I wasn't sure what to expect. Whether my words would maybe frighten her. Or whether she might scoff.

But instead, she burst out laughing. "Oh, my God. They play games on us."

I nodded. "It would seem so."

"How long have you known?"

I shrugged. "Almost since I moved in. I thought it was me, just being absent-minded, at first."

Absent-minded.

The word reminded me that Paul wanted me to see a shrink, and I looked back down at my phone and swiped the screen. "What you should do," I said, "is keep your eye out. My bet is your pen will show up someplace odd later today. A windowsill, the mantle. Some place like that."

"Is everything okay, Aunt Libby?"

I looked back up, again. "I'm fine."

"That was bad, yesterday, with Paul. Wasn't it."

I nodded sadly. "He thinks I need a medical check-up. You know, maybe I've got a brain tumor."

Oops. Shouldn't have said that. Maisey's eyes went from concerned to wide with alarm.

"Relax, Maise. I don't have a tumor." I stood up. "But I have to do this for Paul. Only I need to find the right doctor. I don't want—"

"Someone who thinks you're crazy," Maisey finished my sentence. "You know what? You should ask Dean. He's lived here longer than we have. He'll know someone. Hang on, let me get dressed and we'll go talk to him."

I jumped up, following her. "Maisey!"

Her bedroom door swung shut. "I told him I was going to go see him today, so he'll be home." Her voice was muffled through the door. "Don't worry! I'll drive us there! That way no campers will follow or whatever."

I stood in the hallway, shuffling from one foot to another. Because on the one hand, I would love to get Dean's advice. But on the other hand, Maisey had no idea what I'd said to him, the last time I'd been at his house—

But on the other, other hand, if I saw him, I'd be able to tell if he was still angry.

Maybe he wasn't still angry?

Maybe if I went over there, and he was still angry, I could apologize...

Maisey's bedroom door swung open. "Ready?" she said, running her hands through her bob to comb it.

I swallowed hard.

Was this a good idea?

I knew the answer to that question. I was pretty sure I should do a better job of avoiding Dean Milbrant.

I caught up to her as she reached the front door.

She opened it a crack and peered out. "Looks like the coast is clear! There's a bunch of them hanging around but they aren't really watching the house."

Maybe he'd forgotten.

Maybe my words hadn't been as hurtful as I thought.

"Got your keys?" I said. My voice sounded funny.

She nodded and patted the pocket of her cargo shorts. "Let's do it."

She pushed the door all the way open with one hand while holding her finger up in a 'shhh' gesture with the other.

We eased the door shut behind us, then trotted down the stairs and across the lawn to Maisey's car.

"Hey!" someone shouted from the direction of the tents. "There she is!"

I glanced over my shoulder.

Campers were heading toward us.

Running toward us.

"Libby! Hey Libby! Can I ask you a question? Where are you going? Are you leaving? When will you be back?"

"We're just going to the store," Maisey yelled to them as we piled into her car. "Chill out, guys!"

She flicked the inside latch to lock the doors. Just in time—a camper reached the car and yanked on the driver's side door handle.

Safe!

No. Not safe.

"They're blocking us!"

Maisey was looking in her rearview mirror, and now I turned around and, sure enough. Campers were pressed up against her rear bumper.

She was parked right up next to that old maple tree at the end of my driveway—the one that had dropped a limb on my Toyota that spring. She needed to back up. She couldn't. We were trapped.

"What should I do?" the teenager gasped.

Our eyes met.

"Be careful," I said through gritted teeth. "But ya gotta do it, Maisey. Just—just go slow. Don't hurt anybody."

She put the car in reverse.

Our eyes met again.

Me thinking to myself, would I be able to do it? If it were me, at the wheel?

She pressed her foot on the gas. Gently, gently.

The car started to move.

Campers began banging on the car.

"Hey, you can't leave!"

It became a chant. "You can't leave! You can't leave!"

"Oh, my God. We'll be home in a little while, you nitwits!" Maisey yelled.

"Ignore them," I muttered, but I was talking to myself. She couldn't hear me over the din.

The car was inching backward. Slowly, slowly. And it was working. The campers were giving way behind us.

"Good, good," I said. "I think you've got it."

And she did. She eased down the driveway as campers gestured and yelled and made faces at us through the windshield.

"You got it, Maise, you got it."

She shook her head. "They're going to their cars."

"Aw, no."

But she was right. Campers were now running down the driveway. Running to the road, where they'd parked their cars.

Were they actually going to give chase?

"We can't lead them to Dean's," I gasped. "Turn the other way! Turn right!"

Maisey pulled out onto the road.

"Go, go!"

And bless that girl, she hit the accelerator and we were off.

"How do we lose them?" she said.

"You've got a good head start. I don't know. Head toward the expressway, I guess. Maybe they'll get bored. How are you on gas?"

"Half a tank."

I swiveled around again to check behind us, then settled into my seat and buckled the belt.

Maisey was watching the rear-view mirror. "Looks like there are four of them." she said. "Oh geez, they're driving fast! Oh! One is passing the others!"

I hunched down so I could watch in my side mirror. "Idiots."

"Aunt Libby—look!"

I straightened back up.

Al Butterman. On his enormous tractor. Driving down the middle of the road.

And we were catching up to him. Fast. Because he was Al. And he was on a tractor. And Al drives his tractor very, very slowly.

I unbuckled my seat belt. "We'll ask him to help us," I said. "Keep it steady, Maise." I pressed the button to roll down my window. "Pull up as close as you can get."

"Oh my God, it's like a movie!" she squealed.

I grabbed the strap above the door with my left hand and stood up so that I was halfway out the window. "Al!" I shrieked, waving with my free hand. "Hey, Al!"

He had a radio on his tractor.

And the radio was blaring.

A talk show. I could hear the host ranting about politics.

"AL!" I shrieked again. "AL!"

He finally heard me.

He turned around in his seat. He stared.

I suppose I looked crazy.

He reached out to a dial on his dashboard, and the noise from the radio died away.

"Al! Do me a favor!"

"What?" He cupped his hand to his ear.

"A favor!"

I looked behind us. The camper's cars were catching up. The driver in the first car had his head sticking out of his window. "Libby! Wait for me!" he was yelling, laughing.

Someone else started honking his horn.

I looked back at Al.

The expression on his face made it pretty clear that he'd formed a not-very-positive impression of his neighbor.

"Please, Al," I yelled. "We're trying to lose these guys. Can you block them?"

"This is a gahdamned circus."

Circus. Dean's word.

"Please?" I said.

His mouth pursed. But then he nodded, a single, quick jerk of his head.

I slid back into the car, fumbling, again, for my seatbelt.

Al made a "pass me" roll of his left arm.

"NOW!" I said to Maisey.

She veered to the left.

Al veered to the right.

I grabbed the dashboard, my heart pounding as the car surged forward.

"We made it!" Maisey said, eyes darting from the road to the rear-view to the road again.

I stretched up and turned around. Sure enough, we'd done it. We'd caught them off-guard, and now Al had the campers trapped behind him.

I watched as the lead car swerved, first left, then right, trying to pass the tractor. But Al was ready. He swerved neatly, at the same time, in the same direction, blocking him off.

"Man. I owe that guy," I muttered. "Big time."

We rounded a bend. We reached the end of the road. "What way should I turn?" Maisey asked.

"Left. Toward the valley."

That girl was nails. She rolled through the stop sign and floored it.

We came to the next intersection. "Go right," I said.

She turned and floored it again.

I looked behind me. We'd lost them.

"You did it. Maisey, you did it." I giggled and held my hands in front of me, over the dash. "Look, my hands are shaking."

"Mine, too!" Maisey said.

"You were awesome, Maise!"

"Should I turn here?"

We'd reached the main road. North would take us toward Rochester, south, toward Dansville.

I picked south. "We can circle back and get to Dean's from the other side of town."

"Gotcha."

Thirty-Nine

We wanted to be certain that we were in the clear, so we wandered around a bunch of back roads for a good half hour.

But a long last, we reached Dean's driveway.

"I love Dean's cabin so much," Maisey said as we pulled in. "It's the most beautiful place in the world, isn't it?"

"Yeah," I said, pushing my glasses up and rubbing my temples. The exhilaration of outrunning the campers had worn off, and I was suddenly feeling a bit nauseous. Was it too late to tell Maisey I'd changed my mind? That we should turn around and head back home?

The driveway was so narrow that tree branches whipped the side of the car.

The piles of brush I'd helped Dean move after the ice storm were half-hidden now, some by brambles and others, in the low, wetter spots, by tall pale clumps of jewel weed.

We reached the cabin clearing.

Bo was on the porch. He stood up, alert, watching our car as Maisey parked.

"There's Dean," she said.

My stomach tightened. He was rounding the corner of the cabin, carrying a hacksaw. He set the saw on the porch and drew off his work gloves as he watched us get out of the car.

"Hiya, Dean!" Maisey called out.

My feet felt heavy as I started toward the cabin.

"What can I do for you ladies today?" Dean said. Very politely. Too politely.

"I hope we're not intruding." I cleared my throat.

Maisey was looking at me. I could feel her looking at me.

"Have a seat," Dean said, turning and climbing the steps to his porch.

There were two Adirondack chairs at one end of the porch and on the other, a loveseat-style swing. Maisey pushed past us and chose the swing, calling to Bo as she sat down.

I perched nervously on the front edge of one of the Adirondack chairs, hands on my knees.

"What do you need?" Dean said in that same polite tone of voice as he sat in the other chair.

"Well, I was hoping—well, you know this whole situation."

"Not sure I follow, no."

Maisey was stroking Bo's head and cooing at him.

"The situation with the fairies." I shifted my weight on the chair. "Paul—"

"Paul?"

"My boyfriend." I swallowed. "He's worried about me. He thinks I may have something going on medically."

"Ah."

"So I've agreed to see a doctor." I rubbed my hands against my knees. "Only, since I haven't lived here that long, I was hoping maybe you'd know someone here in town who—"

"Who won't think she's crazy," Maisey interjected.

I swallowed again and nodded.

Dean stood up.

For an awful moment, I expected him to ask me to leave.

But he didn't.

He went inside.

Bo got up and watched through the screen, ears pricked, and Maisey settled back in the swing, pushing off against the floor of the porch to make it move. "Gosh, it's gorgeous here, isn't it, Aunt Libby? So green. Hey, what's that bird singing, just now? There. That one."

"That's a wood thrush."

"It sounds like pipes, kind of."

We shouldn't have come. I shouldn't have agreed to this.

I needed to leave Dean alone. That's what he wanted. He didn't need an annoying neighbor dropping in and asking for help all the time.

The screen door opened, and Dean handed me a slip of paper. It had a name on it, Theresa Grande, and a phone number.

"Thank you," I whispered.

I needed to get out of there.

But as I was about to stand up, Maisey interrupted. "Hey, Dean, okay if I use your bathroom?"

Oh, crap.

Dean and I were now alone on the porch.

The paper with the doctor's name on it felt damp from my hand.

My mind went blank.

I needed to say something.

But what?

A slight breeze had come up. The thrush had fallen silent but now an oven bird called from the undergrowth: *tee-cher tee-cher tee-cher...*

I cleared my throat. "Dean?"

He didn't answer.

"I'm really sorry." My voice was husky. "I shouldn't have said what I said. The other night. About you and—"

"Don't worry about it."

I stiffened at the words.

He was angry at me. No doubt about it. He sounded so cold.

Whatever we'd had, at one time? That little fragment of a friendship we'd once felt?

Gone.

Only—

I stole a quick glance at him.

Was that a quiet sigh I'd just heard?

He was looking off at the trees. "Libby."

I held my breath.

"I shouldn't have interfered in your life."

"But I—"

He made a quick motion with his hand, cutting me off. "You know what's best," he said. "For your situation."

No, I don't.

But I didn't get a chance to say that out loud, because Maisey came back through the screen door. It was time for us to go.

ψ ψ ψ

Miraculously, considering the pandemonium earlier, only a couple of the campers noticed as we pulled back up my driveway.

We sprinted to the door and got inside before they reached us.

But my reprieve was short-lived. Gina was waiting. "You're home! Finally! Come up to your office. We've got some website designs for you to review."

Website designs.

So this was really going to happen? I was really going to turn this— this craziness—into a business of some kind?

Apparently I was, because sure enough, a minute later I was standing behind Ty as he tapped out a URL. "See?" he said, moving the mouse and clicking on links. "Here's the FAQs. And this page isn't working yet, but it's got a shopping cart and everything."

"For your merchandise," Alexa said. She was standing next to Tyler.

"Merchandise?" I asked.

Maisey hadn't followed me. I looked over my shoulder toward the door. Where was Maisey? She would want to see this too, wouldn't she?

"By merchandise, Alexa means seminars," Gina was saying. "Workshops. We'll have guest lecturers, too, like at Findhorn. And you'll write a book. You're a writer. It'll be easy."

"Tyler did a fabulous job, didn't he?" Alexa said. "Tyler, show her the contact form." She put her hand over Tyler's on the mouse and moved the cursor up to a button that said 'Contact Libby' and when she clicked on it—or Tyler clicked on it, hard to tell—a shower of sparkles cascaded over the screen and dissolved into a new screen with prompts for 'name' and 'email' and 'message.' "Isn't that cool?" she said, smiling at Tyler.

"Yeah," I said. "Very cool. Thanks, you guys. But it's been a long day and I should probably get some stuff done."

"Libby," Gina said. "You're on board with us doing this, right?" she said.

Was I?

You know what's best. For your situation.

"Give me time." I sighed. "Just give me time. I need to get used to it, is all."

Forty

It was overcast.

It was also broiling hot. The kind of hot that descends in high summer, as the first cicadas begin singing in the treetops and the goldenrod buds start to swell and turn yellow.

I was weeding.

I wasn't alone. A contingent of campers had followed me up the hill and now sat cross-legged in a circle and joined hands.

I worked down a row until I reached the end nearest to Dean's property.

I considered a bull thistle that was growing next to one of the brussels sprouts plants. Should I pull it? Or leave it? I decided to pull it and probed at the base of the thistle with my weeder to loosen the root.

A movement in the hedgerow caught my eye and I looked up, and as I peered through the foliage, I saw one of the little men. And then another, and another. Seven altogether, walking along a deer path that followed the stone wall.

They didn't look in my direction.

I checked on the campers. Still there.

The troop of little people climbed over the wall and disappeared into the woods.

Would I ever have privacy to speak to them? Ever again?

And was I really so lonely that my best friend was a little man dressed in crinkly brown like a paper bag?

I turned to the next bed. Green beans. My glasses were sliding down my slippery nose and I stopped to adjust them. The sky was white with moisture. This was thunderstorm weather.

Back to weeding. I tried to focus, to work as if the little man was helping. Feeling my way. Pretending it was a kind of rhythm. Leave this one, pull that, leave three, pull two, leave three, pull three.

The thistle I'd tossed into my basket was already wilted in the heat.

I studied a dock plant. Its broad, coarse leaves looked like they might smother the bean plant next to it. But would it? Plants are funny creatures. They like growing next to each other, sometimes. They sometimes get along.

The ground in front of me darkened suddenly.

I looked up. Maisey was standing there, blocking the sun. I couldn't make out her face.

"What's up?" I said.

She didn't answer.

I stood. "Is something wrong?"

She gave her head a quick shake.

A faint rumble of thunder rolled across the valley. A breeze licked my cheeks and the air suddenly smelled different, the faint smell of rain mixing into the tang of hot ripe greenery.

I pulled off my gloves, glancing again at the campers. "Hey. Let's go for a walk."

We started up the hill through the heavy air, but a moment later and here they came. A three-person camper delegation was headed toward us. "Damn it," I muttered. "Hang on a sec, Maisey."

"Hey," one of the campers called out. "'Sup, you guys?"

"Nothing important." I forced a smile. "Just having a private conversation with my niece."

They looked skeptical. Apparently, my attempts to sneak outside without them noticing—and outrun them in low speed car chases—had given me a reputation for being less than trustworthy.

Fortunately, Mother Nature intervened. A stab of lightening split the western sky, followed by another faint drumroll of thunder. I took immediate advantage, gesturing toward the valley. "Well, guys," I said. "I hate to say this, but I'm protected from lightning. By, you know, the fairies. But you're not."

The thunder, cooperating fully, rumbled again.

"What about her?" One of the campers pointed at Maisey.

"I'm pretty sure she's protected, too," I said. "But you guys? Seriously. We'd hate to see you get—" I made a swift chopping motion with my hand—"zapped."

Another flash of lightning cracked the sky overhead, and that was all the convincing they needed. The camper delegation turned and started back toward the others.

They were moving pretty quickly.

"Okay," I said to Maisey. "What's going on, really."

"I didn't realize this would happen, Aunt Libby."

I frowned. "That what would happen?"

"These people. They're awful, aren't they?"

"They're not so bad," I said. "They can't help it, I guess."

"They've ruined your life."

Wow. Who would have thought it? Of all the people in my little circle, it was Maisey who actually felt a little sympathy for what I was going through. Well, Dean perhaps did, too. But Dean wasn't really in my circle.

"It's okay," I said. "I'm getting used to it."

"It's all my fault."

"Oh, no!" I exclaimed. "Not at all, Maisey. I don't blame you. I don't blame Tyler. I don't blame anybody. It's just what happened."

"What are you going to do?"

I shrugged. "I don't know, yet. But Paul's calmed down, at least, since I've agreed to see a doctor. Maybe Paul can help me figure something out."

"Mom said he'd break up with you over it. She says Paul is too uptight to deal with stuff like this."

I winced. "That's not true. Paul's got a lot on his mind. Ever since Cal4 got bought by Dormet Vous, they doubled his workload. And he doesn't really get the whole organic farming thing. He thinks it's too fringy. So he's been kind of cranky for a while now. But he'll be okay. And he's smart. He'll help me figure it out."

We'd reached the end of the first field and I led Maisey through the hedgerow.

"Mom's going ahead with launching that website," she said as we stepped back out into the open again.

I sighed. "I'm fine with that, Maisey. She's got her vision, and..." I trailed off.

"Do you think Paul would like you to just sell the place?"

"Oh, I wouldn't say that," I said.

But I was thinking, *ah, Gina. Trust Gina to guess exactly what Paul wanted.* Not that he'd said so to me. Not directly. But I could tell. He'd wanted that ever since—

Ever since it was too late to want me not to buy the place at all.

A fat drop of rain struck my head.

"We'll be okay, right?" Maisey said. "From the storm?"

"Most likely."

Another rumble of thunder broke out as I spoke, and I flashed a quick grin.

She flashed a grin back, but then the smile died away and her lower lip began to tremble.

"Something's bothering you, Maisey. What's bothering you?"

Another drop of rain struck, this time hitting the back of my hand.

"Tyler," Maisey said.

And I knew what was coming next.

"Tyler. And Alexa."

And you know what? I wasn't surprised. It had felt funny to me, the way Alexa seemed to focus on Tyler. The way he seemed to like her attention a little too much.

"Okay," I said, thoughtfully, as we began to walk again. "Let's think this through. Is there for sure something going on between them?"

"I don't know. Tyler's says there isn't. But it's the way they act around each other. He forgets I'm there."

"Have you talked to your Mom? What's she say?"

A tear rolled down Maisey's cheek. "I haven't really talked about it with her. She and Alexa. They've gotten kinda close. You know?"

I felt an unreasonable flash of anger toward Gina.

I pushed it away.

The sky darkened even more. The wind was picking up and a few more drops splattered down around us, although it wasn't raining really, not yet. These were stray drops, blown in from the thunderclouds that were piling into thick, boiling columns on the far side of the valley.

We reached the highest point of my property.

We turned to face the valley.

A fresh shard of lightning stabbed across the dark purple sky.

"Wow," Maisey said, and I felt it, too. The first edge of the thunderstorm's real power.

A loud BOOM echoed across the valley and the wind lifted my hair.

If I'd been a kid, I'd have raised my arms in that moment. Because it felt like if I just raised my arms the wind would take me. I could just let the wind lift me up, up...

On the other hand, being out here on a relatively open field during a lightning storm probably wasn't very smart. Fairies or no fairies.

I touched Maisey's elbow. "C'mon," I said. "We'd better head down. Let's go this way, next to the woods." I started thinking out loud as we walked. "Okay," I said. "Tell you what. Let's look at this objectively, okay? Like scientists. We'll start with the facts."

I considered what to say next. I didn't want to come right out and ask the obvious. Are they having sex? This was, after all, the same girl whose braids I'd once done up with ribbons for her fifth birthday party. "You haven't, like, seen them, you know, kissing or anything?"

"No. I haven't."

"And Tyler—he hasn't said any of the things guys do, sometimes? 'I need some space'? Anything like that?"

"No."

"So what you have now is that they seem to be friends. They have a connection of some kind."

"Yeah," Maisey said. "Like, he smiles at her a lot. And he pays attention to her. Like, when we're talking about the—about your website, and if I have an idea, and Alexa has an idea, it's like, her idea is always better than mine."

Because, Maisey, you're actually a decent person at heart. And maybe sometimes decent people get overshadowed by the not-so-decent.

We reached the trees. Their branches were whipping in the wind, their leaves flipped over to show their silvery undersides. The fat, stray raindrops were falling more thickly.

"Aunt Libby," Maisey said suddenly. "I don't want to mess this up. I love him so much. I don't want to lose my Tyler."

"I know. And you are caught between, you know, your pride and your love."

We started walking back down the hill. Me, trying to figure out what advice to give.

Only for some reason, all I could think about was Paul. How important it was to compromise, in a relationship.

"Well, Maise, I'm not sure but—but maybe you should try just ignoring it. I mean, you love him, right? So here's the thing. You raise a fuss, confront him or whatever, and all of a sudden you make it a big deal in his eyes, and in Alexa's too, if she gets wind of it. So, you know? It may be that they don't even realize it's going on. Know what I mean?"

"Yeah. I guess. You know what's funny?"

"What?"

"I was in Mickey D's the other day, and someone had left a registration packet for Geneseo on the table there."

Geneseo? "The college?"

"Yeah."

"Oh." I wasn't sure why that had come up.

"I wondered if it was a sign."

"Oh. Well, I'm a biologist, Maisey. We don't believe in signs."

Maisey laughed. "Aunt Libby, you talk to fairies."

I raised my voice to carry over the wind. "And look where it got me!" I rolled my eyes dramatically for the comic effect. "See? It illustrates my point perfectly. We're better off relying on good, practical common sense."

"Aunt Libby?"

"Yeah?"

"Did you know it when Wallace was cheating on you?"

I winced for the second time that conversation. "Towards the end, yes."

"I don't think Tyler is cheating on me. I don't think of it as cheating. At all."

"That's kind of my point. If it's not cheating, and you make a scene like it *is* cheating..."

We'd reached the lowest field, the one with my growing beds. "I'm going to grab my stuff. Wait here by the trees."

I trotted over to where I'd left my tools and the basket of weeds.

And there was my little man, sitting and looking at her.

"Hi!" I said happily. "Everything okay?"

He nodded.

I tried not to grin too widely. "Anything I should be doing?"

"Leave the purslane," he said. "When you weed."

"Okay."

"The hail will do some damage, but most of your plants will survive. Except your lettuce."

What? My lettuce? My fall lettuce crop? The plants were all just seedlings. Babies. And I'd timed them so they'd be maturing right as the weather cooled. "Is there anything I can do to protect it?" I said.

"No." He turned and walked away into the weeds.

Maisey was waiting for me under the edge of the tree line. "You were talking to one of them, weren't you?"

I nodded.

"What did he say?"

"That we're going to get some hail," I said. "We'd better hustle, Maise. It's gonna be a wild one."

And then the first sheet of rain swept over us. So that by the time we got down to the house, we were both drenched to the skin. And because Gina was home, I kept my voice to a whisper when we stepped inside. "Sometimes women have to be patient. Keep our cool, let the men sort out their little problems. Tyler's a good man, Maisey. You take it easy, it'll sort out."

Maisey nodded and went to her room to change.

Forty-One

I sat on a stool in the little exam room. The doctor's assistant had done the usual stuff. Taken my blood pressure, my weight, asked me a bunch of questions. But when she asked me why I was there, I refused to answer. "I'd rather just speak to the doctor, if you don't mind."

The assistant didn't like that very much, even though I'd made a point of thanking her for working me in on a Saturday morning. She made a face and explained that everything I said was confidential.

But my recent adventures had strengthened my stubborn streak, apparently. I pursed my lips and shook my head no.

I would wait for Dr. Grande.

The assistant gave up and left me alone.

I sat on the stool and read the posters on the wall—how to tell if you've got Lyme, who to call if you're a victim of domestic abuse—until, finally, the doctor knocked and entered the room.

"So how are you feeling?" the doctor asked. "Any headaches? Nausea?"

"I get headaches, tension headaches, once in a while. No more than I used to, though."

"Change in sleep habits?" she said, noting my answers on her laptop.

"No."

"And you say you're not using any stimulants." Dr. Grande had picked up one of the forms I'd filled out. She flipped it over to scan the back. "You're not on any prescription drugs. No anti-depressants."

I shook my head again.

The doctor set her clipboard on the counter behind her. "Okay. You have a worried boyfriend. I can understand how this would upset him. But absent any physical symptoms, I really don't see the point of ordering any tests. You say these—"

"Little people." I felt my face color slightly as I said the words.

"These little people you're seeing. They don't frighten you?"

"At first, yes. But now, no. I've adjusted to it."

She nodded. "And you've put here—there's no history of schizophrenia in your family."

"Yes. That's right."

"Well, Libby. Generally speaking, if there's a psychiatric problem, the patient will exhibit emotional problems. Agitation, paranoia. That kind of thing."

I nodded.

"If you're feeling at all anxious about your experiences, I can recommend a therapist."

"I don't."

The doctor stood up. "Then tell your boyfriend I said you're fine."

I'm not crazy.

I collected my paperwork and paid my co-pay and walked out to my car in the clinic parking lot.

I turned on the engine and the AC and sat a moment, thinking.

Because I had no idea what those cryptic little humanoids were. I had no idea why they appeared to me and nobody else. But they were part of my life, and I'd come to welcome them. I'd come to feel that, somehow, they deepened my connection to the land.

And now, I'd been checked out by a bona fide medical professional who'd said I wasn't crazy.

So okay. I wasn't living the life I'd once imagined. I'd imagined that I'd be a cool-headed, data-drive biologist using science in a rational way to grow organic vegetables. That my farm would be an ongoing scientific experiment, with every factor, every decision fully visible and measurable at all times.

But that had changed the moment the little man stood up in the ditch and called me by my name. I'd become something different. The edges of what I was and what I believed had shifted and dissolved.

Part of the shift was in how I worked. I was starting to work my land by feel, instead of what I'd once called science.

But there was more to it, even, than that. This experience—these peculiar entities—had come to embody my connection to the land. They were making my connection to the land come alive.

And now, for the first time, I let myself feel how right that was. I let myself wonder if maybe I had a future working my farm under these new, extraordinary, unexplainable conditions.

I started driving.

I felt like I could handle anything. I was light as a balloon bobbing along in the air.

I could even handle explaining it all to Paul.

I was heading into the city, that afternoon, for a dinner date. I'd been dreading it a bit. But now, I was ready. I knew what to say, and how to say it, so that the man who loved me would truly understand.

ψ ψ ψ

I took my time after I got home. I showered and fussed with my hair until it finally succumbed and settled around my shoulders in beautiful, well-behaved waves. I did my nails. I put on a new outfit that I'd found online, on sale. Very cute. Pale blue skirt, matching floral print top.

I was dressing up. Playing up the girlfriend stuff. Because I might have been newly certified as sane, but I wasn't kidding myself. It was going to take some work to get Paul to come around completely.

He needed to know that I cared for him. That I appreciated him. That even though I was wrapped up completely in my farm—and my farm had taken a turn that neither of us expected—I was invested in our relationship and our future.

I could hear voices from downstairs as I dabbed my lashes with mascara. But I wasn't prepared for what I saw when I walked past the living room.

I did a double take.

Maisey on the over-stuffed chair. Gina on the couch. And what the—?

Sitting next to Gina?

Jade.

The woman who'd barged into my house earlier that summer to talk about The Work.

"Hullo," I said warily.

"Libby!" Gina said happily. "This is Reverend Jade."

Jade stood up.

She was wearing a purple and gold sarong, which made her look kind of monk-like in a psychedelic way.

"Uh, we've already met," I said as Jade came over and clasped my hand in hers. "Good to see you again, Jade. But you'll have to excuse me, I'm on my way out."

"Can you spare a minute, Libby?" Gina said. "You look great, by the way. You should listen to what Reverend Jade has to say. She's pretty incredible. She's a clairvoyant. She's been in contact with your nature spirits."

Oh. Now they're 'nature spirits.'

I must have looked skeptical, because Jade spoke up in a reassuring voice. "This is a highly charged quadrant," she said. "It's relatively straightforward for any sensitive to establish a bridge under these conditions."

This woman was after something. She had some sort of ulterior motive. Don't ask me why I thought that, but I did. "Fine," I said. "Bridge away. I'm on my way to the city. I have a date."

Jade stretched her neck slightly and lifted her chin. "Libby, you need to accept this aspect of yourself. You've been fighting it. This is about your inner growth."

My inner growth.

"This won't take long, Libby, I promise," Gina said. "We won't make you late. Jade, tell Libby what happened yesterday."

I suppressed a sigh and double-checked the time on my phone as Jade repositioned herself on the sofa.

A minute ago, I'd been feeling so happy and light. A brightly colored balloon with wavy brown hair totally under control, for once, and a cute new skirt to wear. Now I was feeling like a balloon with a slow leak. Was there no escaping these people? And my vision from earlier this afternoon? Of me working quietly on my land, communing with those impossible beings?

It was never going to happen.

I could see that, now. There were too many other people involved, and they wanted too many things.

The smile on Jade's face had dissolved into a terribly serious expression. "The energies that you perceive are becoming restless," she intoned. "They need you to understand that you were chosen for a reason, and when you resist them, the positive vibrations become inverted, with potentially harmful consequences."

Maisey was moving restlessly in her chair. And was she avoiding looking at me?

"They haven't mentioned any of that to me," I said, turning my attention back to Jade.

"They can't, if you're resisting it," Gina said. "That's what resistance is."

Jade held up her hand. "Wait a minute, Gina." She looked at me again. "You may have noticed your resistance, Libby. Are you getting headaches? Vertigo? Pressure right here?" She touched the spot between her eyebrows.

I shook my head. "No."

"I thought you said you get headaches?" Gina said.

"Headaches can be a blessing, actually." Jade shut her eyes and began speaking in a measured voice. "You were chosen because of certain alignments. You were first called to this property in—I'm getting the number nine—but you chose at the time to pursue other avenues. You weren't quite ripe yet, in a manner of speaking. Then came a point about a year ago when the energies here attempted to contact you again, this time through the dream state, and at that point..."

She believes what she's saying. She's completely sincere, in a way. And yet there's definitely something off about her. Is there a such thing as a semi-charlatan?

Also, I needed to get out of there.

I wondered if Jade, eyes closed, would notice psychically that I was sidling toward the door.

"...pick the proper quadrant and continue the communication from there."

She opened her eyes.

I froze in place. "Okay," I said. "Thanks for that and everything. But I really have to leave, so—I don't mean to be rude—what is it that you want, exactly?"

"Your destiny is not in your hands," Jade said earnestly. "Do you understand that?"

I felt another sigh of air escape my once-bubbly balloon.

"You've been chosen, Libby Samson. You need to accept that." Pause. "You say you're able to speak to these spirits. You call them, as well?"

"Call them? I don't know. I guess so. But they—they're—"

I broke off.

This was impossible.

It wasn't even what Jade was saying so much as how she was saying it. How could she be so sure of herself? It's not like we had a fairy in a dish in front of us to test and weigh and measure. I was having these experiences, yes, and they were certainly real to me. But what did that have to do with what Jade was trying to say?

"Libby," Gina said. "Jade is here to help. We're here to help."

Help?

This was *help*?

I couldn't take it anymore. I lost it. "Help? You want to help?" My body began to shake. "How about you take over! You know, do it all! The communicating with the spirits, dodging those people out there, having no privacy, having no LIFE. You do it!"

I clamped my mouth shut.

My chest heaved.

All I could hear, for a moment, was the sound of my own breathing.

Then Gina spoke. "You know, Jade, that might not be a bad idea," she said thoughtfully.

And something about her voice. She sounded almost rehearsed. I whipped my head back around to look at Gina so fast, I'm lucky I didn't sprain my neck.

I suddenly knew what they were up to. They'd discussed that very idea. Gina and Jade. They'd discussed taking over my life and making it into this "business" Gina had concocted. They'd discussed running everything the way they wanted to run it, whether I agreed or not.

Whether I participated or not.

What had just happened was actually more an ambush than an offer to "help."

Alrighty, then.

They could have it. They could have all of it. But not with me as part of their scheme.

I was getting out. No matter what the cost.

I drew another deep breath to quiet my churning stomach. "Good," I said. "We're in agreement, then. You two are taking it over. The whole thing."

"Sure. You go talk to Paul. He'll love the idea," Gina said soothingly. "We'll start by redoing the website. And Jade will need a place to sleep. Libby, don't leave just yet—just a couple of things. Jade will need a place to stay, and obviously it will have to be on the premises.

There's enough room in your office, I'm thinking, for a single bed, we'll just need to move the love seat out—"

"You don't understand," I interrupted. "She can sleep anywhere she likes. All she needs to do is come up with the money to buy the place."

"What?" Gina said, and now it was her turn to whip her head around in shock.

"I'm putting the place up for sale. You guys want to run a cult? Fine. Buy the place and do it. Run your cult."

I marched to the front door.

My heart was pounding, and the sweat from my hand made the metal handle feel slick as I yanked it open.

I broke into a run, taking the steps two at a time and then sprinting to my car. To get out before I got chased again by campers.

And that idea—the idea to just sell my farm—had never crossed my mind. At least not consciously. But didn't it make perfect sense?

I'd sell the farm. Take the money out. Move back to Rochester.

Paul and I would get back on track.

I'd get my life back to normal again.

A perfect solution, right?

And how excited Paul would be when I told him! Like I was serving my boyfriend a good news sundae. Whipped cream and a cherry on top.

But is that really what you want to do, Libby?

I bit down on my lip.

Did it matter? What I wanted?

I needed to solve this problem.

Selling my farm solved this problem.

I passed Al's place.

And I was so wrapped up in what had just happened that I almost didn't notice the van that passed me, heading the other way.

Only it wasn't just any van. It had a satellite transmitter dish affixed to the roof.

I slowed down.

I eyed the van in my rearview mirror.

There was no reason whatsoever for a television news crew from Rochester to be driving along my road at 3:00 p.m. on a Saturday afternoon.

None at all...

Forty-Two

You know what I wanted to do?

I wanted to pretend I'd never seen that van. I wanted to drive right on to the city like I'd never noticed that van.

But I made a U-turn.

Just to check. Because that news crew? They were probably lost. They were probably on their way to an annual corn festival in Bristol or something and had gotten lost. They'd lost their GPS signal unexpectedly. Maybe their GPS had been knocked out by an unexpected solar flare.

I'd just follow the van, and by the time I got to my house they'd be a half mile past it, out of sight where the road curls around Dean's property and starts its descent back down into the valley.

Then I reached my house, and the news van was parked in my driveway.

A bunch of campers were crowding around it.

Gina emerged from the front door and descended the steps like a flower girl preceding the towering Jade in her flowing purple and gold.

I got out of my car.

Gina and Jade reached the van and Gina shook hands with the driver—a short, casually-dressed man with thick, tousled hair—while the guy who'd been sitting on the passenger side opened the vehicle's back door and lifted a video camera and tripod.

Gina had seen me.

She waved at me to come over.

You could just jump in your car, Libby. You could just drive off.

I'd just told Gina and Jade they could have this whole silly operation. And I was the introvert. The person who would rather do just about anything than speak to strangers.

I edged closer.

The camera man strolled by, tripod over his shoulder, accompanied by a knot of campers. He stabbed the tripod in the ground and pointed his camera in the direction of the tents.

Now tousle-headed guy had noticed me. "Libby Samson?"

Must be my deer-in-the-headlights expression indicated "yes."

"Great!" He smiled broadly. "Thanks so much for agreeing to talk to us. I'm Howie Southman, Channel Eight News."

"S-sorry?" I managed to stutter. "What did—who?"

"Remember, Libby?" Gina broke in with a nervous laugh. "The television crew. I told you they were coming to—you know." She laughed again, weakly.

Howie looked at Gina.

He looked back at me.

He gave a little cough.

"Howie!" Gina touched his arm to get his attention. "How would you like to interview the Reverend Jade here? Reverend Jade is in full communication with the little people, and as a matter of fact, she and I are purchasing the farm and—"

Howie's brow furrowed slightly. "I read that it's Ms. Samson who sees them."

"We, uh, have more than one person in communication with them," Gina murmured hopefully, but Howie was looking at me, not her.

My knees were wobbling.

My mouth was dry.

An image rose into my mind. An image of what it looks like when a camera crew tries to pursue a reluctant interviewee on one of those muckraker shows, a 60 Minutes-type show, some crank trying to evade the journalist and how lame it looks, the shots through the car window, the reporter banging on the windshield, "Ma'am, ma'am, why won't you answer a few questions?"

"We'd really love to interview you, Ms. Samson." Howie was fixing me with an utterly charming smile.

"I, uh—I'm not really prepared," I stammered. "To be honest, nobody told me—I had no idea."

"Ah! But that's fine. Really." Howie's voice had turned soothing, supple. "There's no preparation necessary! I'll ask questions, you answer. We can re-record if you're not happy. It won't take long. Fifteen minutes, tops."

I could see Gina's face over Howie's shoulder, mouthing the word "please?" at me.

I willed my legs not to buckle.

"Okay. Okay. I guess," I said.

Paul's going to find out about this. There is no way Paul will NOT find out about this.

"Okay, got some B-roll of the tents." The camera man had re-joined us. "Where's the crops? How about we set up the interview by the crops?"

"They're that way," one of the campers called, and they started up the hill toward my growing beds.

My hands shook as I texted Paul to tell him I was going to be late.

And that I'd explain why when I got to the city.

⚜ ⚜ ⚜

We cancelled our dinner reservations and got take-out, instead, and went to Paul's condo to eat.

We switched on the television.

My interview aired in a local news "Our Community" feature that could have been subtitled "Local Weirdballs."

They'd edited out the parts where I'd said I'd never intended for this to become public. And they used a clip where I'd actually said,

"Stories about fairies have been with us forever" but they removed the words "stories about" to make it sound like seeing fairies was normal or something, which couldn't be further from the truth. And they knitted together some other bits of me talking about my encounters, making it sound like that's all I did. All I did was hang out communing with supernatural beings.

They used clips from campers, too. One gushed about the high vibrations and another explained she saw fairies there just about every day.

Ugh.

Then it was over, except the lingering smirk on the face of the anchor when the camera cut back to him, sitting behind his desk.

Paul shut off the television.

"I'm sorry," I said for the eightieth time.

He wouldn't look at me.

"I'll call my realtor, Paul. The property will be sold by fall, easy."

Still no answer.

"You never know," I said. "Maybe this will make the place more valuable. Maybe I'll make a real estate killing."

"Who'd want to own a property crawling with side show freaks?" Paul muttered like he was talking to himself. But then he looked at me and added, quickly, "I don't mean you, Libby. I mean those other people."

The knot in my stomach was still there in the morning—too tight to be undone by anything Paul could offer.

Not his lovemaking.

Not his apologies.

Forty-Three

I spent the next few days trying not to think, too much, about my decision to sell my farm.

I left a voice mail for my realtor.

I wrapped up a new issue of *Skin Tones*.

I called Susan to let her know I'd have a load of beans for her CSA. Green beans and yellow beans and the bi-colored ones with the purple spots.

Susan hadn't seen my interview, but she'd heard about it.

I told her I'd tell her the whole story on Saturday.

ψ ψ ψ

After we transferred my beans to David's truck, I followed Susan into her kitchen. She was making green tomato jam. I sat at the big, wooden table in the middle of the room and watched as she filled a kettle with tomatoes and lit her stove.

Her sons outside playing with some neighbor kids. They were shouting, and every few minutes a ball would *thunk* the side of the house. And I felt, all at once, horribly nostalgic for my own childhood, for what it felt like to wake up on a summer day and the first thing you think of was *let's get outside and play*, just gulp down some sugary cereal drenched in cold milk and you're ready for your day.

"This whole thing has been hellish for you, hasn't it," Susan said as she handed me a cup of coffee.

I nodded. "Go ahead and put it in your newsletter, Sue. Really. I don't mind."

Susan and David pass out a newsletter with their weekly deliveries, and her customers had been asking about me and the fairy thing. Naturally. Since it had been on television, everybody in Western New York was asking about it.

"You're sure?" Susan said.

I laughed ruefully. "A month ago, I would have been mortified. But now that I've been humiliated on local television, an article in a CSA newsletter barely registers." I sighed. "And I'm sorry I didn't tell you about it ages ago." *Thunk* went the ball against the house. "I wanted to believe the whole thing would just go away."

She nodded sympathetically. "I can understand that." She reached over and patted my hand. "I was wondering something else, too, Libby. Have you considered the possibility that the national press will get wind of this and show up, too?"

I nodded. "That's one reason I decided to sell the place."

Susan grimaced. "Are you sure you want to do that?"

I knew why Susan asked the question. She knew how long I'd dreamed about having my farm. And the idea of doing anything else but farming was anathema to her. It was her life—hers and David's.

But me? I hadn't put roots down. Not yet. Well, itty bitty shallow ones, maybe. Easy enough to yank out. "It's for the best," I said.

"What's Paul think?"

"Oh. Paul." *Paul can't wait for me to sell.* "You know Paul. He was never a fan of me moving so far away."

"That must be hard."

"It's part of the equation," I said, trying to sound more light-hearted than I felt. "Things have been a bit strained between us. I'm hoping this will help."

Susan nodded and for a moment I thought she was going to say something, but instead she stood up and went to her stove. Steam had started to trickle upwards from the kettle, and she stirred the tomatoes with a long handled wooden spoon.

I caught a whiff of the tomatoes' sour, pungent greenness.

"He's a good man," I said, and then immediately wished I'd just let it drop. I sounded defensive. And how could Susan really understand why I'd defend my relationship? It was so different from hers. She and David wanted the same things. It's easy, when two people want the same things. But I was committed to Paul. That's what mattered. We just had to find new things, together, to want. As a couple.

I wondered what Dean would think when he found out I was selling.

"Well." Susan said over her shoulder as she tapped the spoon on the edge of the pot to knock the last drips of hot tomato juice back into the kettle. "There's something else you should know." She set the spoon down on the stove.

"What's that?"

"I thought it would be good news, before you told me you wanted to get out." Susan sat back down at the table. "You know the Bedlows? They have that CSA out in Hamlin?"

"Yeah."

"Well, they're retiring. Moving to Virginia to be closer to their son."

My heart began to pound. I knew what this meant. Come next summer, their subscribers would be looking for a new farm to join.

"We're already getting calls from their customers, asking if they could join our farm next year. And, you know we can take a few. But we could take more if you were going to stay in it. Ramp up, even, to supplement what we grow."

"That's awfully nice of you," I whispered.

Thunk. Ball hit the house again.

"It would probably be enough that you could scrape out a living. Or close to it."

The very thing I wanted. The door opening now to the market I need to make a living with my farm...and it's too late...

"Thank you, Susan, for offering. But I've made my decision. It's really for the best—"

And Paul would freak out, if I went back, now, on my decision.

My cell phone rang. Gina.

"I should take this," I apologized to Susan and then tapped the Answer icon on my phone. "Hi, Gina."

"Libby. Is Maisey with you?"

My grip on the phone tightened. "No. Why?"

Susan heard the alarm in my voice and her eyes met mine.

"She's gone," Gina said. "And, um, all her stuff is gone, too. Well. Not all of it. But a lot of it. Her clothes. And Ty says he hasn't seen her since yesterday afternoon."

Yesterday afternoon?

My mind whirled. Something had happened. Something with Maisey and Tyler and Alexa. And Gina didn't have a clue. Gina was too busy scheming with her new buddy Jade to assemble their we-see-fairies empire.

"I'm sure she's fine," Gina was saying in the tone of voice people use when they are hoping you'll agree with them. "She's done this kind of thing before."

"I'll be home as soon as I can," I said. "Have you talked to that friend of hers in Rochester?"

"Good idea, I'll do that," Gina said. "Oh and before I forget, a producer from some cable talk show called. They want to have you on, they think you'll—"

I groaned. "Please don't talk to them, Gina."

"They called my phone. My number's on the website, remember? You didn't want to be the contact."

The website.

Argh.

"What's going on?" Susan asked as I set down my phone.

"Maisey. She's gone missing. Boyfriend trouble."

"Oh, dear," Susan said. "Just what you need. Any idea where she is?"

And my first thought was "no." But then I suddenly realized that I did know. Or anyway, I had a pretty good idea.

My guess was that Maisey was at Dean's.

Forty-Four

Gina wasn't exactly frantic about her missing daughter.

I found her and Jade in my office when I got home. Jade had used her psychic abilities to check on Maisey and explained that she seemed to be perfectly safe. She seemed to be staying at a girlfriend's. They were drinking something—tea or wine, Jade wasn't sure which—and Maisey had been crying but now she was fine.

And, Gina reminded me, Maisey had done this kind of thing before. She always got flakey around her time of month. And anyway, you can't file a Missing Persons report until the person's been gone for 48 hours. Also, would I be able to take a reverse mortgage on the farm?

"No," I said. "I'm not a bank, Gina. I need to get my money out. Paul and I are going to buy a house together."

"Paul? Really?" Gina rolled her eyes.

I excused myself and went downstairs to fix myself a sandwich.

ψ ψ ψ

I wondered if it was possible that Jade's psychic reading was right— which would mean my hunch about Maisey's whereabouts was wrong.

But there was only one way to be sure. And since Maisey had confided in me, not her mother, at least for now I couldn't break that confidence.

I texted her. *Maisey. We're worried about you. Where are you?*

She didn't answer my text.

Dean didn't have a phone. So if she wasn't going to answer me, my only other option was to slip away and sneak through the woods to his house.

I put together my supplies. Compass, because the last thing I needed was to end up wandering around in circles in the woods. Flashlight, in case I ended up leaving after sunset.

Gina and Jade had moved into to the living room and were streaming some documentary about Atlantis.

I hovered.

I pulled a paperback off the shelf and went up to my bedroom and read.

I listened.

They were still down there, talking.

I yawned. I read. I yawned again.

I sipped water to try to stay awake.

It was almost midnight when I finally heard the door slam and the sound of a car in the driveway. I listened to Gina's footsteps as she climbed the stairs and walked down the hall to Maisey's room. I closed my bedroom door soundlessly behind me and tiptoed down the steps. A few minutes later was climbing out of my trusty dining room window.

ψ ψ ψ

It was chilly.

I should have grabbed a jacket.

Too late for that.

I started up the hill.

Ahead of me, a three-quarter moon was untangling itself from the treetops and heading up the eastern sky. So there was a little light.

And this time I didn't have anyone hunting for me.

I paused at the edge of my property.

If I kept to a southwest trajectory, I'd eventually hit Dean's driveway, if not his cabin.

I stepped over the tumbled stone wall and flicked on my flashlight. The beam illuminated a tunnel of branches and leaves. The effect was disorienting and otherworldly, and I considered calling out to my little people.

It was worth a try, right? "Hey," I called quietly. "If you guys are around, I could use a bit of help right now."

But instead of the little man I heard the whoo *whooo*, whoo *whooo* of a great horned owl floating spookily through the trees.

Perfect. A little B-movie creepiness to make my journey even more pleasant.

I took a few more steps. Spider webs brushed against my face. Because in late summer in the country, there are spiders all over the place. And as soon as the sun sets, they come out en masse, crisscrossing the forest with their creepy wispy little guy-lines.

I shuddered and wiped my face. I shined the flashlight back down onto my compass and pulled my cell phone from my back pocket to check the time.

I sighed.

At this rate, I'd make Dean's sometime around 4 a.m.

I climbed over a huge limb left from the spring's ice storm.

Something outside the reach of my flashlight beam made a high-pitched snarly noise and I stopped in my tracks, feeling my heartbeat as I listened to whatever-it-was run off through the undergrowth.

I checked the compass again.

I reached the edge of the first of three gullies I'd need to negotiate. I peered down. The bank was frightfully steep. And I'd have to put my flashlight away so that I could hold onto tree branches with both hands.

On the other hand, coming to a gully was a good news sign. It meant that I was headed in the right general direction at least.

ψ ψ ψ

Okay, so going southwest meant I'd be headed in the "general direction" of Dean's cabin. Give or take a few degrees. Meaning that, after an hour's worth of nighttime bushwhacking, I came out on the road.

Some woods person I'd turned out to be.

I stood on the berm, listening.

The coast was clear.

At least I knew which direction to walk now.

I'd gotten away without any campers noticing.

And I wasn't far from Dean's driveway.

ψ ψ ψ

I stood beneath the window of his loft. "Dean!"

Inside the cabin, Bo woofed.

A minute later the door opened, and Dean stepped out, lantern held high. He was barefoot and wearing a white tee shirt, the sleeves tight over his biceps.

"Well, Libby," he said. "I thought you might turn up. Although I didn't expect it would be the middle of the night."

"Is she alright?"

"Yes, she's fine. What did you do to your face?" He lifted the lantern and touched the scratch across my left cheek.

Our eyes met.

"Ran into something, I think?" I whispered.

His fingertips kept going when they reached the end of the scratch.

They dropped and brushed the side of my neck.

And then they dropped again, and his hand was behind me, and he pulled me in and put his mouth on mine.

And I didn't mean to. And I hadn't planned to.

But a moment later I found myself following Dean indoors.

We walked past the kitchen and through the living room, past the couch where Maisey was sleeping.

We reached the ladder to the loft.

I put my foot on the rung.

What are you doing, Libby?

I set my foot back on the floor and turned around and looked up at Dean. My eyes, accustomed to the dark after my time in the forest, could just make out his face.

"We don't have to do this, you know," he said quietly.

I reached back with my hand, searching for the ladder, and caught it, steadying myself. "I—I can't, Dean," I whispered. "It wouldn't be—I can't."

It felt like the air between us was trembling. And all I wanted to do was fall forward, fall into Dean's arms.

But I couldn't do it.

"You don't have to walk me back," I whispered. "I'll go by the road."

Dean shook his head. "You came to talk to Maisey. You might as well stay, now."

A moment later, I peered down from the loft as Dean, sleeping bag under his arm, crossed the living room, heading toward the front door and his porch. To sleep outside.

Forty-Five

I dreamt the whole thing. Right? Right?

Wrong.

I opened my eyes.

I was in Dean's cabin.

I was in Dean's bed.

I heard someone moving downstairs and crept to the edge of the loft and looked down. It was him, rolling up his sleeping bag on the floor of the living room. Shirtless. In the soft light of the cabin, morning light filtered by the trees outside, I could make out the slope of his shoulders, the muscles of his bare back...

I crawled silently back to the bed and shut my eyes again and lay still, pretending to be asleep, listening to his footsteps as he walked back across the room to the kitchen.

I heard him say something.

I heard Maisey answer.

I sat up.

My face felt hot. What would Maisey think? Had she seen the sleeping bag? Would she believe that nothing had happened between me and Dean last night? Maybe I could just hide up in the loft. Maybe, if I hid long enough, she'd leave the cabin and I could sneak out and sneak home and nobody would know.

Nobody would know, except me and Dean, how close we'd come to—

And what about Gina? What if she decided it was late enough, I must be awake, and banged on my bedroom door with some inane question about her budding wee-folk empire?

I needed to get back. If she was up, I'd just pretend I'd been out for a morning walk. I'd been out checking on my crops.

And I could trust Maisey, right? She'd learned her lesson about what happened when secrets get out.

I needed to trust Maisey.

ψ ψ ψ

They were in the kitchen.

Dean, standing by the coffee pot, saw me first and took a second mug down from the cupboard. Maisey, in her bare feet, was pouring herself a glass of water from a pitcher. And she may have done a little double-take when she turned around, but I'm not sure, because honestly, I was so nervous as I slipped into the room that I didn't dare look at her closely.

And if she was surprised, she got over it quickly. "Hi, Aunt Libby," she said.

Maybe she thought I'd just gotten there that morning? Okay. Okay. I'd go with that. I let myself breathe again and lowered myself into a chair at the little kitchen table.

Dean set a mug on the table in front of me and pulled out a chair.

I took a sip of coffee. "I'm just glad you're okay, Maisey," I said, sounding as natural as I could. "I was awfully worried about you."

"It didn't take you very long to find me." She sat down now, too, and flashed a little smile, but then her face turned somber again.

"It was a lucky guess," I said, avoiding looking at Dean. I took another sip of coffee. "Maisey. You shouldn't have run away."

"I wasn't running away."

"Oh?" I shot her a skeptical look. "What do you call it? You disappeared. We didn't know where you'd gone."

"I just couldn't stand it anymore." She looked up from her water glass. "Do you know what Mom said to me when I told her I was breaking up with Ty?"

Oh dear. What had Gina done? I shook my head.

"She said, 'Well about time. I was sure you were turning into another Libby. You don't own him, you know. Men like to have fun. Give Alexa a turn.'"

I set my mug down. "What did you just say?"

"She's worried I'm turning into you."

"No," I said. "The other bit. About Alexa."

"She said I should give Alexa a turn," Maisey said. "At Ty."

I'd heard Gina say almost that exact same thing myself, one time.

"That's an interesting choice of words," said Dean.

I'd dropped my hands in my lap and now I looked down at them, at how they'd clenched into fists.

She'd said it about Wallace.

I felt Dean looking at me, studying my face, as Maisey went on with more details about what had happened, about her going to see Tyler and Gina showing up with Alexa and—

"Libby? You okay?" Dean said.

"I'm fine." I loosened my fists and made myself pick up my coffee mug.

Act natural. Whatever had happened between Gina and Wallace, it didn't matter anymore, did it?

"Maisey," I said. "I'm sorry about all of it. It's an awful mess. But you should have said something to someone before taking off. We were worried about you. Your mother—" I cleared my throat. "She's worried about you."

"No, she isn't." Maisey set her jaw. "Mom thinks I'm always fine, no matter what I do. And anyway, you're running away, too. You're running away from your farm."

I frowned. "No, I'm making a difficult decision. Running away means taking the easy way out. I'm not taking the easy way out." I glanced at Dean, steeling myself. "I don't know if Maisey told you, but I've decided to sell."

His eyebrows shot up. "Oh? Really?"

"And I'm not a minor child," Maisey said, defiantly. "And Mom's not going back to Hawaii either, you know. She's staying here. Indefinitely. She wants you to go to Hawaii for her, to help her boyfriend with the pineapple thing."

"I'm not going to Hawaii. I'm moving to Rochester. I'm—"

I stopped myself. I'd been about to say *I'm moving in with Paul.*

"Did you know she's gotten quotes on putting in a Visitor's Center?" Maisey said. "A Visitor's Center. On your property."

I forced myself to emit what passed for a laugh. "You're kidding me. And my body not even cold yet."

I wished it didn't feel like Dean was always studying me.

He couldn't be that surprised at my decision to sell, could he?

"Anyway, Dean says I can stay here for a few days," Maisey said. "Then, I dunno. I'm thinking maybe Florida."

I looked up. "Why Florida?" I asked.

"I dunno. They don't get snow."

I shook my head. "Do you really think that's a good idea? What about college? You were thinking about college, weren't you?"

She shrugged and the conversation died. We all three sat in silence, each moving off into our own private thoughts.

Did Maisey have a point? About me? Was I running away?

I took another sip of coffee. "Maisey," I said quietly. "You're right. I am running away." I turned my face and met Dean's gaze full on. "But I don't see what else I can do. Even if I toss Gina out this morning, I still have a huge publicity mess. And she's not going to quit, she'll just work it from town. She sees this as her ticket to fame and fortune."

"It might be a bit deeper than that," Dean said.

"Whatever," I said sadly. "It doesn't matter what her motivations are. She's not going to give it up. And I didn't buy this place to star in a sideshow."

"That's pretty defeatist, isn't it, Libby?" Dean asked.

I felt a quick spark of temper. "It's not defeatist to be realistic about my situation."

"Realistic? You've convinced yourself you're trapped."

"I *am* trapped."

Dean leaned toward me. "Only if you think you are."

"If you guys are going to fight," Maisey said. "I'm going for a walk. C'mon, Bo."

"What's your point, Dean?" I said as the screen door banged shut behind Maisey. My voice had an edge to it.

"I'm trying to help," he replied. There was a little edge to his voice, too.

"By insulting me?"

He set down his coffee mug and his next words were low, but urgent. "I didn't insult you. I made an observation. You know, this may surprise you, but I like you, and I'd like you to have what you want. I'd like you to be happy."

"You want me to be happy? Alright. You want to do something for me? Talk to your sister. And Tyler, too, while you're at it."

"Tyler?"

"Maisey loves that kid," I said, gritting my teeth. "And no offense, but Alexa needs to be told—she needs to back off. Tyler is—Tyler's making a huge mistake. And Lord knows, Gina will never intervene on Maisey's behalf." I glanced toward the door reflexively, but Maisey was well out of earshot, over by the edge of the clearing around the cabin.

Dean stood up, taking his coffee mug to the sink. "Sorry, Libby. I don't see what you want me to do."

"Talk to Tyler. Have a man-to-man with him."

"Men don't have 'man-to-mans'," he said as he rinsed his mug and set it on the drainboard. "That's a myth."

I glared at him. "Is that right?"

"Look, Libby. I've been on the receiving end of that kind of BS—"

The Iranian princess.

"—and I'll be damned if I'll ever interfere that way in peoples' lives."

"I'm not asking you to break them up," I said.

"You're asking me to tell a guy that he doesn't know his own mind."

"Forget it. Forget I asked." I stood up. "I have to go. I have to get back before Gina and Jade—"

The screen door slammed again. "You guys done?" Maisey said. "Oops, I guess not."

"Look, Maisey." My mouth tightened. "There's something I need you to understand. I can't cover for you. You need to tell your mom where you're staying."

Maisey's face crumpled.

"I'm sorry, hon," I said, avoiding Dean's gaze. "But she's your mother, and she's worried. And I have to go."

But I should have known I wouldn't get off that easy.

I'd only made it as far as the edge of the clearing when Dean caught up to me. "Hey." He grabbed my arm. "What are you doing, exactly?"

"What do you think I'm doing?" I pulled my arm away, refusing to look at him because of what I might see in his eyes. "I'm going home."

"You know that's not what I mean."

"I have no idea what you mean." I wasn't being entirely truthful. Because I did know what he meant. "I just need to go home. Please, Dean."

There were brambles growing along the tree line, and they tore at my clothes as I forced myself through them and into the woods.

Dean didn't follow me, of course. Because life isn't like the movies. Except maybe the part about how hard it is to see when you're trying not to cry.

Forty-Six

There's no point in revisiting the past. That's what they say, right?

And they have a point. It's over. You can't change it.

But I couldn't stop myself.

I managed to evade Gina. I managed to evade the campers, for the most part. I changed my clothes and grabbed my tools and went up to my planting beds.

The air was crisp, and a few bright white clouds were starting to slide across the blue.

There wasn't a lot that needed to be done, for my crops. It was the time of year when everything I'd planted was reaching maturity. No weed could compete. The roots of my crops were deep enough to find water even without regular watering.

I threaded my way between my planting beds. I'd have Swiss chard ready to harvest this weekend. And sweet onions…

ψ ψ ψ

It was after Wallace and I'd gotten engaged.

And of course Wallace and Gina were friends. They'd been friends for years before she introduced me to him. But then Gina started acting oddly. She would tell me how glad she was for me, what a catch Wallace was, what a hunk he was. But she was acting strange around me.

No, around him. When it was the three of us, out somewhere.

Gina couldn't possibly be envious of me, could she? The woman who was always the center of attention? Who dressed like a jeweled butterfly? Who was funny and charming and always had men flocking around her?

And why did it bother me so much when she joked about Wallace? When she said, "You've had Wallace awhile now. You should give me a turn, Lib."

It was just Gina, being silly, right? Cracking one of those jokes I couldn't really get because I was so unlike her.

She hadn't actually slept with my fiancé, had she?

And what about after we'd gotten married?

And oh, crap. What had I just done? I groaned aloud.

I'd stepped on one of my pumpkin plants. I knelt to check the damage. The main stem was broken clean through. "Stupid Libby," I muttered. "Watch where you're going."

I collected the ruined vine with its tiny, unripe pumpkins and carried it to my basket.

A threesome of campers walked past. They'd been further up the hill, apparently. I hoped they weren't using my upper field as their latrine, now.

I looked around for the little man. Did the little man know I'd just killed one of my pumpkin vines?

Gina wouldn't have slept with Wallace. She was my friend. She introduced us. She thought Wallace was great for me.

I looked down the hill at the campers as they disappeared into the hedgerow.

I hadn't talked to Wallace since the divorce was finalized. But I knew right where to find him.

⚜ ⚜ ⚜

I picked out Wallace's car right away. It was parked in the "Employees Only" space closest to the dealership's staff entrance. Silver, slung low to the ground, a two-door sports coupe.

I went into the showroom, and when a portly guy in a sports jacket asked if he could help me, I told him I was there to see Wallace. He said he'd check to see if he was available, and a few moments later Wallace walked out, a fake smile pasted on his face.

"Libby! Nice to see you."

"Yeah." I kept my tone super polite. "I have a quick question for you. In private."

He led me into one of the little rooms where they seat people to discuss their financing options.

"If this is about money, forget it, Libby. You got your half of the house. It's over."

"No. It's not about money. I just need to know something."

He hadn't dropped the smile, but I could almost smell how uncomfortable he was. "I've got two minutes," he said.

Right. "Just tell me if you slept with Gina."

He puffed out his cheeks and his eyes darted around the room. "Who?"

"You know who. Gina. Our good friend, Gina."

"Libby, you called me out here for this?"

"Just answer."

"No. No, of course not. I wouldn't—I wouldn't do something like that if my life depended on it, Libby."

He smoothed his moustache as he was talking. It struck me, suddenly, that he always did that when he was lying.

Time to give Alexa a turn, indeed.

"Thanks, Wallace, you liar. You *did* sleep with her. And I got exactly what I came here for."

His eyes slid nervously toward the door, but he needn't have worried. I was done with him.

For good, this time.

Forty-Seven

I didn't go straight home after I left Wallace's car dealership. I needed some space to think. Someplace where I wouldn't be interrupted by other peoples' problems.

So I drove east, to Mendon Ponds Park.

It's a place I knew well. I used to go there a lot back when I was married. Hike the trails, center myself, and picture myself living someday in the country. Someplace quiet where I could get away from people once in a while.

How'd that work out for you, Libby?

I sighed, and parked, and chose a trail that winds around Hundred Acre Pond.

There were a few other people there.

I avoided eye contact.

I'd done the right thing. Because Paul and I had never officially declared ourselves a monogamous couple. But as escape clauses go, that was a pretty lame one. Paul wasn't seeing anyone else. I was pretty sure of that. I was pretty sure he didn't have time for anything other than work.

Plus he'd stuck with me through my divorce...

The air smelled rich and warm and swampy.

I passed through a little swarm of midges dancing in a shaft of sunlight. I stopped to watch a hawk circle the sky.

And what did I know about Dean? Not much. He was perceptive and kind to strangers and new neighbors. And good-looking, with that body and those eyes and that soft, curly beard. Good-looking enough (*admit it, Libby!*) that I couldn't look at the guy without starting to fantasize about what it would feel like if he ran his hands over me...

But on the other hand, there was a ton I didn't know. How could he afford that land and that cabin, for instance? He wasn't working, obviously. He could be some kind of crook, for all I knew.

People let sexual attraction make their decisions for them. Wallace had. Gina had.

Tyler was, most likely.

I wasn't going to be like them.

I reached a spot where I could see the far side of the pond. A black lab stood on the distant bank, waiting for his human to throw a stick into the water. He pranced back and forth, barking, until the stick splashed in the water, then jumped in to fetch it.

It wouldn't be right to toss away everything I had with Paul just because I found Dean attractive. It wouldn't be right.

I turned around and started back to my car.

I had one thing in common with Dean. One, single thing. We were neighbors. And I was going to sell my place. Which meant the only thing I had in common with the man would be gone. And then what? I couldn't exactly see him driving up to Rochester to take me to dinner. Not Mr. Holed-Up-In-His-Cabin.

No. My future was with Paul. And if my relationship with Paul had been a little stressed, that was understandable. And all that would be fixed, as soon as I got rid of my property.

It would work out. I'd sell my place, move in with Paul, and I'd never be around Dean's temptations again.

Problem solved.

🌱 🌱 🌱

"There you are, Libby!" Gina said. She'd been in the living room on her phone, chitchatting excitedly.

I was in the kitchen, doing a quick inventory and making out a grocery list. "Was that Maisey?" I asked quietly. "How's she doing?"

The teenager was still staying at Dean's. But she and her mother were talking, at least.

"No, it was Jade," Gina said. "But Maisey's fine. And anyway, I did the same thing when I was her age."

"What do you mean, 'you did the same thing'?" I said in a dangerously low voice. "You mean when you ran off with Mr. Jeffers? Because that was not the same thing at all. Maisey isn't with her dad's golfing buddy."

"Well, she's run off to stay with some man. What's the difference?"

What? I felt the blood run from my face. Dean? Did Gina think Maisey was sleeping with Dean?

"Because that's what women do," Gina said, grinning. "Come on, Libby. You know it's all about our sex drives."

I felt my jaw tighten. *Is that how she justified sleeping with Wallace?*

"Anyhow," she went on, "what I wanted to tell you is that Jade found an investor. Isn't that fabulous? He's fronting us the money to buy your place."

"Ah," I said. "Do you really think Jade's legit, Gina? She comes across, sometimes, like she's full of it. At least, to me."

"Jade's a great person. She's the real thing," Gina said. "She met this investor during a retreat at Findhorn. He's a multi-multi-millionaire."

You told me Wallace was a great person, too.

The sink was full of dirty dishes, and I reached for the detergent. I'd wash the dishes and hear Gina out, and let the Wallace thing drop. Because it was a long time ago. And Gina wouldn't understand why I was upset about it.

Just let it drop.

"He's completely on board with our plans, Libby." Gina tossed her head happily, making her dangly earrings flash and sway. "He's going to turn this place into a resort. There will be, like, a retreat for alternative healing, and there will be seminars. He says it's going to be huge, Libby. Bigger than Deepak."

"That's great, Gina."

She was an old friend. She was getting what she wanted. So that made one of us.

"Isn't it nice?" she was saying. "You don't even need to list it. That's good, right? You won't have to deal with strangers tramping through your house." Gina grinned. "He's going to fly in. We think he'll be here a week from Monday. We'll have the paperwork all ready when he gets here."

I rinsed a glass, flipped it over, and set it on the drying rack. It was nice to know that, maybe, the sale would happen quickly—and with minimal bother.

But then she touched my arm. "But Libby, there is one thing. I know how much you hate doing press interviews."

I glanced over. There was a pleading look on her face.

"But he really wants you to keep on doing them, for now. He doesn't want us to lose any momentum. The more publicity, the better! He was pretty adamant about it, Libby."

She paused. Waiting for me to say something.

I rinsed another glass. "You're sure he's the real thing? He's really going to buy the place?"

I saw her, out of the corner of my eye, nodding vigorously. "I'm positive. And so, what I wanted to talk to you about—we have a couple things we're lining up." She started talking more quickly. She was in full sales mode, now. "One is a newspaper, that's local. But there's also that cable show person who called before. I'm SO sorry, Libby, but Jade says our investor went nuts when he heard about that. He specifically requested that you do that interview. We'll make it worth your while, Libby. This guy, this investor, he'll pay what this place is really worth. Not what you'd get if you sold it as a farm. He's having his lawyer draft a memorandum of understanding with all the details about doing press. They'll email it to us."

"Fine," I said. "I just want to get it over with."

I didn't sound very happy.

But Gina was.

And okay, it was really going to happen. I was giving up my farm.

But if I made a quick sale and got a price above market?

Not a bad consolation prize, right?

ψ ψ ψ

The newspaper that wanted to do a story on me turned out to be an outfit that publishes a string of local weeklies.

And I suspect Gina had already told them I'd do the interview, because the reporter—a tall, balding fellow carrying a voice-activated recorder—was on my doorstep the next morning, accompanied by a photographer. She was a woman in her mid-thirties, dark hair with a premature gray streak down the left side of her bangs.

The reporter asked me the usual questions, and then we walked out back—trailed by a pack of curious campers, naturally—so they could pose me for photos.

I pretended to work around my pie pumpkin plants.

"I know your neighbor," the photographer said as she knelt and pointed her camera at me. "Dean Milbrant, right?"

I wonder if they're dating. "How do you know Dean?" I said, half to be polite and half, I admit, to find out if they were dating.

"I was a beta-tester for a software company he once owned. It was years ago. But I was at his cabin, right after he built it. It's gorgeous. Can you turn your head a little to the right? And tip it up a little. Good."

We finished with the pumpkins and I sat for another set of pictures, perching on one of the rocks from my tumbled-down wall.

"Are the fairies around now?" the reporter asked for the umpteenth time.

"It's not like that," I said wearily. "I can't explain it, really. But I'm not in the right state of mind to see them. Not with—" I gestured at the crowd of campers assembled around us.

"If we move away, would they appear?"

I shook my head no, but the reporter herded everyone to the other end of the field anyway.

The photographer switched lenses on her camera, and I sat on the rock where I'd once seen the little man, feeling foolish.

But it was almost over, right?

So I went along. I went through the motions, looking around, saying, "Hey, you there?" to the empty air every few minutes.

But, of course, nothing happened.

I stood up.

I heard the camera clicking as I made my way around the growing beds.

Bo suddenly bounded out of the woods, and the photographer took a couple of photos of me with the dog, too.

Then we walked back down to the house, and the reporters left, and the retinue of campers slowly dispersed, again.

One interview down.

I felt a little wave of relief.

And maybe that would be the last one. Maybe that cable thing wouldn't happen after all.

Because if I was going to give up my farm, I knew exactly how I wanted to spend my last few weeks.

By myself. On the land. Touching it, smelling it.

Saying good-bye to it.

And I'd do it, too. I'd find a way to have some private time in my fields.

Even if it meant I had to sneak up there at night, again. Or start getting up before dawn.

Forty-Eight

Monday morning.

Had something wakened me?

The alarm in my phone hadn't gone off, yet, but it was morning all right. Strips of pale light shone in around the edges of the curtains.

I sat up and swung my legs over the edge of the bed. I'd need a jacket. It would be cool outside, this early.

I reached for my glasses on the nightstand and yawned.

And then I cocked my head, listening.

Rapid footsteps downstairs.

And now Gina suddenly yelling from somewhere, "HEY. LIBBY. PAUL'S HERE."

What?

"LIBBY!"

What the hell would Paul be doing here on a Monday morning?

I grabbed my robe and cinched it around my waist as I went downstairs.

Paul was standing inside the front door. He was dressed in coveralls.

"Paul?" I said. "Is everything okay?"

"Surprise!" He grinned at me. "I've got the week off and I'm going to help you paint."

"Help me paint?" I said, my brain struggling to catch up.

His grin widened. "Your house. It will boost the resale value, right? And besides." He came over and put his arms around me. "I've been thinking. I haven't been very supportive. I should be more—"

"But what about work?"

"That's the thing." He gave me another quick squeeze and stepped back. "HR's been bugging me. It's been almost four years since I took any vacation, do you believe it? And if I don't take it now, I'll lose it. So I left a message for Josh this morning and told him I had a personal emergency. I said I was taking a week off."

It was chilly. I re-cinched my robe. "You, uh, think painting my house will take a full week?"

"Probably," he said cheerfully. "Four or five days at least, I expect."

Four or five days.

"Well, uh, Paul? About selling the place? I don't think we need to paint. It looks like I already have a buyer."

"Seriously, Libby?" He looked confused. Pleased, but confused. "But have you signed anything? A contract?"

I shook my head. An email from Jade's investor had come in the night before. And the subject line was Memorandum of Understanding, which sounded promising. But I hadn't looked at the actual email very closely.

"Well! No contract, no offer." Paul smiled again. "No more arguing, babe. Anyway, I already bought all the paint. Primer and exterior latex. White. That's okay, right? White? And blue for the trim, like it is now? You can put up with me for a few days, right? Babe?"

A few days.

So much for my plans to spent time, alone, with my land.

But he had such an anxious, please-let-me-please-you look on his face. And just because he was here didn't mean I couldn't find a few minutes to check on my fields, right? He'd understand.

"Are you sure about this?" I said. "Painting houses—it's not really your thing."

"Hey, what's a boyfriend for? Besides, you'll help." He pulled a painter's cap out of his pocket and yanked it down over his head. "How do I look?"

He was being nice. That's what was important. "Dashing," I said, stretching up on my tiptoes and kissing him lightly on the lips.

"I'm going to go get started, okay? You have a ladder, right?"

"In the shed. You want coffee?"

"Nope," he said. "Stopped at Mickey D's. This is a big job, you know. We really ought to get moving on it."

I watched him open the trunk of his car and start unloading cans of paint. And a big fat duffel bag of clothes.

Four or five days...

"Well." Gina had come over to stand next to me. She was stirring sugar into a mug of coffee. "That's a very nice thing for your Paul to do." She licked her spoon and took a sip, and then jabbed my arm lightly with the spoon.

It was warm from her coffee.

"What's the matter, anyway?" she asked. "You've been acting strange, lately."

"I'm fine."

"You blame me for Maisey, don't you?"

I blame you for a lot of things, Gina. "I'm sure Maisey's fine."

"I'm sure she is, too. Kids have to go off, do their own thing. It's Tyler's who's having regrets."

"Oh?" Now, this was news.

"Yeah. I can't understand why, really. Maisey said he's into Alexa, and between you and me, I know Maisey's my daughter and everything, but if I were a guy, it would be Alexa. The more experienced one. Definitely."

What kind of mother are you? "I'm going to get dressed," I said.

This will be over soon.

But how was I going to get alone time on my land with Paul here?

ψ ψ ψ

I could hear him bumping a ladder against the house. Apparently, he'd decided to start scraping the old paint on the west side. And sure enough, a minute or so later, the bumping sound stopped, and I heard the rhythmic noise of the scraper against the siding.

That's the side of the house that faces the valley, not the fields.

Gina was in the shower.

Would he miss me, if I slipped out for a few minutes?

I peeked out of my office window at the tents.

It was still pretty early. Nobody else seemed to be up and about.

If I go now, I could grab a few minutes.

I threw on my clothes. I tiptoed downstairs. And I crawled out the dining room window and sprinted across the grass.

All I needed was fifteen minutes.

That's all.

Fifteen minutes.

ψ ψ ψ

The sun was still low, so the hillside was still cloaked in pale shadows.

The air felt cool on my face.

I stood, listening to the distant murmur of highway traffic.

The first rays of sunlight brushed the highest tree branches at the top of the ridge, and a little flock of chickadees tittered as they flitted through the hedgerow. Looking for insects—or maybe playing tag. You never knew with chickadees.

My feet were wet from the dew.

I picked my way through the prickly stems of my pumpkin plants that crisscrossed the path between the beds. The pumpkins were base-ball-sized, now, pale green amid the vines' broad, dark leaves.

And then I saw them, at the end of the bed. The little man and the little woman, looking at me with bemused expressions.

I realized I was there to see them. I was there because I hoped I would see them.

My heart pounded.

I forced myself to walk calmly as I approached them. "Hi," I said.

They nodded.

"It's been awhile," I said softly. "I don't get much privacy anymore."

"You don't have any now," the woman said.

I turned around.

Paul. Paul was on his way up the hill. And toward my little people.

Nobody else could see them. Nobody else had ever seen them.

But what if Paul could? How would he react?

"Libby!" he shouted. "What the hell are you doing?"

"Checking on my planting beds," I said in a weak voice as he got closer.

He was breathing hard. He wasn't in very good shape, and the climb to where we now stood was a steep one.

"You weren't looking at your planting beds," he said in an accusing tone.

And I couldn't help myself. I turned to see if the little man and little woman were still there.

But they'd vanished.

I looked back at Paul.

He hadn't seen them.

And, oh, how I wish he had! How I wish he'd seen them, even if it meant he would have freaked out. Because that would have made the whole thing right. I'd finally be sharing this whole thing with the man I hoped to spend the rest of my life with—

But he hadn't seen them. And now he was glaring at me. "You were looking for those—things," he said.

"No," I lied.

Great. Just great. It wasn't even a successful lie.

"And you snuck out of a *window*? To come up here?"

I bit my lip. "It's—it's the only way I can get up here alone."

"Libby, is this any way to live?"

"I'm not crazy, Paul."

But I could see, in his eyes, that wasn't sure that he should believe me. "I don't understand this," he said. "I came here to do you a favor. It's a big job. Are you going to help? Or not?"

I followed him down the hill.

He walked pretty fast, considering that he still hadn't caught his breath.

And why? Because he was angry? Or afraid?

Or both?

Forty-Nine

Paul handed me a paint scraper, then re-climbed the ladder and began scraping, grunting slightly with each stroke.

Chips of paint skittered and whirled to the ground like flakes of snow.

I went to work a few feet away. But I could tell he was watching me closely now. I could tell he was going to watch me every second.

The campers were awake. One wandered over to see what we were doing, then wandered away again.

🌿 🌿 🌿

The sun got higher. Beads of sweat gathered on my upper lip.

"I'm gonna get my water bottle," I said. "Want one?"

Paul frowned but nodded.

At least he was going to trust me to go fill water bottles, unsupervised.

🌿 🌿 🌿

Gina was crossing the kitchen toward the door when I stepped inside, and we nearly collided—she was heads down, tapping a text into her phone, and my eyes were still dazzled from the sunlight.

"Hey, guess what!" she said. "We just heard from the guy who wants you for that *Hey! America* cable interview."

I suppressed a little groan. I'd so hoped this one would just go away.

"Jade's investor knows the producer, as it turns out," Gina was saying. "Everyone's very excited."

I held my hand under the tap water, waiting for the tepid water that had been sitting in the pipes to give way to the water cold from the well.

She was watching me, waiting for me to say "yes."

Or to try to wriggle out of it.

Could I wriggle out of it?

"Aren't they based in Manhattan or some place?" I said weakly. "I can't afford to fly to Manhattan."

"You don't have to. You'll go to the Rochester affiliate. They do it from there."

So much for that escape hatch. I swallowed hard. "So, uh, when is this all supposed to happen?"

"Friday."

I looked up in alarm.

Friday? Paul would still be here on Friday. And it upset Paul enough that I'd done some local news shows. But *national* news? And me so close to getting rid of the place, putting all this behind us?

"It'll be fine, Libby," Gina said. "It'll only take a couple hours. And this is the last one you'll have to do. And we've talked about it, remember. You promised to do it."

What could I say? Gina was right. I'd promised to do it.

But Paul wasn't going to like it. Not one bit.

ψ ψ ψ

"What we really need is a second ladder," Paul said when I returned with his water bottle.

At least he was speaking to me again. And I really should mention the cable interview to him. Sooner, rather than later. But now was not the time. Not when he was just getting over being mad.

I held the water bottle up to him. "We could get a ladder at the Wal-Mart."

"Can't you borrow one from somebody?" He took a swig, then handed the bottle back down to me. "Don't you country people do that sort of thing?" He laughed.

"Al's probably got one," I said.

Paul paused his scraping. "Who's Al?"

"The farmer who plowed my garden this spring."

"Why don't you ask your next-door neighbor, that Dean guy?" Gina said, and I turned around, surprised.

I hadn't noticed that she'd followed me.

"Dean's closer," she said.

"I'll call Al," I said.

But when I fetched my cell phone and dialed Al, he didn't answer.

I went back outside and suggested, again, that I buy a ladder from Wal-Mart.

But Paul grunted. "Not a good use of our money, Libby. What about the other guy?"

"Dean? I can't ask Dean. He—he doesn't have a phone."

"Doesn't have a phone? What kind of person doesn't have a phone?"

I cleared my throat. "He's a—a back-to-lander, sort of."

Paul stopped scraping and turned around to look down at me. "Is that the guy you stayed with this spring? Then he'll lend you a ladder. Can't you just drive over there? The paint is peeling ten times worse up here by the eaves. We really need you up on a ladder, too, if we're going to finish this job this week."

If he only knew what a bad idea this is.

At least he was letting me go by myself.

☙ ☙ ☙

Dean must have heard my car, because he was standing on the porch when his cabin came into view.

My heart was racing.

You've made your decision. It's Paul. You're staying with Paul.

"I'm sorry to bother you," I said, forcing myself as best as I could to sound casual. "I was wondering if you have a ladder we could borrow."

We.

"Step or extension?" His voice was as stiff as mine.

"Extension, please."

He folded his arms, studying me, and I wondered if he would even say yes. He might say no. He might hate me so much that he'd just say no.

My cheeks felt hot. "So, uh, where's Maisey?"

"Maisey moved out."

"Oh?" I forgot, momentarily, how uncomfortable I was. "When? Where is she?"

"You'll have to ask Tyler," Dean replied in a dry voice. "I believe the two of them have moved into a place in town."

"Tyler!" My heart jumped. "They're back together?"

"How do you plan to get that ladder to your place? Carry it?"

I hadn't thought of that. Neither had Paul. So much for being logical scientists. "Top of my car?" I said weakly.

"I'll bring it over in my truck. Give me ten minutes."

ψ ψ ψ

I took deep breaths as I drove back to my place.

I'd done it. I'd talked to Dean.

And I'd survived.

And I wouldn't have to deal with him one-on-one ever again.

And anyway, the important thing was that the two kids were reunited. That was one bit of unfinished business that was taken care of, at least.

Fifty

Paul was sitting on the ground eating a ham sandwich when I got back.

Three of the campers were hanging around him, which probably explained why, in addition to being sweaty and red-faced, he also looked pretty annoyed.

There were paint chips stuck to his sweaty skin.

The forecast that day was for the low 90's, and it was already so humid that the sky was white at the horizon.

"It's all set," I said. "Dean's bringing the ladder over in a couple of minutes. Any ham left?"

I went inside to make myself a sandwich, telling myself that eating something would settle me down a little. I'd get through this.

But as I was taking the mustard from the fridge, I heard Paul yell.

Oh, dear God, he's fallen off the ladder.

I ran outside and around the corner of my house, panic clutching my chest.

I came to a screeching halt.

Paul hadn't fallen from the ladder.

He'd run up it.

To get away from Bo. The dog was jumping up, bellowing his huge excited WOOFs as his enormous paws landed on the rungs of the ladder, making it shake.

I ran over and grabbed the dog's collar. "It's okay, Paul. It's Bo. Dean's dog. My neighbor's dog."

"He shouldn't be off leash," Paul snapped.

"He's friendly." And suddenly I had to fight to keep myself from laughing. No, giggling. That same hysterical giggle that had come over me the night I ordered Thai take-out was suddenly threatening to burble up again.

"Monster got half my sandwich." Paul no longer looked hot and merely annoyed. He now looked hot and deeply irritated. "Where's his owner?"

I heard the rattle of Dean's extension ladder behind me and turned to see him coming around the corner.

"Right here good?" he said and leaned the ladder against the side of the house.

"Thanks," I said. "Bo startled Paul."

He glanced up at my boyfriend. "I see that. C'mere, Bo."

I let go of the dog's collar and he trotted over to Dean.

"You ought to keep that animal restrained," Paul muttered as he backed down the ladder.

"Bo won't hurt you, if you haven't done anything wrong," Dean said. His face was upturned. He was scanning the siding of my house. "Hey, you've got a big job, here. I'd be happy to stick around for a while and give you a hand."

He was talking to Paul, not me.

My body tensed.

What the hell is Dean pulling here?

"That's very kind, Dean," I said, "but we couldn't possibly—"

I broke off. He wasn't listening. He was still looking squarely at Paul. And surely, Paul wouldn't agree to Dean's offer? Would he?

But Paul was wiping his sweaty, beet-red forehead, and his eyes were darting at Dean and then back at the house.

Dean waited, scratching Bo's neck.

"Well, you know," Paul said, "if you have the bandwidth. We could pay you."

"No need," Dean said. "I'm happy to help a neighbor."

I couldn't believe what I was hearing.

I turned on my heels and went into the house and opened the mustard jar, but then I set it down and gripped the edges of the counter with both hands.

What the hell was Dean trying to pull?

Breathe, Libby.

And then something else occurred to me.

If Dean helped, we'd get the job done more quickly.

Maybe even quickly enough that Paul will be back in Rochester before Friday.

Which would mean I could avoid the sticky subject of that cable show interview.

I was due for a change of luck. Maybe this was it.

ψ ψ ψ

Some change of luck.

Dean was up to something. He was following me. Every time I finished a section of clapboard, he climbed down from his ladder and moved it along the wall to be near to me again.

Paul, on his ladder at the other end of the house, hadn't seemed to notice. But I sure had. My stomach was in knots.

And now Dean was next to me again, so close I could smell him, the soapy smell of his skin. He jiggled his ladder to make sure it was nested securely on the ground and then bent toward me. "That's what you looked like, you know," he said in a low voice. "When Bo treed you."

"I did not look like that," I hissed. "Why are you following me around?"

"Yeah, you're right. You're a lot cuter." He laughed.

My face flushed crimson. "Stop that," I hissed again.

"Nope." He paused. "You're too good for him, you know."

"Stop it." I glanced surreptitiously at Paul to see if he'd heard.

He hadn't. He was wiping his face with the arm of his tee shirt.

I waited until he was scraping again.

"You need to stop it, Dean," I muttered. "You need to stop interf—"

But at that moment, the window next to Paul slid open and Gina's head popped through. "Hey, guys, guess who just phoned?"

"The President," Paul said.

Gina made a face. "Maisey."

I avoided Dean's eye.

"She and Tyler are back together, Libby, so that should make you happy. They've got an apartment in town. And they've invited us to dinner in their new place tonight. You too, Dean."

Oh, great.

"They asked you to bring the vegetables, Farmer Libby," Gina said.

Fifty-One

Tyler and Maisey's place was a second-floor apartment on Main Street, over an insurance agent's office. It was narrow and dark and grubby. But they were as proud of it as if it were a palace.

"We're having fondue for dessert!" Maisey grinned as I handed her a bag of baby zucchini. "Chocolate. And Ty's made his famous chicken enchiladas."

She linked her arm in mine and pulled me into the kitchenette. "Thank you soooo much, Aunt Libby!" she said into my ear.

"What did I do?"

"You got Dean to talk to Ty, of course!"

My eyes widened in surprise, but I didn't get a chance to answer because right then Paul walked in. "What's burning?"

"He's joking," I said to Maisey. "Can I help you cut up the squash?"

ψ ψ ψ

They didn't have enough space in that little apartment to seat six, so they'd set up a folding card table in the living room, then dragged their bistro table and stools from the kitchenette and squished them into the hallway leading to the bedroom.

"Maise and I will sit here, at our table for two," Ty said, adjusting the bistro stools.

He'd set out pillar candles on both the tables, and now he lit them and flicked off the light switch.

"The enchiladas smell delicious, Ty," I said.

"Dean. I could use a drink," Gina said from the couch, and I did a double take.

She was running her eyes over him. Like the drink she wanted was a glassful of my neighbor.

Of course. Pineapple Man was a long way away. Why would Gina "it's all about the sex drive" hold back if another man caught her eye?

"We aren't 21, Mom," Maisey said. "We don't have any alcohol here."

"We've got wine glasses, though," Tyler chimed in.

"There's a liquor store across the street," Dean said. "White wine okay? We'll have to chill it."

"That would be divine," Gina said, and then after he'd left, she murmured, "wow, he's nice on the eyes," to nobody in particular.

You've picked Paul. It's none of your business if Dean wants to—

But I couldn't help hoping that if Dean wanted to date, it would be someone else.

Anyone but Gina.

ॐ ॐ ॐ

The food was on the table, and Gina had shifted her chair so that her shoulders were angled toward Dean. "So tell me, Mystery Man," she said as she spooned rice onto her plate. "What do you do, all by yourself out there in the woods?"

I shrank down into my chair. How could anyone have the nerve to ask Dean such a direct question? And wouldn't he hate it?

But he smiled. "For a living, you mean?"

"Oh, a living, or for fun." Gina stroked her wine glass as she spoke. Her fingers were supple-looking and covered with rings. "Alexa says you've been living by yourself in that cabin for what, six, seven years?"

"Well, originally, my intention was esthetic, more or less," Dean said. "There's something pleasing about stripping life down to its essentials, don't you think?"

"Assuming the essentials include pleasure, of course."

I'd cut up my entire enchilada into bite-sized pieces. Without even realizing it. Like a mother might cut up a serving of meat for a child.

"But now," Dean continued, "I know what I was actually doing was waiting."

He looked right at me as he said it.

"Hey, Libby, take it easy," Paul said, patting me on my back. "You need some water?"

"I'm okay," I gasped. "Just swallowed wrong."

"I'll take another splash of that lovely vino." Gina held out her glass. "Esthetics aside, Dean, what do you do for a living? Or are you one of those independently wealthy bachelors we women are always dreaming about?"

Dean reached for the wine bottle. "Not hardly, but I'm able to live off investments at this point."

Paul was scooping another enchilada onto his plate. "Day trader?"

Dean was still holding the bottle. "No. More wine?" He was asking me.

I shook my head in a quick no.

"I knew a guy who claimed he made a living day trading," said Paul, chewing as he spoke. "Last time I saw him, he was standing at a bus stop downtown. Something must have happened to his BMW." He laughed.

"So, Dean, what kind of investments?" Gina asked.

"High tech, mostly. I co-founded a software company. Image processing software, stuff that lets people email photos, post them to websites, that kind of thing. It did pretty well."

"Oooh. Smart." Gina held her wine glass up in a congrats gesture, then took another swallow.

"No. Lucky," Dean answered. "My partner and I had a disagreement—not work-related—so we parted ways."

"You mean, you cashed out," Paul said.

Dean shrugged. "Something like that. It was play money to my partner. Big oil family."

"So what was the disagreement about?" Gina said.

"Gina!" I yipped. It came out louder than I'd expected, and now everyone was looking at me. My face, already warm with wine and the spiciness of the food, felt even warmer.

I cleared my throat. "Uh, maybe Dean doesn't want to talk about it?"

Gina laughed. "I guess if he doesn't, he'll say so, right, Dean?" She turned back toward him.

She had her hair in a French braid that night, and I noticed how striking her face looked in the candlelight, with her hair pulled back that way. She had one of those faces that make people think *good bones.*

"No problem," Dean said. "I don't mind discussing it. It was over a woman. His sister."

"Oh!" Maisey was listening from her table, now. "The princess!"

Dean laughed.

"A princess!" Gina said. "And you were in love with her?"

Dean laughed again. "It wasn't a princess. Alexa gets a bit creative with the truth, sometimes."

I dropped my eyes back to my plate.

"My partner's family was Middle Eastern. Long story short, his sister liked me, but not as much as she loved her home. So when she had a chance to go back and marry someone else, she took it."

"When you said oil money, I figured Texans," Paul said.

I was forcing myself to eat. *Put bite in mouth. Chew. Swallow.*

"So let me guess," Gina said. "The brother found out you and his sister were lovers. He lost it. Threatened to kill you unless you broke it off—"

"I think I will have some more wine now, Paul," I said. "Could you pass the wine?"

"You guys are going through that bottle pretty fast," Maisey said. "Ty, I think they're going to need the other bottle."

"Actually, you're way off," Dean said to Gina. "The brother wanted me to fight for her. He wanted her to stay here. If anything, he saw me as a way to keep her in America—"

"Enough, enough!" I yipped again.

Everyone stared at me.

I gestured weakly at my glass. "I—I was talking to Paul," I said. "I only wanted a little more wine and he—"

Somehow, my face was burning even hotter than before.

"You're so funny, Libby!" Gina smiled and turned back to Dean. "So did you take her brother's advice and fight for her?"

"No, I didn't," Dean said. "She'd made her decision. She knew what she wanted. I had to trust that."

"Well sometimes that's how it works, with couples," Paul said. "Right, Libby?"

I startled.

They were all looking at me again.

I laughed nervously. "I guess so. Depending on the, uh, circumstances."

Dean lifted his wine glass, looked at it, and set it back down on the table. "Well, it's ancient history now, anyway."

"You've moved on," Gina said.

"Yeah, something like that," Dean said.

Gina sighed. "It's really a romantic story though, isn't it?"

Ty had fetched the second wine bottle from the kitchen. Maisey stood up when he re-entered the room and said, "Here you go, guys," taking the bottle from him and putting it on the table. Then, as she went back toward her seat, she asked Ty if he wanted any more enchilada. "Nah, just more Maisey," he answered and pulled her in for a kiss.

I wondered if Dean realized how happy he'd made them.

I stole a glance in his direction to see if he'd noticed.

He was picking up the wine bottle to open it. His eyes met mine.

I looked quickly away. The last thing I needed was another choking fit.

Fifty-Two

A line of thunderstorms came through while we were eating dessert, and the room darkened, making the yellow light from the pillar candles even more dramatic. But the storm didn't last long, and when it was time to go and we went back down the worn, wooden staircase and stepped outside, the sun was out and everything was gleaming.

"Mmmmm, that cooled things down," Maisey said. "Ty, we should go for a walk."

"Sure," Tyler answered, and the two of them started up the sidewalk behind us. But I was watching Gina. She'd driven to town with Paul and I, but now, instead of waiting for us, she'd picked up her pace and fell in step next to Dean. "Dean," I heard her say in a breathy voice, "Could you give me a lift home?"

"Sure," Dean answered. "Heading that way anyhow."

I felt a tug on my sweatshirt.

Maisey. I slowed down, and she linked her arm into mine so that I was walking with her and Ty instead of Paul, and then I felt her breath on my ear as she leaned into me. "Is Mom making a pass at Dean?"

I didn't answer.

"Like *that'll* work." Maisey giggled and leaned into my ear again. "He's totally crazy about you, Aunt Libby."

I stopped walking abruptly—my eyes on Paul—which jerked both Maisey and Tyler to a stop as well. "That's not true, Maisey!" I whispered. "And you need to shush."

"Okay," she sighed. "I'll shut up."

We started walking again.

The air smelled like wet pavement.

Paul, walking more quickly than us, was now a half block away, and Maisey started talking, again, in a low voice. "Anyway, speaking of Dean," she said, "Ty and him and me were talking, and we really think you're making a mistake, selling your place."

They've talked about me—with Dean.

"It's your dream," she said. "Isn't it your dream?"

I shook my head. "It may have seemed like my dream, once. But it's not. Not really. It was—it was something I veered off into, after my divorce."

"You once told me that it was the only way you could make any sense out of your divorce—by taking what was left of your marriage and using it to do something you love. Something worthwhile."

I'd said that? "Being with Paul is what makes sense."

"But don't you love Dean?" Maisey had lowered her voice to a whisper again. "That morning when you were there—"

"Maisey!" I hissed, shaking my head vigorously to get her to stop.

Paul had reached his car. He stepped off the curb and went around to the driver's side, and I waited until he slid into his seat before I spoke again. "Nothing happened between me and Dean that night, Maisey. I was there to find you. We didn't—"

"Hey, guys!" someone called out.

We turned around.

It was Alexa.

Maisey's arm was still linked in mine and I felt her tense up.

"Whatcha doing?" Alexa said as she walked up to us. "Hi, Tyler!"

"Hey, Alexa," Tyler said. "We're just going for a walk."

"Can I come, too?" Alexa said. "I've got something to tell you guys!"

"Coming, Libby?" Paul had started the car and had lowered the passenger side window.

"It's okay, it'll be okay," I whispered quickly into Maisey's ear, and then looked across the street.

Gina was climbing into Dean's truck.

"Come on, Libby," Paul called again. "Let's get going."

I turned back to say good-bye to the kids.

Alexa had stepped between Maisey and Tyler, and the three of them were heading down the pavement.

"Come on, get in!" Paul said.

ψ ψ ψ

Three hours later and Gina still wasn't home.

I laid in bed, listening to Paul snore, until I couldn't stand it anymore.

I slipped out from under the covers, tiptoed downstairs, turned on a light and opened a paperback.

Where could they be?

ψ ψ ψ

3:12 by the clock on the kitchen stove when I finally heard the low roar of a pick-up truck engine in the driveway.

3:22 by my cell phone when the front door finally opened, and Gina tumbled in.

She didn't notice me at first.

Not until I stepped over to intercept her at the bottom of the stairs.

"Well, hiya, Libby."

"You guys took a detour on the way home," I muttered.

"We went out for drinks. That man is—" She licked her lips and leered conspiratorially.

"Do you really think that's a good idea, Gina? What would your boyfriend think?"

"Oh, him?" She laughed. "He's fine. He's got his wife."

My jaw just about dropped. "His *wife*? Your boyfriend is *married*?"

283

"Dean is so smart! We had so much fun," Gina said, taking no notice of my question. "First we went to this college bar in Geneseo. Dean told me the funniest story about one time when—"

"I want you out of here, Gina."

It was like the voice came from someone else.

But it wasn't someone else. It was me. I'd finally had enough.

"Tomorrow morning," I said. "I want you out of here."

Gina's head tilted as if she were unable to comprehend my words. "Out of here? What? Why? What's the matter, Libby? What have I done?"

"Has it ever occurred to you what you're doing to your boyfriend's wife? His *wife*, Gina. The woman who is *married* to your *boyfriend*."

"I don't understand what that's got to do with—"

"You slept with WALLACE!" I snapped.

Her mouth dropped open, then clamped shut. "That was a long time ago," she said peevishly. "It didn't mean anything."

"It means something to me," I said.

"You didn't even know. Besides, you weren't right for him."

She was never going to get it. "That's not the point, Gina," I said. "And this conversation is over. Pack your things in the morning and get out."

I listened to her footsteps as she climbed the stairs.

And then I went weak and rubbery and collapsed onto the couch.

Fifty-Three

"What'd you say to Gina last night?" Paul asked.

I should have felt marvelous. I should have felt like a possessed person the morning after the demon had been confronted and cast out. I should have felt lighter, free, empowered.

But I didn't. I felt shattered. I felt like I'd swallowed a bomb, and it had gone off, and now there was nothing left inside me except shards and grief.

And I felt like I needed sleep, hours and hours of sleep. The rims of my eyes stung, and my muscles ached, and my brain felt like mush.

"Libby?" Paul prompted me.

We were in the kitchen getting ready to cook breakfast. "Is she gone?" I said wearily.

"Yeah. Maisey came and picked her up. What happened?"

So he'd slept through our argument. That was fine by me. I was by the stove, and I lowered the flame under the frying pan, grateful I had an excuse to avert my face as I spoke. "It was time. She's been here for weeks."

"She can be a bit hard to take." He'd been buttering a piece of toast, but now he put down the knife and came over and pecked me on the cheek. "You look like hell. No offense."

Great. "I had trouble sleeping," I said.

He frowned slightly. "You going to be able to work?"

I'd asked myself the same question more than once that morning. "Yeah. A cup of coffee, and I'll be fine."

Truth was, I wanted to work. As exhausted as I was. Anything to keep myself from thinking.

His brow smoothed again. "Good. We can start with the primer coat today. We'll have this baby sewn up by Saturday, easy. Sooner, maybe, if Dean comes back."

"Right," I said, thinking to myself, *please, please, please don't have Dean come back.*

⚘ ⚘ ⚘

But my little prayer or whatever it was didn't work. I was upstairs putting on my sneakers when I heard the sound of Dean's truck in the driveway, and the image of Gina climbing into it the night before flashed through my mind.

"It doesn't matter, Libby Samson," I scolded myself. "He's allowed. He can sleep with whoever he wants."

And at least today, he'd leave me alone, right? None of this following me around, continually making some pretense to work near me.

I heard voices—Paul and Dean were talking—and I crept to my office window to listen. Dean was saying he'd finish the last bit of scraping on the north side of the house. Good.

"I'm going to primer," I said to Paul a minute later.

I pried open a paint can and picked up a brush and got to work. On the south side of the house. As far away from Dean as I could get.

⚘ ⚘ ⚘

My plan worked for a couple of hours. But by 11:00 or so, the scraping was done, and of course Dean began to help with the primer. And once again, I found him next to me.

I made a point of ignoring him.

"You look a bit under the weather," he said as I dipped my brush into the primer can.

I didn't answer.

"You know I took Gina out to be polite," he said in a low voice. "Not because I'm interested in her."

I sucked in my lower lip and bit it, hard, letting the pain keep my focus where it needed to be. "I'm glad you had a nice time," I said in a firm voice—a voice loud enough so it would hopefully carry to Paul. Then I dipped my brush in the can again and side-stepped down the wall and away from Dean.

✲ ✲ ✲

It wasn't as hot as it had been the day before.

The breeze was coming in from the north, and I could smell new-mown hay.

Al leased a field in that direction. I turned my head to listen, and sure enough, I could make out the faint noise of his tractor.

Mowing while the sun shone.

I brushed away a drip that had fallen on the clapboard below the windowsill where I was working and realized Dean was next to me again.

"Libby, can I ask you a question? Do you really want to sell this place?"

I bit my lip again and focused on smoothing the primer against the siding. Back and forth with my brush.

"Pretty clear your boyfriend would like you to," Dean said. "But what do you want?"

He wasn't getting the message. "It's not a question of what I want, Dean."

"Sure, it is."

"Okay, maybe it's something I *did* want, past tense. Maybe I *did* want to get a place in the country and start a little organic farm," I said. "But that didn't happen. Instead, I ended up with a circus. Your word."

"So you're saying, if we could get rid of these jokers—"

"No use playing with 'if's,' Dean."

"I'm just saying—"

I cut him off again. "I've made my decision. I've got a buyer." I glanced at the corner of the house, where Paul would reappear any moment. "I'll be getting my money out, plus a little extra. It's a good deal. The best I could hope for, under the circumstances."

"But you haven't signed anything, right? And what if I told you I could get rid of them? These tent people? For good?"

Was that possible? Was it possible that Dean—

No.

I shook my head. "There's no way that will happen. They think I'm holding the answers to the cosmos. Tyler tried to stop it. But like he says, its gone viral. It's all over the 'net. For every one of them who gets tired and leaves, two more show up."

"I've thought of a way."

I shook my head more vigorously. "No. No, Dean. I know you mean well, but—"

"I don't want to lose you, Libby."

I forced myself to keep painting.

The brush was shaking in my hand.

I needed to put an end to this. I needed to make Dean understand, for once and for all, that there would never be anything between us.

"There's nothing to lose," I whispered.

"Do you really mean that?" he said quietly.

"Yes."

Something rattled inside the house.

Dean caught my wrist in his hand and pulled it away from the siding.

My brush dripped primer onto the grass.

"Libby, look at me."

I looked at him.

He intended to kiss me. I was sure of it.

But something in my face stopped him, and he dropped my wrist, picked up his can of primer and disappeared around the corner of the house.

Fifty-Four

I stood over the bathroom sink, scraping primer off my hands and arms with my fingernails, running only a thin trickle of water because Paul was in the shower, and if I turned the faucet any higher, he'd get blasted by cold water.

And even though it was late August, Paul was taking a hot shower. To get rid of the aches, he'd said. So my glasses started to fog, and I took them off and wiped the steam from the mirror.

I must have brushed up against the house. The hairs around my right temple were frosted white from primer and gummed together at the tips.

Condensation started to re-form on the place I'd wiped clear, and through the film of moisture the paint made it look like I was graying at the temples.

"Hand me my shampoo, would you?" Paul said. He'd left it on the side of the sink. I passed it to him around the edge of the shower curtain.

ψ ψ ψ

I'd just changed into clean clothes when my cell rang.

Gina. I almost didn't pick up. But it could have been something about my place. About selling my place.

"Well, Libby," she snapped when I answered. "You're so smart, why don't you talk to Maisey? Here."

Huh?

Muffled noises. And then Maisey was on. "Aunt Libby?"

She sounded terrible.

"Maisey? Maisey, what's happened?"

But she couldn't talk. She was crying.

"Where are you? Are you at your apartment?"

She made a sound that passed for "uh huh."

"I'll be right there."

⚜ ⚜ ⚜

"Got a cig?" Gina said to her daughter.

Why Gina needed to smoke, I had no idea. As far as I knew, Gina hadn't smoked for years.

"They're in the bedroom," Maisey said in a little voice. She was curled up on one end of her drab little couch, a throw pillow clutched to her chest.

I took a seat on the other end. "Maise, what happened? Did Tyler—is it Alexa?"

She nodded.

Gina was back, unlit cigarette dangling from her lips. "I need something to eat," she muttered out of the corner of her mouth.

But she didn't leave. She stood on the other side of the scratched coffee table and looked at me, then took the cigarette out of her mouth. "So, Libby. Are you happy, now? Are you happy? Look at her."

I looked at Maisey. Her hair was falling, scraggly around her face. Her eyes were swollen and red, and she was scrunched up and small, curled around the pillow like that.

"What do you have to say for yourself?" Gina glared at me. "You think you're so smart, you think you can walk into Maisey's life and start handing out your stupid advice. You think I don't know what's going on? You told her to go back to him, didn't you?"

I swallowed.

Because yes. That day Maisey and I had gone for our walk—the day we'd walked up the hill and got caught in the thunderstorm—I'd told Maisey to go back to Tyler. And then I'd gone to Dean, asked Dean to help patch them up...

"Your Mom's right, Maisey," I whispered, "and I was wrong. You deserve better. You deserve a boyfriend who adores you so much he'd never dream of—of going off with someone else. You should have walked away from him."

Maisey let out a deep, ragged sigh. "It's okay, I know." She looked up at me. "I don't want him back. I hate this, I hate all of it. I thought I loved him. I thought he loved me. I thought we'd be happy together. Forever."

"Good job, Libby," Gina said, and picked up her purse.

The door closed with a bang, and her feet thumped down the stairway to the street.

I slid down the couch and touched Maisey's shoulder. "Come home, Maisey. Move back in with me." And then I remembered. I was selling my place. I swallowed. "At the farm, for now. And then you'll come with me to Rochester."

"But what about Paul?" Maisey whispered. "If I come live with you, what will he say?"

Paul? I leaned over and stroked Maisey's cheek. "I'll tell you 'what about Paul'," I whispered. "It doesn't matter. That's what."

"But you—"

I shook my head. "Certain things are more important than other things, Maisey. And I love you, and care about you, and I'm going to support you in any way I can. And that's up to me, alone. It's got nothing to do with Paul."

She looked up at me. Her eyes were wet. "All I wanted was Tyler," she whispered.

"I know. But you don't need him. You need yourself. You need your own strength. I love you, Maise. We'll see it through together, okay?"

She nodded. "I love you, too." Then a thoughtful look came over her face. "But Aunt Libby? There's one other thing—"

"Yeah?"

"I was thinking about college. I've sent out some applications. To a bunch of places, actually. And I got accepted, Aunt Libby. To almost every place I applied." She looked down at her lap. "It was a sign."

I scooted over the rest of the way toward her and took her in my arms. "You are so right, Maisey," I said. "You are *so* right. It *is* a sign. I'm so happy for you. I'm so *proud* of you."

She dropped her head on my shoulder. "Thank you, Aunt Libby." And then, in a lower voice, "I wasn't sure—me and Ty—it seemed like we couldn't come to an agreement about what to do. But now—"

I tightened my arms a bit more around her shoulders. "Do what's right for *you*, Maisey. That's what you need to focus on."

We sat a moment, and then I stood up to go. And I was about to say something else, but Maisey's eyes were drooping. They were almost closed.

I hoped Gina would be quiet when she got back. That she'd eat her take-out quietly in front of the little television and leave her sleeping daughter alone.

Fifty-Five

For the first couple days, we'd made pretty good progress, painting the house. But on Wednesday, we had a couple of setbacks.

Dean didn't show up. And about 11:00 Josh called, and after Paul got off the phone he was pacing and stressed. The FDA had objected to some marketing copy Dormet Vous Lustre had developed for a new cream. They'd need to change some of the product claims. All the collateral needed to be rewritten.

So much for Paul's vacation. And so much for getting the house done. Paul disappeared inside with his laptop and was gone for hours.

Thursday went a little better, but by mid-afternoon it was clear we wouldn't be finished by the weekend.

Although I had to admit that the part that was finished looked awfully nice. And Paul was so proud. After we put the paint away that afternoon, he put his arm around me, and we stood, admiring our handiwork. "Sure is coming out nice, isn't it, Libby?"

"Yes, Paul. It is."

"So you going to list it, when, Monday?"

I felt my body stiffen. I still hadn't told him about that cable show.

"Libby?" He'd picked up that something was wrong, and now dropped his arm from my waist and fell back a step, fixing his eyes on my face. The poor guy. Waiting for some fresh shock. "You're still planning to sell, right?"

"There's something I need to tell you, Paul. I mentioned that I may have a buyer."

He nodded.

"Well, it's Gina and her friend, Jade."

He rolled his eyes.

"Yes!" I said. "It sounds crazy. "But here's the thing, Paul. If the deal does go through, I'll get more than market for the place."

That got his attention. "Oh, really?"

So I told him the whole story. How a multi-multi-millionaire investor wanted to finance the purchase, and Gina and Jade would turn the place into a retreat, so it would be an actual money-making venture instead of a break-even farm.

"I dunno," he said. "It sounds pretty far-fetched."

"Come on," I said and led him to my office and turned on my computer and Googled "Findhorn." I clicked on the Findhorn Foundation's website. "See? Like this."

He was frowning. "Never heard of the place."

"It's in Scotland. It was originally a farm, and then people—" I hesitated. The whole fairy idea was such a sore point with Paul that I couldn't quite bring myself to say it. I couldn't say, "then people started seeing fairies."

But he knew what I meant. "You're kidding me," he said. "What a scam." He took the mouse and began clicking around on the Findhorn website. "So Gina thinks she's going to buy your place and turn it into a retreat for whackos."

"I wouldn't put it that way."

He smirked. "Well, I suppose as long as the whackos are showing up anyway, you might as well figure out a way to part them from their cash." But then his smirk turned back into a frown. "But Libby, why didn't you discuss any of this with me? Have they given you anything in writing?"

"I've got an email. I printed it out to show you." I pushed some papers around on my desk, found the printout, and handed it to him.

"There are no numbers here," he said, after a moment. "There's nothing about what they think the property is worth."

"No. Just that they understand the property's valuation is based on its use as a business, rather than a farm. I'm pretty sure I'll get my money back out of it, at least. Maybe even a little more."

My money...my divorce settlement...back where I started from...

Paul was re-reading the letter.

"Okay if I keep this? I'd like to have Cliff look at it."

I knew about Cliff. He was a lawyer Paul had used, once, when he'd been sued for leaving a stack of old *Lab Biology Today* magazines on the stairway to his condo. An elderly woman had tripped on them and fractured her wrist.

It was Paul's fault, of course, for leaving magazines there, but on the other hand—a half million dollars?

"We need to make sure you're getting a fair deal, Libby," Paul pointed to the third paragraph of the letter. "And what's this bit mean here? About you promoting the place?"

I felt my face color slightly. We were finally to the subject I'd been avoiding. "The thing is, Paul, the more people know about my, uh, experiences here, the more the place is worth. Gina and Jade won't be offering workshops and stuff until next summer, but it's important to start raising awareness now. You know. Build demand."

"I see." Paul nodded thoughtfully. "So let me ask you this. Once they take over, you're done, right? It will be someone else claiming to see these—fairies?"

"Yes. Jade, I guess. She says she can communicate with them."

He rolled his eyes. "Whatever. But the main thing is, you are done. Once the place is sold, you don't have to be involved."

"Right."

"No special guest appearances." He looked at me sharply. "You never have to come back to this place again."

I nodded. "That's the idea."

I dropped my head and blinked back my sudden tears.

How awful this whole thing was. How glad I'd be when it was over.

"Okay," Paul said. "I guess if that's the deal, that's the deal. I'll have Cliff look at this. And I'll have him look into this so-called investor. Let's get as much money from that sucker as we can."

"Paul?" I took another deep courage breath. Now was as good a time as any. "About doing publicity? They want me to go on *Hey! America*. That morning cable news show."

"That figures. When is this supposed to happen?"

"Tomorrow."

"Geez, Libby. Is there anything else?"

"I'm sorry, Paul. There was never a good time to bring it up. There's been so much going on. And I wasn't even sure, really, if it was going to happen. And—this whole thing—the whole fairies thing. It hasn't exactly been easy for us to discuss it. We really need to work on it, a little bit—our communication."

He sighed. "This is national television, Libby. It's going to get back to Josh. You realize that, right? I mean, put yourself in my place. Do you realize I'll be a laughingstock?"

"Put yourself in my place?"

Did he not realize how hard this was for me?

I struggled to keep myself under control. "Look, Paul. I know what you want. You want an easy answer. You want for me to get out of this whole situation, and believe me, I want that too. I hate it as much as you do, being paraded around like a sideshow freak." I paused for breath. "But I'm working on it. I have a buyer for the property. The last thing in the world I should do now is mess it up."

Paul looked a little shocked. But I'd gotten through to him. "Okay, Libby. Okay. Point taken." He nodded. "At least your name is off the *Skin Tones* masthead. Maybe I'll have our software guy look into getting it off any cached versions, too. You know. As a precaution. I think he can do that. What time is the interview?"

"They're picking me up at 5:45."

"Picking you up?"

I nodded. "They're sending a car."

Fifty-Six

They sent a limo.

It couldn't have been more out of place, that long black luxurious car, crawling up my gravel driveway. I imagined the driver wondering who the hell this Libby Samson person was, and how could anybody living this far out in the sticks be important enough to warrant this kind of treatment.

I'd decided to wear a suit.

It was one I'd bought years ago so I'd have something appropriate for biology conferences and was the most expensive outfit I owned.

I wanted to look like a professional.

Paul didn't get up, just rolled over when the alarm went off and went back to sleep.

I closed the front door softly so I wouldn't wake him, and turned the key to lock it.

From the stoop, I saw one of the campers' heads peeking up over a tent.

I trotted to the limo.

"Morning, miss," the driver said as he opened the limo door.

The interior of the car smelled of leather and the driver's cologne.

I looked down at my hands. I could have used a manicure. My fingernails were short and scuffed from a summer working outside, and my cuticles were stained white from primer.

Well, my hands wouldn't show on TV.

"Hi. I'm Kendra. Libby, right?"

Kendra looked to be about Maisey's age although she had to be older. She was wearing a magenta scoop neck top and a chunky gold necklace, and as I followed her back to the studio where the interview would take place, I marveled at how glamorous she looked.

"Sit down and we'll have them do your make-up," she said.

"Do I need make-up?"

"Yep. Here's Jack. Your cameraman."

Jack shook my hand. He was tall and gaunt with a receding hairline and smelled faintly of garlic. "Have a seat." He gestured at an upholstered office chair near the back wall.

Another young woman came in and started daubing powder on my face.

"Okay, let's get you wired," Jack said, when the make-up person was finished, and he clipped a microphone to my lapel and handed me an earpiece. "Your IFB," he said.

"IFB?"

"Interruptible feedback."

I'd begun to feel nervous during the drive. It was getting worse, now.

I wondered how many people would be watching, and told myself it was the lowest-rated morning talk show, and, anyway, I wouldn't be able to see the audience, so I could just pretend there was no audience, and it would be over fast, right? When you're stressed out time passes quickly...

Kendra left the room, and Jack fiddled some with the microphone. I couldn't tell what he was doing, only that he couldn't seem to get it right.

"Is there going to be anyone else here? In the room?" I asked.

"Nope. Just you and me."

I swallowed. "How will I know when my interview starts?"

"They said 7:30, right? I can turn the IFB on at quarter after if you like. You'll be able to hear the show. But you know sometimes people get bumped. You might be sitting for a while." He was at his camera now. "When it starts, when you hear Dave and Jillian introduce you, just look right at the lens."

"Okay."

A bright light suddenly came on behind me, and I swiveled my head around to look. A surreally vivid image of the Rochester skyline glowed on a screen behind my chair. "Oh!" I said. "Is that what people will see behind me?"

"Pretty nice, huh? Backdrop rear projection."

"How's it going?" Kendra was back. "Everything okay?"

Before I could answer, my earpiece suddenly switched on, and I was hearing disembodied voices—a lively conversation led by the *Hey! America* hosts, Dave Swindon and Jillian Bates—and I began to listen, fascinated. Dave was talking to someone about his business start-up, some sort of hybrid between Starbucks and Hard Rock Café. A bar specializing in alcoholic coffee drinks and pop culture décor. With free wireless access and terminals embedded in the tabletops.

"I just spoke to the producer," Kendra said. "Looks like we're good to go for 7:30. Jillian will be doing the interview. They have another guest on to talk about the photos."

Photos?

"I'm sorry?" I said. "What did you just say?"

"I just spoke to the prod—"

"No," I interrupted. "Something about photos?"

"Those pictures of you with the fairies," Kendra said. "You know."

I yanked the earpiece from my ear. "I'm sorry. I don't think I heard you right. What pictures?"

"Hang on." Kendra left again.

"You'd better put that thing back on," Jack said.

My hands had started to shake.

I'd been feeling nervous before. I was beyond nervous now.

Photos? Photos of what?

Kendra popped back through the door. "Here you go. These."

She handed me a sheaf of glossy paper and I stared at the sheet on top. It was a black and white printout of a web page. And right there in the middle of the page was a photograph of me, crouched down next to one of my planting beds, and right next to me, a little elfin figure in a striped tunic, wearing what looked like a knit cap. Looking up at me. His mouth open as if he was about to speak.

My stomach lurched. "I—I don't know what this is," I said, looking up at Jack and Kendra and then back down again.

"Better get that earpiece back in, Ms. Samson," Jack said.

I flipped to the next page. Me, again. I was standing by the wall between my property and Dean's, and four elfin figures, also dressed in stripes, were standing in a semi-circle in front of me. One was pointing at me with the mouthpiece of a little pipe.

I looked back up at Kendra. "I don't know what these are." There was a panicked note in my voice. "I've never seen them before in my life."

"Well," she said doubtfully. "That's you. You're in them."

"I can't do this interview." I started to stand up, but my knees gave out and I sat back down.

"Three minutes," Jack said. "You need to get your earpiece in, Ms. Samson. They just did the teaser."

Kendra took the earpiece out of my hand and inserted it in my ear. "Don't worry, Jillian's nice. There. That feel okay?"

Jack had walked to a panel of switches near the door. He touched one and suddenly the room was dark except for the bluish light cast by the projection screen. "Remember to look right at the camera," he said.

"I don't know what to do," I said to Kendra. "I can't talk about these photos. I have no idea where they came from."

"Just be yourself," she said.

"I'll do this when you're on the air," Jack said, making a chopping motion with his arm.

"See you after," said Kendra and when she opened the door the room lightened for a second, then returned to its disorienting bluish half-light.

Jillian's voice cut in. "And now: Modern Fairy Tale, or Age-Old Fraud?"

Oh, no. I suppressed a groan.

Jack, standing behind his camera, slashed the air dramatically.

"Our first guest is Libby Samson, an organic farmer from Upstate New York who claims that she sees, and talks to, fairy folk. Good morning, Libby."

"Hi," I said, hoping the grimace I was directing at the camera lens would pass for a smile.

"So tell us, Libby, what are the fairy folk like? How did you come to meet them?"

"They're—well, I'm not sure what they are, exactly. They appear to be humanlike, but of course, they're small—"

"How small, would you say?"

"About two feet tall."

"I see!" Jillian said brightly. "And you see them on your farm?"

"Yes." My tongue was dry. Sticking to the roof of my mouth. "I bought this place with a farmhouse and about ten acres of land—"

"And what do you and these fairies talk about?" she interrupted.

"They, uh, give me advice for my crops. What to grow, that sort of thing."

"And their advice. Is it good advice?"

I had the sudden impression that Jillian was desperately bored. "You know what I think?" I said. "I think I'm somehow picking up energy from the land itself—from the plants and the soil—and somehow it's taken the form of—"

"And what we all really want to know, of course, is—have they got a pot of gold? Just kidding, Libby! Just kidding. Now, your story first took off when these encounters you're having with these fairies appeared on the Internet."

"Yes." I swallowed, miserably, while also somehow keeping that grimace-smile fixedly in place.

"And more recently, there have been some photos as well."

"Yes, but—"

"Here, for our viewers to see!" Jillian's voice was now decidedly lively. "There's Libby talking to one of the fairies. Here she is talking with them. Cute, aren't they? Libby, these photos are quite extraordinary."

"Yes, but, those aren't—Jillian, they don't look anything like—"

"We have, joining us now, photography expert George Wales. George is director of the Photodocumentation Institute in Miami. Welcome to *Hey! America*, George."

A gravelly man's voice came through my earpiece. "Thanks for having me on, Jillian."

"George, based on your analysis of the photos of Ms. Samson with her fairies, would you say they are genuine?"

George's rattled out a chuckle. "No, Jillian. On the contrary. They are most definitely fake. They're not even as good as the Cottingley fairy photos of 1917—a pretty successful hoax at the time. Pre-digital, of course."

I wished, desperately, that I hadn't eaten that morning. Because those eggs? They wanted to come back up.

"What makes you so certain they're fake?" Jillian was saying.

"Keep looking at the camera," Jack whispered urgently. "They may cut to you."

I stared again at the camera. As if it were possible to look relaxed and unconcerned while being pilloried on national television.

Because not only was it impossible, it was dreadful to have to even try.

"...mismatch of illumination," George Wales was saying. "Note how the lighting on the so-called 'fairy' is more diffuse than that on Ms. Samson and her surroundings? You can also see variations in image contrast..."

I wanted to break in. Shout, of course they're fakes! I never said they were real! They aren't my photos!

But, how could I? Like Kendra had said, I was right there. I was in the photos. They'd come from somewhere—

I jolted suddenly. Jillian had said my name. "...admit they're pretty realistic."

"I—I've never said that the, um, fairies were 'real' in the same way that, you know, this chair is real." I leaned forward slightly and tapped the arm of my chair, then realized it was probably out of view of the camera. "I'm not sure they are—I think it's more that—"

"So are you admitting that you faked the photos?" Jillian asked. The boredom in her voice had completely vanished.

"Oh no! I did *not* fake them!" My voice rose. "What I'm saying is—"

"The angle of the lighting on the figure's jacket is irrefutable," George, the Photo Sleuth, cut in. "These aren't only fakes. They're *bad* fakes."

Jillian laughed heartily. "So there you have it, folks! They're real, they're fake, both sides of the story. But Libby, if they do lead you to that pot of gold, give us a call, and we'll have you back on, okay? And thank you, George. Next up. They're cousins. They hate each other. Why do their parents think they should marry? And still to come—"

Jack was chopping the air with his arm again.

I yanked the earpiece by its cord and slumped in my chair while the cameraman unclipped the microphone.

"You did great," he said.

Fifty-Seven

The whole way home, all I could think about was Paul.

Pleeeeeeeeeeease pleeeeeeeeeeease let me find out he spent the morning asleep, or painting the house, or on the phone with Josh.

Anything but watching that awful interview.

The limo turned into the driveway.

Campers huddled in clumps over by the tents.

Do they know? How soon will they know?

And there was an old Ford parked by Paul's car.

Maisey's Ford.

I stepped out of the limo, and the front door flew open.

But it was Gina, not Paul, who was first out of the door. Her eyes were blazing. "Why didn't you tell me you had pictures? How dare you hide this from me!"

"Where's Paul?" I said.

Campers were trickling toward the house. "We saw your new pics online!" one of them called out. "Can we, like, get copies?"

And then I saw Paul. He'd burst through the door and was striding down the steps.

His face was pale.

"Paul," I said, my voice catching. "I don't know anything about those pictures."

He looked furious.

"I swear," I whispered.

"You'll be lucky if we don't pull out of this deal, Libby Samson," Gina hissed from behind me.

I turned around. Gina was flanked by campers, now. "Why would you pull out?" I said sarcastically. "I thought you were gung-ho on publicity?"

"Good publicity. Not *this* kind of publicity. I've been an hour trying to figure out what I'm going to say to our investor. He's not taking my calls, Libby. I can't believe you didn't tell me!"

"I didn't know!" I howled. I looked at Paul again. "Paul. I don't know what they are except that they are fa—"

Gina's hand clapped over my mouth.

I felt the campers' eyes on me, staring.

"Gina," Paul said. "You and your friends need to leave. Libby, we have to talk."

"We have to talk, too, Libby," Gina muttered.

But I ignored her. I followed Paul.

He went straight up the stairs to my office.

ψ ψ ψ

"They're fakes," I said.

"Of course, they're fakes," Paul said angrily. "That's not the point. The point is that every time things seem to calm down, you find a way to stir them up again."

It was almost more than I could take. "But I didn't *do* anything!"

Paul had seated himself at my computer and gestured at the screen with one hand while maneuvering my mouse with the other. "Look," he said harshly. "Look."

I gasped.

It was like the original outbreak all over again. Website after website displaying those horrible photos.

Paul turned and opened his mouth to say something more, but then he saw the tears streaming down my cheeks and stopped himself.

I pulled a tissue from the box on my desk and wiped my eyes.

I heard him sigh. "I'm sorry to get mad at you, Libby," he said in a calmer voice. "But try to think. Where could these have come from?"

He picked up a sheet of paper from my desk. He'd printed out copies of the photos. "Obviously you posed for them."

I shook my head. "I was so shocked when they first showed them to me in the studio. But then on the drive back, I realized. It's the day I was interviewed for that newspaper article. I mean, they're different shots from the ones that ended up in the paper."

I picked up the printouts and shuffled through them. "They're different," I said. "I've never seen these specific photos before. But they were taken on that day, I'm sure of it."

"You're sure that's who took them?"

"I'm positive. If you compared them to the newspaper photos, you'd see. I'm wearing the same clothes. Those shorts, my pink long-sleeve top with the polka dots."

"Okay, but here's the thing. I can't see someone from the paper doctoring photos like this."

I shook my head. "No. Me either. At least I would hope not."

"It had to have been someone else. Someone who got their hands on the photos. Gina?"

I frowned. "Why would Gina do something like that? And she was furious."

We were quiet a moment, and then his cell phone buzzed. "That'll be the systems admin from Cal4. I asked him to look into it."

I took another Kleenex from the box and listened while Paul and the computer guy talked. At one point Paul looked at me and made writing motions in the air to signal he wanted a pen and paper for making notes, so I pawed through the stuff on my desk and handed him what he needed. He jotted down some notes and nodded and finally hung up. "Okay. He traced one of the sites back to the IP address of a web hosting company called Jeepers Hosting. We are so going to sue the sonofabitch who did this."

"Oh!" I said. "Oh, no! That's the company Ty used when he set up the website!"

"You must be kidding me." Paul stood up. "He did this?"

"Paul, maybe it's just a coincidence," I said. "I'll talk to him."

"No. I'm gonna talk to him. And it'll be a conversation he won't ever forget. Maisey knows where that punk's staying, right?"

"Paul!" I ran after him down the stairs. "Paul, I don't think—"

He wasn't listening. He'd reached the front door.

"Paul! Please let's talk about this!"

He was halfway to his car by the time I got to the stoop.

He stopped to root through his pockets for his car keys as I took the front steps two at a time and—

Dean?

What was Dean doing here? Standing, holding a paint brush?

"Paul!" I yelled again and started running toward the driveway.

But Dean's hand caught my arm, stopping me. "What's going on?" he said.

"Let me go! Paul, you need to calm down!"

"Libby! What is going on?" Dean's hand was still on my arm.

"Some photos! Some photos turned up," I gasped. "And Paul thinks that Ty—Paul!"

Dean dropped my arm. "It wasn't Tyler," he said in a loud voice.

Paul turned.

He looked at Dean.

He started walking back toward us. "What did you just say?"

His jaw was jutting out, and his eyes were narrowed.

"You want to punch somebody?" Dean said. "Then you can punch me."

"Dean!" I gasped. "What are you saying?"

"It was me, Libby," Dean said. "I posted the photos." He waved his hands at the campers who had gathered around us again. "I hacked into your website, downloaded the photos, and posted them. To prove to all these people, here, what a fake you are."

"You S.O.B.," Paul snarled.

His fist jabbed through the air toward Dean's face.

I screamed.

Dean's right hand flew up and deflected Paul's punch as easily as if he'd swatted a fly.

The campers gasped and backed away.

I could hear Paul's breathing.

And then Dean was speaking to Paul in a low, hard, even voice. "I did it for Libby, you idiot. Because I happen to care about her."

"So you publicly humiliate her. That's your idea of—"

"That's all you think about, isn't it, Paul," Dean growled. "What people might say. Not whether she's happy. And you claim you love her? You don't have a clue."

I'd never seen Paul so furious.

He probably didn't even realize he was punching out at Dean again until he'd done it.

But this time, Dean just stood there, and Paul's fist connected with his jaw, hard enough that Dean's head snapped back.

I screamed again, then clapped my hand over my mouth in horror.

And we stood there, the campers behind muttering "whoa!" and "holy shit," and Paul looking at Dean and then at me.

Paul's face was purple, and his breath was fast and hard. "There," he said. "There."

Then he turned and walked to his car.

"I'll call you later, Libby," he said over his shoulder as he slammed the door.

He turned his car around and went down the driveway, and then when he was on the road and pointed toward Rochester, he jammed the gas hard. His tires squealed and gravel spurted up and pinged off the campers' cars.

And then he was gone.

"I didn't have to let him hit me," Dean said.

He was rubbing the red mark on his jaw.

"Well then," I spat. "Why did you?"

"Because he needed to hit me more than I needed to duck."

"I see." But I didn't see.

Why had Dean done this to me? Of all people, why would he do something that would make my awful situation even worse?

I turned on my heel. "Suppose you get out of here."

"Libby."

"Just go."

And I left him standing there.

I went into my house, shut the door, and locked it behind me.

Fifty-Eight

Saturday morning. And I told myself that it should be comforting, to be back into my old routine. Up before it was fully light out, dragging baskets out to my gardens, picking produce, packing it in my coolers to drive to Susan's.

But it wasn't comforting. Not really.

I'd hardly slept.

I could barely choke down a piece of toast.

Susan hadn't seen the interview, but she knew about it, of course. Word was getting around. And she was kind about it. She felt bad for me, really bad, so genuine and sorrowful for what I was going through that I wished I dared to ask to move in with her.

Please adopt me and let me live with you forever.

I stayed a little longer than usual, helping her sort and bag produce for her subscribers' weekly pick-up. And then, finally, about 2:00 in the afternoon, I dragged myself to my car and started home.

The first thing I noticed, when I drove up, was that my road was empty of cars.

I turned into my driveway.

I saw my house.

Someone had spray-painted across the front. Across my brand-new paint job. *Hoax, hoax, hoax* and below that *lying bitch Libby* with bunches of exclamation points.

And then I gasped.

Only a single tent remained on my lawn. And it was listing to one side, and the rain fly was torn.

The campers were gone.

☙ ☙ ☙

I spent Sunday morning painting over the graffiti.

Then Paul phoned me. We agreed to meet in the city, at Highland Park.

To talk.

I got there first, and parked on Highland Avenue and waited, and then saw him in my rearview mirror, coming up the sidewalk.

He pecked my lips with his.

We hiked up the hill through the lilac bushes to one of the blacktop paths that crisscross the park, and then after a bit we came to a bench and sat down and agreed that it was a gorgeous day.

Then we were both silent for a while.

"I spoke to Maisey this morning," I said finally.

"How's she doing?"

"She's okay. She's going to see if she can matriculate in January. She's thinking maybe she'll major in special ed. And she's probably going to come stay with me at the farm until she starts."

"Good for Maisey."

"She says Gina's going back to Hawaii."

We sat a bit longer. "So," he said finally.

I waited.

"Sorry I punched your friend."

"He'll live," I said. "How's your hand?"

"I'll live, too."

A couple strolled by. They were walking a dachshund on a little red harness. They smiled and nodded at us as they passed.

"Libby." Paul was looking at his hands. "I don't really want to do this. But Josh—"

"I'm off *Skin Tones*," I said. "It's okay. I'll live."

"It was bad enough before. But now that this has happened? You know how important credibility is. In this game, well—we can't risk that people will think the articles are bogus. Josh was saying—"

"Paul, I'm not a fraud."

He didn't answer.

"I really do see them."

A couple of kids flew by on skateboards. A robin landed on the grass nearby and began hopping about, cocking his head at the ground to look for worms.

"Anyway, I'm awfully sorry about everything," Paul said finally.

Me too, I thought. "I know." I paused. "About us."

He was looking at his hands again. "It would probably be best if we took a little break."

The robin hopped out of sight down the hill.

"Right," I sighed. "Let's not kid ourselves, Paul. It would be best if we just called it quits."

He sighed. "Yeah. You're probably right."

We sat for a while more, and then made our way back down the hill to my car.

We hugged.

And I drove off, leaving him standing there on the grass on the side of the road.

Fifty-Nine

I was moping around the house the next morning when somebody banged on my door.

It was a flower delivery guy. "Libby Samson?"

I took the bouquet, and closed the door, and set it on the kitchen counter.

I opened the card.

No message, just Dean's name.

He got rid of the campers. He told me that he could help me get rid of the campers.

And I didn't believe he could do it. But he did it. He figured out a way to do it.

For me.

I remembered how humiliated I'd felt during the cable interview, being accused by that photography expert of being a fraud.

I tossed the flowers into the kitchen garbage can in the corner.

I moped around the house a bit more.

I went back to the kitchen and fished the flowers back out of the garbage can and put them in water.

After all, it wasn't really the flowers' fault.

⚜ ⚜ ⚜

Next morning.

Same time.

Delivery guy was back with another bouquet.

☙ ☙ ☙

By Friday I'd run out of vases.

By the middle of the following week, I had flowers in canning jars and pitchers and drinking glasses in every room of my house.

He got rid of the campers.

He gave me my life back.

This man who has been offering to help me over and over again for months—even when I told him not to help, told him I didn't believe he could help.

He gave me my life back.

Sixty

I went for a walk up to my planting beds. For no particular reason. Just to be outside, and smell the air. Listen to the cicadas. Feel the sun on my face.

The nights were turning almost frosty, but the days were still summery. The golden rod and wild asters were in full bloom, and the leaves of the sugar maples, always the first to turn in the fall, were already tinged with orange.

I hadn't spoken to my little friends since that last time. When Paul had been there, and I'd sneaked away...

Although I noticed them from time to time, walking, sometimes alone, sometimes in groups.

What were they doing?

Tending to things. Tending to the land.

I sat next to one of my beds and leaned back on the straw covering, lowering my eyelids against the brightness of the sun.

And then I opened my eyes again, and suddenly it was as if the colors had all doubled in intensity—tripled in intensity—the yellows and purples of the wildflowers, the shimmering horizon, the azure sky deep as infinity overhead.

And I suddenly felt so much a part of it, so that somehow the intensity was inside me as well as outside, and I realized also how much bigger it was than me, the pulsing energy of nature and of life, and how much bigger it was than the petty failures people mourn, our silly failures that we snatch to our hearts from the teeth of our silly fears and our silly angers.

"So that's it, then," I murmured.

Thinking to myself, who would have thought that me, Libby Samson, the biologist, would be sitting out here having a mystical experience.

Because that's what it was, right?

Mystical?

And then it began to fade.

And everything looked the same as it had before—

Except still achingly beautiful, and crystal clear through my tear-cleansed eyes...

I shivered, stood up, and walked back down to my house.

Sixty-One

The next morning I finished my coffee, rinsed the mug, pulled on my sneakers, and set off down the road.

I turned into Dean's driveway, walking slowly, watching.

Listening.

They were there. I could feel them. The little people were on Dean's land, too.

I rounded the last bend and paused.

Dean was sitting on the swing on his porch, Bo curled up near his feet.

I felt his eyes on me as I walked up. "You can stop sending me flowers," I said.

He stood up, and the look in his eyes was one I'll never forget.

The relief and the longing and the love.

"Libby."

II walked up the steps.

Dean put his arms around me.

Bo's tail thumped against the porch's floorboards.

Dean's was holding me like he thought if he let go, I might vanish into thin air.

"I'm not selling my farm," I whispered into his shirt. "I'm not going anywhere."

A movement caught my eye.

The little man, walking, making his way through the trees.

"I'm not going anywhere," I repeated, and then I turned my face up and offered my lips to Dean's.

More by Kirsten Mortensen

Once Upon a Flarey Tale

Her new apartment is a Tower.
Can her Prince be far behind?

COMING FALL 2020!

Fo Fum Flarey

She thinks she's got her Prince. But when Fairy Tales are real?
You'd better watch out for Thieves…